Love Finds You™
IN
SUNDANCE
WYOMING

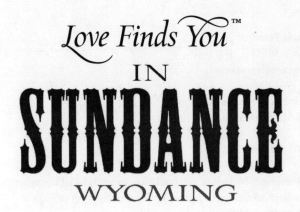

Love Finds You™ IN SUNDANCE WYOMING

BY MIRALEE FERRELL

summerside
PRESS™

Summerside Press™
Minneapolis 55337
www.summersidepress.com

Love Finds You in Sundance, Wyoming
© 2011 by Miralee Ferrell

ISBN 978-1-60936-277-5

The town depicted in this book is a real place, but all characters, other than known historical figures addressed in the Author's Note, are fictional. Any resemblances to actual people or events are purely coincidental.

Cover Design by Garborg Design Works | www.garborgdesign.com

Interior design by Müllerhaus Publishing Group | www.mullerhaus.net

Scripture references are from The Holy Bible, King James Version (KJV).

Summerside Press™ is an inspirational publisher offering fresh, irresistible books to uplift the heart and engage the mind.

Printed in USA.

Dedication
....

This book is lovingly dedicated
to my best friend
and a horsewoman in her own right—
my daughter, Marnee.
I love you and am so blessed you're my daughter.

Acknowledgments

....

So many people have contributed to making this story what it is today. Family, friends, editors, agent, critique partners, and prayer partners who offer an ongoing covering have all been such a help and blessing during the writing and editing process.

Special thanks go to my critique group. Kimberly Johnson, Sherry Kyle, and Karen O'Connor made suggestions that helped strengthen my book from start to finish. Each one is a talented writer, and I'm blessed to be on the same team. To Kristy Gamet and Tammy Marks who both read my books in advance—I appreciate your valuable input. And special thanks to Debbie Fluit and Barb Dorscher, for their unwavering prayer support during the writing of this book.

I especially want to thank my agent, Tamela Hancock Murray, for her help, encouragement, and prayer support throughout my growing career, and to the people at Summerside Press for giving me another opportunity to write for them. And thank you, Susan Lorher, for your help with the Italian and Spanish phrases I needed.

My family has stood beside me through all the times I've pushed to make deadlines and struggled when the words wouldn't come. Allen, thank you, dear husband, for loving me and understanding when I didn't have time to cook. To my kids, Marnee and Steven, and their wonderful spouses, Brian and Hannah—I love you all. You are the joy of my life and make everything I do worthwhile. Mom, I love you. Thank you for believing in me.

Special thanks go to Pam Halter, who serves on the board of the Sundance Museum. She was a wonderful asset in giving me information on the town as it was during the late 1800s.

And, of course, all praise, honor, and glory must go to my Lord. For without His hand on my life, this journey would be useless. I pray that each story I write will point back to Him—then I'll truly know I've accomplished what He put me on this earth to do.

To my readers, whom I choose to think of as my friends, thank you. If it weren't for you, there would be no more books. I love hearing from you and enjoy knowing what you think, feel, and experience as you read my stories. Drop me a note, or visit my website, www. miraleeferrell.com, or my Facebook page. I'd love to meet you there!

Sundance, Wyoming

LOCATED IN THE NORTHEAST CORNER OF THE STATE, SUNDANCE, Wyoming, is a picturesque small town nestled in the Black Hills, named after Sundance Mountain to honor the Native Americans and the sun dances they performed on the mountain south of the town site. Albert Hoge, who owned and operated the local hotel and store, founded Sundance in 1879 during the Black Hills' gold rush. He carefully surveyed the land and in the beginning sold lots only to future businesses and county and city government, as well as eating establishments and saloons. His vision laid the foundation for what Sundance is today.

Sundance is most famous for Harry Longabough, also known as the Sundance Kid, who later teamed up with Butch Cassidy. Harry took his infamous name after bragging about his stay in the Crook County jail located in the town. He'd stolen a horse from the VVV ranch and was captured by Sheriff Ryan, serving eighteen months in the local jail. Later he teamed up with Cassidy and the Wild Bunch, and their fame grew as they robbed trains and banks. The name Wild Bunch was misleading, as Butch Cassidy always tried to avoid hurting people during robberies. He ordered his gang to shoot at the horses, rather than the riders, when being pursued by posses. Cassidy always proudly bragged that he had never killed a man.

With a population of just over 1,100, the small community of Sundance boasts unparalleled scenery, adventure, and history. Nestled between Devils Tower and Mount Rushmore in the heart of the Black Hills, Sundance offers natural beauty, breathtaking monuments, and many recreational activities.

Miralee Ferrell

Chapter One

....

Texas Panhandle, 1887

Angel Ramirez woke with a start, her heart pounding a rolling beat in her chest. Someone was in her room.

Inching her fingers under the edge of her pillow, her hand brushed against the cold steel of her Colt revolver. She eased the gun out and waited, allowing her vision to adjust to the partial darkness of the muggy August night. Uncle José had taught her to wait, never to rush when confronting an intruder—the first shot might be her only one.

Rolling over onto her side, she pointed the gun at the door. "Who's there?"

A half moon sent tentative fingers of light through the small window near the foot of her bed, and a dark form stepped forward. "It's José. Put your gun down, *m'ija*." Her uncle's accented drawl was absent—the words short and clipped. "Get dressed and meet me outside. Hurry now." He slipped out the door and closed it carefully behind him.

Angel drew on her trousers and long-sleeved shirt, tugged on her boots, and shoved her sombrero onto her close-cropped curls. After a quick look around the room, she grabbed her rifle and headed outside. José raised his hand for silence and drew her into the nearby stand of trees, not far from their small, three-room cabin. "Keep your voice down. I don't want any of the men in the *banda* to hear."

The hair on the back of Angel's arms stood on end. "What's wrong?"

"Another cattle raid. I won't leave you behind. It's not safe for you here."

"With the men?"

"Yes. Bart Hinson's up to something."

Angel sucked in a breath between her teeth. "Hinson. He's the worst of this bunch. I don't like the way he looks at me."

José stifled what sounded like a curse and gripped her arm. "If anything happens to me tonight, promise you'll ride out of here and never come back."

Her heart rate accelerated, but she patted his hand. "Nothing's going to happen to you."

He swung her toward him and leaned close, dropping his voice. "I don't trust Hinson. An outlaw *banda* is no place for a girl, even if you *were* raised here. You're eighteen and can take care of yourself away from this place." Her uncle pointed to the rifle near her knee. "That rifle will take you far—you shoot better than most men. Keep dressing like a boy and get work on ranches as a hunter or horse wrangler."

She tried to laugh off his concern, but the effort nearly choked her. "This is my home. You've had these feelings before, and you've always come back safely."

José placed his arm around her shoulders and squeezed. "I wish I'd made other choices years ago, m'ija. If your parents were alive, they wouldn't have chosen this life for you. I should have sent you back to your mother's people in Italy." He dug into the pocket of his denim jacket and removed a small bag. "There's gold in there—enough to keep you a couple of years, if you're careful and work when you can."

She drew back, hating the thought of taking it. She'd never considered where José's money came from, but accepting a bag of gold procured from other people's loss didn't sit right. Besides, her uncle's words implied he might not be along. "You're scaring me."

He closed her fingers over the handful of gold. "I plan on living for a long time, m'ija, but you must be ready." He swung away from her and called softly over his shoulder. "Saddle Bella, bring a bedroll, and put whatever you value most in your saddlebags—quick. And whatever you do, stay close to me on the trail."

* * * * *

Angel swung into the saddle and picked up Bella's reins, her black Spanish-Arabian mare. She shoved the Winchester lever-action rifle into the saddle scabbard and tugged her hat over her forehead.

The pale moon shone over the encampment, offering little in the way of light, but the deep reaches of the sky were lit by myriad stars sparkling against the dark backdrop. Dust rose as the outlaws' horses stamped their hooves and pawed at the churned-up ground. Sweat trickled down between Angel's shoulder blades. A horse bumped against Bella. Angel tightened her reins and turned sideways in her saddle.

Bart Hinson swiveled toward her and leered, his narrow lips tipping up the corners of his sun-baked, flat face. "Finally gonna become a true outlaw and help us rustle some cattle, hey, Angel?"

She raised her chin and backed her mare a couple of steps. "I rustle nothing. José asked me to come, but I'll not take part." Deliberately she touched her spur to the mare's flank and swung away from the man.

"Think you're too good for us, do you?" He laughed, and a shiver of apprehension ran across Angel's skin. "Once you ride with us, you'll share all that we stand for."

She'd lived among these men and their wives since she was eight years old, and had never been on a cattle raid before—for that matter, she'd never felt fear until recently—and then, only around a handful of the outlaws. Hinson's attentions had increased over the past couple of months, and she'd done her best to stay clear of the man. A sudden understanding of her uncle's concern coursed through her. Hinson wasn't a typical outlaw. He emanated something dark—a hint of evil deep at his core.

José moved up alongside her, inserting his sorrel gelding between Bella and Hinson's mount, effectively blocking the man's view of Angel. She was glad to have Bart's hawk-like scrutiny removed. She wanted to sink into a washtub and scrub the evil away.

José pressed his horse closer. "You all right, *pequeña?*"

Angel nodded. "*Sí.*" She kept her gaze averted from Hinson as he spurred his horse the opposite direction.

José dropped his hand to the butt of his rifle. "Good. Let's pray this night will go well and we'll be back in our beds by nightfall tomorrow."

"Pray, Uncle? You think God in heaven smiles on what we do tonight?"

"Maybe not, but we pray just the same, sí?"

* * * * *

An hour later Bella snorted, sidestepped, and shook her head. Angel stroked the neck of her jigging black mare and stared out over the herd of restless cattle. José had insisted she stay back in the brush line, within sight of the men moving close to the herd but not near enough to be in danger.

Dust rose from the milling cattle. Calves bawled and their

anxious mamas lowed as they searched for their young among the constantly moving melee. Angel struggled to see her uncle through the gloom as the approaching dawn withheld its gift of light. Ghost-like figures rode shadowy horses along the edge of the scrub brush, circling around and returning strays to the herd.

A shout rang out. A rider spurred his mount and charged after a bull racing away from the perimeter with three longhorn cows following close on his heels. The bay gelding stretched his neck and lengthened his stride, his one white stocking flashing against the dark background. His rider pushed the horse harder, leaning forward in his saddle. The pair leapt ahead of the bull, and the man swung his mount ever closer to the wicked horns, pushing the animals in a wide arc toward the rest of the cattle.

José reined in beside Angel, pushed his sombrero back, and wiped his sleeve across his forehead. "It's warm, and the dust makes it worse."

Angel rested her hands on the pommel of her saddle, her reins draped loosely against Bella's neck. "What now?"

"We move the herd north into New Mexico." José dropped his voice. "You must leave tonight."

"Leave? I don't understand." She'd never known anyone to leave the outlaw band. "What about you?"

"This is my life." He shrugged. "And I must stay here to make sure you can get away."

"It's gotten so bad?"

"Sí."

"I won't go without you."

"You must promise me, little one."

She hesitated, but the determination bathing his face left her no room to argue. "I promise."

A shout went up from the fringe of the herd, and José swung his horse. "Stay out of sight, and don't return to the cabin." He peered back over his shoulder. "Angel?"

"Yes. I hear. Nothing will happen. Now go, before the men get angry at your absence."

He laid the big rowels of his California spurs to the flank of his gelding and cantered across the clearing, rejoining the ever-shifting herd.

Angel turned Bella and followed along parallel with the apex of the jostling cattle, watching the swift riders with grudging respect. These men were some of the best riders and ropers in Texas, and most of them were excellent shots. They had to be—their lives, not to mention their livelihood—depended on their horsemanship and speed with a gun.

The hours dragged as the men, horses, and cattle moved north and glimmering predawn colors appeared in the eastern sky, heralding a clear, hot day. Angel dropped back along the flank of the herd. She slipped her bandana over her nose to block the billows of dust rising from the dry streambed. She'd spoken to her uncle not long ago and knew the men were concerned about the lack of water.

The thirsty cattle bellowed, and restlessness crept through their numbers. A dozen cows and calves raced for freedom on the far side, seeming intent on returning the way they'd come. The animals had been traveling for over six hours now with no water, and the youngest started to lag. She wanted to urge Bella forward and help the men tighten the herd, but José wouldn't approve.

A glance over the heads of the jostling cattle showed her uncle riding not far from Hinson, with Junior Bailey just ahead.

Dust drifted on a light breeze, bringing with it the scent of sweat, manure, and fear. Angel drew Bella to a walk and moved off to the side. Tension knotted her stomach, and unease seemed to wrap itself over the atmosphere like a dark, looming thundercloud.

The other five men were spread from the point of the herd to the rear, hats drawn low and bandanas snugged up over their noses. All were alert, their posture in the saddle tense, and at least two had their rifles out of their scabbards.

She could see nothing moving in the rear. No. Wait. A dust trail rising in the east in the morning sun. Was that what had the men spooked?

José waved his arm and shouted. "Angel. Go. Hurry!" He reined his horse away from his position along the far edge of the cattle and broke into a hard trot. "Remember—"

An explosion of rifle fire severed his warning.

Five men rode into sight a hundred yards back on the cattle's flanks. They leaned low over their horse's necks, rifles extended in front of them, and Angel could see a flame erupt from the muzzle of the one in the lead.

Hinson let out a war whoop. "Rangers!" He aimed his six-shooter off to the side and let loose, firing a steady stream at the men approaching them at a ground-covering gallop. "Get the herd moving." Hinson turned his head and stared at José racing his gelding along the flank of the herd toward Angel. "Ramirez, get back to your post!"

José dug in his spurs and lashed his horse with the end of his reins, his attention fixed on Angel. "Get into the mesquite, pequeña. Hide!" He closed the gap to within ten yards of Angel and pointed toward a thick stand of brush. "Go, now!"

Angel hesitated, but her uncle's expression brooked no disobedience. Gripping Bella's reins, she leaned forward in the saddle and grazed the mare's side with her spurs. Bella leapt forward, digging in her haunches and catapulting over the ground.

Another shot sounded and Angel turned her head, gazing back toward Hinson. He'd holstered his pistol and removed his rifle, aiming toward the Ranger and the posse. She ducked into the brush, reined Bella to a halt, and turned back toward the action unfolding before her.

Hinson sighted down the length of his rifle and squeezed the trigger. A loud report echoed across the hills, and Angel swung in the direction he'd aimed. She froze. Her uncle lurched in the saddle, blood soaking his arm. He gripped the saddle horn with the other; the reins lay useless on his horse's neck.

Another report erupted from Hinson's rifle and an explosion of sound followed, as Rangers, posse, and outlaws emptied their guns across the expanse. The rifle in Hinson's hands bucked, and the lead Texas Ranger tumbled from his horse's back, disappearing under the hooves of the stampeding cattle.

Angel sat frozen as her uncle's horse made his way toward her, seeming intent on reaching his pasture mate. Bella neighed, and Angel broke from her stupor. She dismounted, tossed her reins over her horse's neck, and stepped to José's side as Rio drew to a stop.

"Uncle! How hard are you hit?" She caught Rio's reins.

"Not bad. Leave now, while they are busy with the posse." Blood oozed from between his fingers.

Angel yanked open her saddlebag. She withdrew a clean shirt and moved close to Rio. "Let me tie this around your arm. You're losing too much blood."

He grunted, held out his hand, and wrapped the shirt around the wound. "Knot it for me." He raised pain-filled eyes.

She tugged at the end of the fabric. "There. Promise me you'll be careful."

José gave her a tight smile. "I'm too tough to kill, m'ija. Your mother called you that. Do you remember? She always said that she named you Angel after taking one look at your sweet face on the day of your birth. And your papa, he called you pequeña—little one. Remember them, and remember me—your family."

"I won't leave you. I'll go back to the banda, and we'll stay away from Hinson."

"No! Hinson grows too powerful among the men. He fears me, but he's the kind of snake that will strike when your back is turned. If the posse wins this battle, you would go to jail along with the rest of us." José fixed a firm gaze on her. "Ride fast and go far. Stay on the path the cattle have made for now, then veer off when you hit rocky ground. I'll keep an eye on Hinson—make sure he doesn't follow." He laid his spurs into Rio's sides, and the big gelding bounded forward.

The renewed gunfire and the shouts of men brought her back to her immediate danger. She eased her horse deeper into the brush, knowing she should leave. *Uncle, be safe.*

Hinson had moved to the far side of the herd, engrossed in a gun battle with two men from the posse. Three of the outlaw band tried to head off stampeding cattle, two lay sprawled on the ground, and the sixth crouched behind a stand of mesquite, firing at another Ranger.

Angel's gaze returned to her uncle, trotting his horse across a small clearing, his rifle raised. She wanted to pull her own rifle from its sheath and turn it on Hinson, the good-for-nothing who'd turned her life upside down. But she'd made a promise, and she'd keep it.

"Come on, girl." She nudged Bella forward, then slumped in her saddle, numbness permeating her body. She laid her knotted reins on her mare's neck and rested her hands on the horn, trying to still the shaking.

Her uncle had been her only family for the last ten years. She had memories of her parents, but not many. José had raised her like his own daughter and showered her with love and attention. Spilling blood wasn't new to her, but the memory of her uncle's wound caused bile to rise in her throat. She pushed it down and picked up the reins. This wasn't the time to grieve.

Angel headed toward the rising sun, praying the intense rays of early morning light would blind anyone who looked her direction. Hopefully the men were too engaged in staying alive to notice her weaving through the brush several hundred feet from the action.

The men's shouts grew fainter, and she could no longer see anyone from the posse or the outlaw band. Only a small number of straggling cattle milled about when she bent forward over Bella's neck, urging her into a canter.

Angel glanced at the sun. At least an hour had passed and nothing appeared behind her on the horizon. Grief slammed into her like a herd of stampeding horses. Everything she'd known lay behind her, and an unknown future beckoned.

Alone.

She had the gold, her rifle, and José's instructions. Somehow she'd make it. But what should she do next? Angel straightened her shoulders and raised her chin. She'd not let Hinson find her.

Time to change direction. On the first leg of her journey, the goal had been escape. Now, she added another element.

Survival.

Over the past month, Hinson had dogged her steps in the banda. He wouldn't let her go without a fight. Every bit of the training she'd received from José would be bent on one thing—hiding her tracks as she moved toward country where she could disappear. If she didn't, her life wouldn't be worth living.

* * * * *

Bart Hinson holstered his gun and grunted with satisfaction. His men had killed the last of the posse as he tried to race away, hanging low on his horse's neck, undoubtedly to alert the rest of the Texas Rangers about their dead compadres. No way could they allow a man to return and sound the alarm, not after Bart had shot the Ranger heading the posse. They'd be hunted soon enough when the men didn't return, but no one knew who'd fired the shot that brought the Ranger down. No one but Angel Ramirez.

Bart scowled and spat to the side, then swung around to the nearest man. "Where's the girl?"

Barnes tugged at a torn strip of cloth he'd knotted around a flesh wound in his arm. "Gone. Saw her ride off close to an hour ago."

Bart sprang at the man and backhanded him across the mouth. He leveled his pistol at Barnes's head. "You let her go? Give me a reason I shouldn't kill you now."

Barnes lay on his back, clutching his arm and groaning. "I'd just got winged. Weren't nothin' I could do to stop her."

"Why didn't you tell one of us?"

"Didn't think about it." The man's voice changed to a whine. "She ain't no account. Why you worried about her, anyway? We got most of the cattle."

Bart lowered his weapon, leaned over the man, and snarled a curse. "She saw me plug that Ranger, that's why." He jerked his head at the remaining four men. Two others had fallen in the battle, and José had been wounded and slipped away at some point. "José go with her?"

"Naw. He limped off a different direction not long ago. Bleedin' pretty bad. He probably won't make it."

"I want two of you to go after him. Hunt him down and kill him."

They'd take time to bury their dead. Their women wouldn't be happy that the bodies of the men weren't returned to the camp, but he refused to cart stinking bodies along the rest of the trip.

Once that was done, the men would start after José. Bart himself would find the girl. José must have schemed to fool Bart by going the opposite direction, so Angel would get away. Bart's lip curled in contempt. No woman could hide her tracks well enough that he couldn't find her. He smirked, thinking about Angel Ramirez wearing men's trousers. He'd always fancied he'd have her one day.

He'd suspected Angel's uncle intended to take her away. When the bullets started flying, he knew—José planned to disappear, leaving the men to fight without him. It was one thing to be hunted as a cattle thief, but a Ranger's death would increase the intensity of a posse's search. No one walked away from this gang unless they were dead.

Angel would agree to be his woman, or die.

Chapter Two

....

Wyoming Territory, 1890
Three years later

Angel Ramirez was tired of being alone and sick of posing as a man. In fact, living a lie these past three years had wearied her beyond measure.

Hunkered on her belly on top of a bluff, she stared at the herd of cattle in the distance, wishing she'd followed her impulse to get a dog. "Talking to myself is just *one* of the things I'm tired of," she muttered under her breath.

Accepting the puppy offered by a family making their way west a few months ago would have helped pass the lonely hours, but it wouldn't have solved her more urgent problem. She couldn't just change into a dress and announce to her boss that he'd hired a woman.

Heaving a sigh, she pushed to her feet. All appeared well, with no gray shadows skulking along the edges of the grazing cattle, seeking to pull down a lone calf.

Angel tugged off her sombrero, loosened her braid, and ran her fingers through her tangled black curls. She shook out her hair and rubbed her scalp, enjoying the feel of the breeze. But she'd best get it braided again and tucked back under her hat where it wouldn't be seen.

She'd finished breaking the last mustang from the small band they'd captured a few weeks ago, and the rancher she worked for was teetering toward letting her go.

Not that she cared, but she had nowhere to go after this short job ended. Angel hadn't minded moving from one ranch to another, but not having a home had started to wear heavily on her.

Angel still missed her uncle José, but he'd made the right decision. Hinson wouldn't have left her alone and probably would've forced her into a marriage she didn't desire—or worse.

Three years was long enough to dress in men's clothing with a tight band around her chest to keep her figure from showing. She'd purposely deepened her voice, speaking mixed Spanish and English, and managed to get by.

She swiped at the moisture dotting her forehead with the back of her sleeve. The sun dipped toward the horizon. Time to toss her bedroll on the back of her saddle and call it a day.

* * * * *

Travis Morgan loped Ranger, his bay gelding, alongside his thirteen-year-old nephew James's buckskin, keeping a constant eye on the boy.

Overall, James had adapted well to the move from San Francisco to Wyoming, though an occasional sullen air hung over him—no doubt due to the death of his father ten months prior. Travis sighed and tugged on his reins, slowing Ranger to a trot. He loved that his widowed sister, Libby, had moved to his home, but sometimes he felt inadequate in helping to raise her son.

"Slow down, James." Travis scanned the grasslands and pointed to the sky. "See those circling buzzards? They've spotted fresh kill."

James turned toward him. Hazel eyes, so much like Libby's, glowed with excitement. "Whad'ya think it is?"

"Not sure. Could be a calf, but I hope not. I'd hate to lose any more stock."

James hunched a shoulder. "But you got thousands."

Travis shoved away his irritation. Until a few months ago, James had lived in a city and didn't understand what it took to survive in this rugged country. "Every calf is important. The ranch wouldn't have thousands if I lost calves every day." Travis kept an eye on the buzzards. Whatever was hurt wasn't too far away.

"Maybe it's something else. Wanna race?" James picked up his reins and leaned forward in the saddle.

Travis grasped Jasper's reins before the boy could act. "Not so fast! In these parts, you look first." He waited for James to relax before releasing his hold on the horse. "Take it slow, all right?"

James nodded, but his lips drooped. "All right." Jasper followed at a quick walk behind Ranger as the gelding moved out.

Travis headed across the open plateau that extended miles to the south. He never tired of this view, even after owning the ranch for six years. Rock cliffs rose in the distance, showing clearly against the clear Wyoming sky. Grasslands that could graze far more than his two thousand head of cattle rose higher than a man's knee over much of this country, and springs and creeks dotted the land.

If only his father would come west to see what he'd accomplished since leaving St. Louis. Had it really been nine years since he'd last seen his only parent? But Derek Morgan was angry that his son hadn't joined his law firm. It still puzzled Travis that Libby had chosen to come to him, but he hated to question his sister as to her motives in this time of grief.

A dark splotch grew more distinct as they drew closer. A black, long-horned cow stood some distance away from a small body lying on the ground. Strange that the mother wasn't standing guard over her baby. A ragged shape rose from the ground next to the lifeless calf, and Travis withdrew his rifle from the scabbard in one easy motion. A gray wolf raised his head and glared in their direction.

James must have seen the predator at the same time, as he sat forward in his saddle and stared. "Is that a wolf?"

"It is." Travis reined his horse to a halt. The calf was dead, so making sure of a kill wasn't vital, but he could scare the wolf and teach James to protect the herd at the same time. "Here." He held his Henry .44-caliber rifle across the open space between the two horses. "Take it."

James stared at the rifle and then up at Travis. "Why?"

"We can't have wolves killing our stock. Take it nice and slow, just like I taught you. "

"Yes, sir." James handled the rifle carefully, keeping it pointed down until he got a tight grip on the stock.

"Good. Aim a little higher than you think you need to."

James nodded, his face alight. "Okay." He placed the rifle against his shoulder and sighted down the barrel.

Travis watched the rangy gray wolf, intent on the feast before him. It was a long shot—over two hundred feet—but it would serve the purpose of scaring the predator away.

James took a deep breath and let it out slowly, just like he'd been taught, then squeezed the trigger. The gun bellowed and jumped in his hands, and James yelped.

A chunk of grass not far from the calf flew up in the air, and the wolf bolted.

"Not bad, son." Travis held out his hand and waited till James gave him the gun. "You just needed to tighten the butt against your shoulder."

James rubbed the sore area and scowled. "Yeah. I got so excited I forgot."

Travis bumped his gelding with his heel and moved toward the carcass. "Let's make sure the mother isn't hurt, and then head home. Don't want to worry your ma."

A lone wolf howled and, seconds later, another voice echoed the refrain. Answering calls resounded as the pack bayed, apparently on the hunt again. He'd hoped this kill was an isolated incident, but from the din in the distance, he guessed his troubles had only begun.

* * * * *

Libby Waters stood at the window in the parlor gazing at the cloud of dust surrounding the two riders approaching the house. Her shoulders slumped in relief as she noted her son bringing up the rear. It was only another hour before sunset. What was her brother thinking, keeping James out so late? She pushed open the door and stepped out, drying her hands on a dishtowel. She worried her bottom lip with her teeth, wondering how much she dare say.

Travis and James reined to a stop in front of the two-story house and swung to the ground.

Libby straightened her shoulders. "I'm glad you're back. I thought something might have happened…" She turned toward Travis. "It's not that I don't trust you with my son." She wrapped her arms around herself and attempted to smile.

Travis nodded. "He won't get hurt, Libby." He looped the reins around the hitching point and stepped onto the porch.

"I'm not used to living so far from town." Her fingers worked at a wrinkle in her skirt. "I'm not complaining, mind you—I love the ranch and I'm grateful to be here—but it's so different from home."

He took off his hat and tossed it onto the porch swing. "It's a better place to raise the boy. And he's always with me or one of my men."

"I know. It might be different if I had another woman close by. It's just so far…"

Nate Taylor, the ranch foreman, strode up to the edge of the porch just as James bounded up the steps, his freckled face lit with excitement. "Ma, guess what?"

Nate tipped his hat at Libby but waited for the boy to finish. The big man had an easy way about him and moved with a fluid grace that didn't mark many men his size.

Libby leaned forward. "I was afraid you wouldn't make it home before dark."

James shook his head and waved an impatient hand. "I was with Uncle Travis." The next words nearly exploded from his mouth. "I shot at a wolf."

Libby stared. "With what?"

The boy rolled his eyes. "A rifle. A wolf killed one of the calves. Uncle Travis let me shoot at it." His grin faded, and he dropped his head. "But I missed."

Travis stepped forward and clapped the boy on the back. "You came close. It was a fine first try."

Libby drew herself up, frowning at Travis. "You let him shoot at a wolf? Why?"

Travis lowered his brows. "Learning to shoot is part of living in the West."

"Fine. Take him out to practice. But teaching him to kill animals?" She glared at her brother. This Western country was hard, and the last thing she wanted was her son turned into a killer—even if his target was a wolf. She'd protected James most of his life, and while she was thankful Travis had taken them in, this wasn't the direction she wanted her boy to take.

Her brother started to answer, but Nate stepped forward. "Boss, I'm sorry to interrupt, but you need to know something."

Travis turned his attention away from Libby. "Let's have it."

"It wasn't just one calf. I was on the west side of the ranch and found two more dead. We've lost at least two dozen this spring, and I'm guessing we'll lose more. There's got to be two or three packs pulling down the young ones." He turned to Libby and withdrew his hat from a head of dark brown hair beginning to show a sprinkling of gray on the edges. "Sorry, Mrs. Waters, but we can't allow critters to kill our stock."

Libby nodded slowly. "I see. I won't say anything more, although I'd appreciate it if you men, rather than my son, did the shooting." She swung toward James. "Take your horse to the barn and unsaddle him."

"But Ma, we haven't had supper yet."

"You need to do your own chores and that includes caring for your mount. It's not Mr. Taylor's job." She waved her fingers. "Go along with you, now." She turned to Travis and braced a hand against the aching small of her back. "I'll reheat dinner. Have you given more thought to hiring household help?"

Travis leaned against a post. "Smokey takes care of fixing breakfast and supper. I can't see why it's too big of an imposition for you to care for your son when he comes in late."

"I do our laundry, cook the noontime meal, help tend the garden, and keep the house clean. I don't understand why you're so against hiring someone to help."

"There are a lot of ranch expenses you aren't aware of, Libby. If it becomes too much of a burden, I'll consider it." He shook his head. "But let's see how things go for a while."

Libby nodded to Nate and Travis. "I'll leave you gentlemen to your discussion." She turned toward the door.

"Evening, ma'am," Nate said as she walked away.

Travis could be so dense at times, just like when they were kids, she fumed. Sometimes she wanted to shake her younger brother.

But now wasn't the time. Why couldn't he understand the stress she felt, moving here from San Francisco? Would it hurt him so much to bring in a woman to help, even part-time? She'd hold on to his promise to consider it and pray he'd agree soon.

* * * * *

Travis shook his head, working to stifle his frustration. Libby's husband had hired more household help than she'd known what to do with, and as far as Travis was concerned, she'd grown soft as a result. Most women in the West would never think of asking for outside help. But she'd been widowed less than a year and never lived this far from town.

Nate placed his hat back on his head after Libby disappeared through the door. He raised his eyebrows at Travis. "Hope I didn't rile your sister too much, Boss, and add to your troubles."

Travis waved at the chair on the porch and took the one near it. "Libby needs a little time, that's all. I'll have to put some thought into what I can do to help ease her mind, but right now I'm worried about the stock we're losing."

"Yes, sir." Nate stretched his long legs in front of him.

Travis tapped his fingers against the wicker arm of the chair. "I don't have the manpower to put a cowboy on it full-time, and finding good cowhands is getting harder."

"I heard some talk from a puncher over at the Broken Bar Ranch. Seems he heard tell of a fella who's good with horses and an expert tracker as well. Mexican man—doesn't speak much English. Might put out word we could use him—see if he'll mosey this way."

Travis shook his head. "If he's already got a job, why would he want to move?"

"Might, for the right money." Nate pushed up from his chair and hitched his belt. "I'll ask around, see what he's used to getting paid."

"Pay him what you have to. The calves we're losing will cost us more than a tracker's wages. He can figure out where the varmints are holed up, and you boys can clean them out. Besides, having another hand with the horses would be a plus."

* * * * *

Angel broke camp, swung onto Bella, and slid her rifle into its scabbard. Thankfully it was payday. A shiver ran across her shoulder blades. Another nightmare had haunted the early morning hours, dredging up the memory of the outlaw who'd made her life miserable just a few years ago. She'd heard word from time to time about the old rustler band. They'd fled Texas after killing the Texas Ranger and his posse and moved their operation to New Mexico. As much as she'd love to see her uncle José, she couldn't take the chance Hinson would hear of a young Mexican man who was a crack shot with a rifle, so she'd gone north to Wyoming. She bumped Bella into a canter. Hopefully Uncle José had left the band and started over.

Angel cantered across an open pasture and slowed her mare to a walk. Several ranch hands milled in front of the barn, and Mr. Granger, the tough-as-dried-leather owner of the Broken Bar Ranch, stood outside handing out the pay envelopes. Good. She reined Bella to a halt.

Granger swung around, and his bushy brows lowered. "Angelo. You got a telegram. Climb off that mare and take a gander. Got your pay, as well." He thrust out two envelopes as she stepped forward.

"Telegram? ¿Quién le mandé?" She kept her words short, her accent strong, and her sombrero low. She hated payday when all the men were here.

"I told you, I don't speak much Mexican." He turned to one of his men. "What'd Angelo say?"

"He wants to know who sent it."

Granger shrugged. "No idea." He gave it to her and turned to the next man.

Angel stuffed the envelope with her pay into the back pocket of her denim trousers. She grabbed Bella's reins and drew the horse a few feet away, stopping in the shade of a wide-spread tree. The telegram was penned in neat script.

Sundance Ranch needs help. Stop. Will pay top wages. Stop. Come soon. Stop. Travis Morgan. End.

She tucked the paper into her shirt pocket, a deep sense of relief washing over her. "Boss?"

Granger turned his head toward her. "Yeah."

"*Nuevo* job. You know Sundance Ranch?"

The big man motioned to his foreman, and the slight, stooped cowhand strode over to join them. "Where's the Sundance Ranch? They want Angelo to work for them. Right, Angelo?"

She dipped her head. "Sí."

The foreman drew off his hat and scratched his head under thinning hair. "Well now, *cerca del Sundance*. You know—the place the Sundance kid hails from." He pushed his hat back onto his head.

Angel maintained a quizzical expression. It would only embarrass Mr. Granger if he discovered her secret now. No sense in allowing him to know she understood every word.

Granger grunted and waved the man away. "Thanks, Sam." He turned to Angel. "I hate lettin' you go, Angelo, but it's your call. Go east. One hour from Sundance." He held up a finger. "*Uno* hour. Sí?"

She grinned and nodded. "Sí. *Gracias*."

"*No tener prisa*." He frowned. "Hope I said that right—no rush. Get some grub and bunk here. Start *mañana*."

"Gracias, Señor Granger. Eat, then ride." Angel headed toward the barn. She'd rub down her horse, give her a nosebag of grain, and hit the trail. The boss had tried to get her to stay in the bunkhouse before, but that wasn't an option. Best ride an hour or so from the ranch where she was still in familiar territory, then get an early start in the morning.

She stripped Bella's saddle and turned her out in a pen to roll. Her horse deserved a short rest before riding out again. This new job had come just in time. No more hiding her long curls under her sombrero and speaking broken English. Once she arrived at the new ranch she'd be riding as Angel Ramirez. She only hoped the desperation in that telegram would last after her new boss discovered he'd hired a woman instead of a man.

Chapter Three

Angel shifted in her saddle to ease the ache in her back. She'd been riding straight through for eight hours now, with only a couple stops to water her horse. A few minutes ago she'd skirted Sundance, loath to meet any strangers. The town was located on the edge of the Black Hills, and the founders had settled in a wide basin at the foot of Sundance Mountain. She'd kept away from towns most of her life and didn't feel comfortable venturing into one now. The ranch lay about six miles northeast of town, not far from the Montana border, so she might be riding on ranch property now. At least she was close; she was thankful for that.

A whisper of her spur against Bella's side moved the mare into a swinging lope. The country had flattened out. This section was cattle country, with grassland as far as she could see, and only an occasional butte or rocky gully marked the land. The grass could easily feed thousands of stock. Of course, more cattle meant an increase in predators.

After covering what must be a couple of miles she spotted a roofline. Reining in her horse, she stood in the stirrups. A cluster of buildings loomed ahead, with a two-story house off to the side. The lane leading to the house had an upright log set in the ground on each side of the hard-packed surface, with a slender pole nailed across the top between the two. Someone had burned the words SUNDANCE

Ranch into a board that hung from the crosspiece. Horses grazed in a pasture to the side of a barn.

"It looks like we made it, Bella." She ran her gloved hand down her horse's neck and picked up the reins. "Let's go see what our new boss thinks of us." The mare broke into a canter and Angel let her go, the pace fitting the pounding of her heart.

Angel wasn't in a rush to reveal her identity. She tucked a strand of hair back inside her sombrero, suddenly glad that trail dust coated her body and that she'd worn a loose-fitting jacket. What if she'd made the wrong decision in coming out of hiding, and this man regretted his offer? She reined Bella to a trot. It might be best to take things easy.

Bella slowed to a stop in the dusty area between the barn and the house. Angel surveyed the empty space, wondering at the lack of activity. She nudged Bella toward the hitching rail in front of the wood-sided house.

The front door gave a slight squeak and swung open. A pretty blond woman stood framed by the doorway. She appeared to be at least ten years older than Angel and wore her hair in a bun. Small flowers dotted her lavender skirt, and gray buttons closed the front of the plain-cut blouse. A quizzical expression tugged at her mouth, but her eyes were welcoming. "Good day, sir. May I help you?"

Angel hesitated, disliking this continued deception. What would it be like to live in a house like this and dress in fine clothes? She wanted to be free of her outlaw past, but tracking varmints and breaking horses was the only life she knew. A slight jerk brought the brim of her sombrero down over her forehead. "Howdy, ma'am. I've come in response to your husband's telegram." Angel purposely dropped her voice a notch, and her sense of integrity dropped with it.

"My husband?" The woman moved away from the door, letting the screen slam shut behind her. "Oh, you mean Travis." She took a step forward and rested her hand on one of the porch posts. "I'm Libby Waters. Would you care for something cold to drink?"

"No. Thanks. Any idea when Mr. Morgan will return?"

"It's near supper time, so he should be here soon. May I ask what telegram?"

Angel wondered if she should tell this woman her business. She decided to risk it. "Asking me to work for him."

"So he's hiring another hand for the ranch. I shouldn't be surprised." Her voice held a bit of an edge.

Angel scrambled to understand the direction the conversation had taken.

"Pardon my manners." Libby shrugged, and sadness flashed across her fine-boned features. "That's not your worry." She shaded her eyes against the sun lying low on the horizon. "Someone's coming."

Five men all riding bay or sorrel horses trotted up the lane and reined their mounts in front of the barn. A sudden panic gripped Angel. She nearly turned her horse and fled. In the three years of living like a man she'd grown comfortable with the role, and the thought of leaving the security it provided choked her.

Then, squaring her shoulders, she faced the riders, watching them veer toward the barn. More than anything she longed to be true to herself. If only she could muster the courage to remove her sombrero and introduce herself properly to this man.

* * * * *

Travis, Nate, and three of the other cowboys dismounted in front of the barn. Travis wiped the sweat from his forehead with the back of his sleeve. It had been another frustrating day with heavy losses to the wolves and no word from his telegram. After supper he'd probably have to deal with Libby's repeated requests for household help and talk to her about James. She continued to interfere with his attempts to turn the boy into a man.

On top of everything else, he'd gotten another letter from his father urging him to "Give up this foolishness and come back to St. Louis." Why couldn't the man understand Travis's need to succeed on his own? It shamed him that his father didn't trust his judgment. His stomach hardened into a knot. *Shake it off.* It wasn't the time to worry about it, with stock dying and the range overrun with wolves.

Libby waved and stepped to the edge of the porch. "Travis. There's someone to see you."

He'd already noted the lone rider sitting a black mare near the hitching rail, a bedroll and set of saddlebags behind the saddle. Slight of build, the man had a sombrero pulled low. A drifter looking for work or his tracker come at last? He handed his reins to Nate and walked toward the rider. "What can I do for you, mister?"

"I'm Angelo de Luca. You sent a telegram saying you needed a tracker."

He nodded and looked the man over but couldn't see much of his face with the sombrero shading it, other than smooth cheeks and chin beneath the coating of dust. "So you're Angelo de Luca. You're younger than I expected. I need someone who can ride, shoot, and track." He narrowed his eyes. "You sure you can do this job?"

The young man stiffened. "You sent the telegram. You must have heard of my reputation."

Travis took a step toward the edge of the porch and rubbed the day-old growth on his chin. "In that case, glad you made it. I'd about given up hope when I didn't get a reply."

De Luca shrugged. "I headed out as soon as I got your wire. Took awhile to get here."

"No matter. That all your gear?"

"It's all I need."

Travis stared for a long moment. Something about this man felt strange. Maybe it was the pitch of his voice or the fact he wasn't speaking Spanish. Someone got it wrong. "Nate will take you to the bunkhouse." He waved toward a single-story building with a wide porch on the front, just to the side of the barn.

Thank the good Lord he'd finally get on top of the predator problem. Maybe one thing would get solved, and he could move on. He'd build his herd to the point where his father *must* recognize his success. The man had seen him as a disappointment for long enough.

He raised his voice. "Nate. De Luca's arrived."

The older man raised his hand. "Be right there."

At least they'd found another experienced hand. He relaxed and smiled. Once he dealt with Libby's needs, their immediate problems were over.

* * * * *

Angel turned in her saddle. Travis Morgan stared into her eyes and her stomach did a somersault. Tall, broad shoulders, dark brown hair. Must be somewhere in his late twenties. She liked his purposeful walk—he appeared to be a man who knew what he wanted. Her muscles tensed as he drew a step closer. She'd hoped to talk to her new boss privately. Maybe land the job, then gently let him know of the—well—altered situation. But no way would she sleep in a bunkhouse with a bunch of cowboys.

She straightened her shoulders and raised her chin. Time to end this. "Do I have the job?"

"You do."

"I won't sleep in the bunkhouse, Mr. Morgan."

The muscles around his mouth tightened, firming his square jaw. The deep blue eyes darkened a shade. "All the men bunk there, unless they're on the range overnight. No exceptions."

Out of the corner of her eye she noticed the cowboy called Nate step closer. He wore a serious expression. She'd not make friends by refusing to bunk with the men. "I'll stay out on the range. Same as I do on every job."

Travis took his time pondering her response. "Not unless you're too far from the ranch come nightfall. My ranch hands eat at my table for the morning and evening meal, and report to me each night. There are a couple of empty bunks, so you're not putting anyone out."

Angel's heart plummeted clear down to her dust-caked boots. There seemed no hope for it—she should have done this sooner. She tipped back her hat to meet Travis's gaze. "I'm afraid there's a slight problem."

She swung off of her horse and removed her bulky jacket, hanging it on the saddle horn. Snatching her sombrero from her head, Angel allowed her hair to cascade over her shoulders.

Chapter Four

....

Travis gazed into the dust-smudged visage of what must surely be a woman. He noted the long black curls and the wide brown eyes. The perfectly formed lips and her now obvious curves contradicted her attire, not to mention the gun strapped to her hip. His gaze strayed downward almost without his permission and flew back to her face, his own burning with shame. He'd never gawked at a woman's figure before, and he'd have to repent for that later. Yes, he could definitely attest that this *was* a woman.

Nate cleared his throat. "Guess I'd best check on the men and horses, Boss." He removed his hat and nodded. "Ma'am." Just as quickly as he'd arrived, he turned tail and ran—like a scared jack-rabbit fleeing from a hawk. The least he could've done was stay and help Travis dig out of this hole. Travis shoved his hat to the back of his head.

He faced the girl again. Large eyes stared up into his. He'd thought his sister's pretty, but these dark pools left him short of breath. "Who are *you*?" His words came out rough, and he noted the sharp intake of the girl's breath.

"Angel Ramirez." She withdrew the sombrero from under her arm and shoved it back onto her black curls.

He waited, sorting through his memory.

She lifted one shoulder and sighed. "Angel *de Luca* Ramirez." She

41

paused another moment. "Angelo de Luca. The tracker and horseman you sent for."

Travis felt as though he'd been bucked from a bronco and the wind knocked from him. He couldn't believe it—wouldn't believe it. Women didn't work for a living and pass themselves off as men. What he'd give to only have Libby's expectations to deal with. He groaned. Now there were two strong-willed women on the ranch, and he didn't feel equipped to deal with either.

* * * * *

Angel stared at the man who held her future in his hands and waited. If she didn't land this job, she was finished. His blue gaze, deeper than a desert spring, made something flutter in her chest. But from his stern look he was none too happy with her information.

Then the stunned expression slowly softened to one of disbelief. "I beg your pardon?" His words held a hint of amusement. "I sent my telegram to a man, not a woman."

Angel stiffened. The last thing she'd tolerate was someone laughing at her. She'd earned her place, and no one would take that away. "You sent your telegram to *me*." She jabbed her thumb toward her chest. "*I* am Angelo de Luca. But my real name is Angel de Luca Ramirez."

A grin creased Travis's face, setting off a dimple in the corner of his cheek. "So who put you up to this? One of my cowboys?" He turned away and stared at the man standing nearby. "Nate. Who hired this girl to pretend to be de Luca? The jig is up, but it was a good joke." He turned to Angel. "They find you in the dance hall?"

Angel's blood thrummed in her ears. The smell of fresh-cut hay permeated the air, lending a false feeling of contentment in sharp contrast to the charged atmosphere.

She uttered a low cry and leapt at the man, swinging her closed fist. There'd been plenty of times growing up where she'd had to fight the boys in the band, and she'd learned to hold her own. Her knuckles connected with the man's chin, and he staggered backward.

He caught himself, rubbed his chin, and stared. "What was that for?"

She kept her hands up for a moment, then slowly dropped them to her hips and glared. "For laughing at me. I'm one of the best marksmen and trackers in this country, and I'll not be slighted like that."

"Sorry, lady. I'm not buying it. You've earned whatever someone paid you. I'll admit, you look like the real thing, and you throw a punch like one, but it's time to come clean."

Nate stepped up and tapped Travis's arm. "Uh…Boss?"

Travis jerked his chin to the side. "Go drag the fella out here who came up with this idea. I've had enough." He waved Nate toward the bunkhouse.

Angel turned and stalked for her horse. Rarely did she allow her rifle to be far from her reach, but running into this man had rattled her. She removed it from its sheath and checked the load. Full. Good. She drew a couple of two-bit pieces and a silver dollar out of her saddlebag and walked back.

She wouldn't lower herself by talking to these men again until they understood. She withdrew her Colt revolver and placed the rifle against a nearby post. Without further warning, she threw the coin as high as her strength would allow, whipped up her revolver, and fired. The handgun boomed and the smell of gunpowder lingered in the air as the silver piece jerked with the impact of the bullet.

"You." She motioned toward Nate, then dug a silver dollar from her pocket. "Put this on edge, face out, on the butt of that branch." She flipped the coin through the air and smirked when he caught it.

"Huh?" The man stared at her like he didn't have a brain.

She waved at the tree that must be at least fifty feet away and pointed at the dead branch positioned just above his head. "Put it against the trunk on that branch." She spoke slowly, turned, picked up her rifle, and walked the opposite direction.

"Hey! What're you doing?" Travis called after her, but she ignored him until she'd paced off another hundred feet. Far enough for a decent demonstration, but nothing like what she could do if she put her mind to it. Right now while shaking with anger was no time to push her limits.

She swung around. Nate stood near the tree. The sun glinted off the face of the silver dollar where he'd placed it. Perfect. "Move away from the tree."

"What?"

She raised her voice. "Move away from the tree. Unless you'd like a chunk of bark in your face." She cocked the rifle and raised it to her shoulder.

The man bolted, taking three leaps and landing not far from his boss.

Silence settled over the clearing, but Angel saw motion from the corner of her eye. She lowered the rifle and swung to the side. Three long-legged, dusty cowboys and a short, scrawny one stood gawking near what must be the bunkhouse. One whistled low between his teeth, and a big grin split the mug of another. Angel turned her head and ignored them.

"Hey, Boss. I'll give you two-bits she makes it," a voice called.

"Shut up, Arizona, or I'll make *you* the next target," Nate growled.

The man obeyed, but another cowboy took Arizona up on his bet.

Angel grinned. Their boss was due for a surprise, and she hoped these men would rub his face in it when she finished.

The door of the house banged open, and the woman who'd welcomed Angel stood on the porch, a boy by her side.

Angel hefted the rifle again and placed it firmly against her shoulder. No time to think of the people watching—she had to make this shot. Her reputation, her virtue, and her very identity had been questioned. She focused on the small, gleaming disk at the base of the branch, drew in a deep breath, and exhaled. Her finger tightened on the trigger, and she squeezed it slowly. The report of the gun sounded loud in her ear, but her focus stayed trained on the dollar. A split second later, the coin leapt in the air and completed a dizzying dance before landing a full stride away from Travis Morgan's boots.

* * * * *

Travis rubbed his chin where the girl's fist had landed as she walked toward him. How had he thought anything about her feminine? Ladylike she was not. More like a wildcat in trousers with a face pretty enough to make most men drop their guard. He stared at her as she lowered the .45-caliber Winchester. She was an excellent shot, he'd give her that. But Angelo de Luca? He shook his head and groaned. What in the world had he gotten himself into?

A sudden whoop split the air, and the four cowboys who'd stood frozen near the bunkhouse door came to life. Charlie, Wren, Arizona, and Bud all raced one another, pushing and shoving to reach the girl first. Smokey, their sixty-year-old grub slinger, ambled behind, a wide grin creasing his sun-bronzed face.

"Man, did you see that shootin'?" Arizona's voice rose above the rest as the blond cowpoke beat the rest of the men to where the girl stood.

Wren caught up and elbowed him out of the way. The man might be built like a banty rooster, but he was wiry and tough when riled.

"Outta the way, men. I wanna shake the hand of the woman who made that shot," he crowed.

Charlie and Bud jostled for a spot beside the bemused girl, who didn't seem able to take in the sudden change in the atmosphere. Charlie leaned close and stared at the rifle. "That one of them new Winchester repeaters I been hearin' about? Saw an advertisement over to the store, but ain't seen one of 'em in the flesh." He extended a hand. "Can I hold it?"

The girl came alive. She jerked the rifle close and took a step back. "No one handles my guns." She turned toward Travis and raised her brows, the rifle cradled in her arms. "Well?"

He crossed the open space with Nate stalking behind. "Well, what? That was great shooting." The words came out grudging and harsh—not the way he'd typically address a woman—but the painful memory of that punch left him on edge. Besides, the girl's claim rankled. Range gossip couldn't have gotten the facts so off kilter, neglecting to mention that Angelo de Luca was a woman.

"Do you believe me? I'm the person you hired." Her expression grew cold. She slipped her hand into her breast pocket and removed a folded piece of paper. "See for yourself."

He reluctantly took the paper. The telegram he'd sent lay exposed on his palm. "How? Why?" He scratched his head.

Nate stepped up and clapped him on the back. "Hey, Boss. Looks like you've hired a crack shot. If she can ride and track like she shoots, I'd say you've got a winner." A beaming grin lit the man's face. He swung toward the girl and his smile faded. "I think what the boss is trying to ask is how do you happen to be a girl, instead of the man we expected."

Angel stared at him like he'd asked something incredibly stupid, then a smile peeked out. "How do I happen to be a girl? I reckon I was born one."

Travis felt a surge of annoyance. He'd wanted to hire a man and got a young woman. "That's not what Nate meant." He folded his arms over his chest and tried not to glare. The cowhands hovered in the background, and by their moonstruck expressions this girl had more than captivated their interest. He swung around. "Find something useful to do."

Arizona's lips drooped, and he kicked a pebble. "Aw, Boss. We'd like to get better acquainted with the lady."

"Now." Travis pointed at the barn and the men scurried away, but more than one cast a glance over his shoulder.

Smokey stepped forward. "Guess I'll rustle up some grub." He tugged at the brim of his hat, smiled at the girl, and moseyed back toward the house.

Nate stood beside him, still staring at the rifle.

Travis held up the telegram. "I'd appreciate an explanation."

The girl sobered. "Fine. I've worked for the past three years under my mother's maiden name, de Luca. I'm using my own name now. Ramirez."

"Why not use your own name to begin with? And why let people think you were a man?"

She bent an intent look on him. "Would you have hired a woman?"

He felt like he'd been punched again and wasn't sure how to answer. He wouldn't have asked a woman to take a man's job and probably wouldn't hire her even now. But her expression silenced him.

She nodded. "That's what I thought. No one else would either. I don't have any formal schooling, so I can't teach. I've never learned to sew, cook, or any of the things women do." She stared at him coolly. "So what kind of job would that leave me?"

Heat rose in his cheeks. Only one occupation remained. "I apologize for my remarks. They were—inappropriate."

She rested the rifle butt on the ground and gripped the muzzle. "They were. But you wouldn't have hired me if you hadn't heard about my ability to track, ride, and shoot. I hope you're not going back on your offer."

He shook his head, regret coursing through him, but it couldn't be helped. "I'm afraid I am, Miss Ramirez. I don't intend to hire a woman to do a man's job, no matter how good a shot you are."

"Why not? I've done it for three years."

Nate shifted at Travis's side. "Boss?"

Travis gave a slight shake of his head. "Just a minute, Nate." He turned back to the girl. "You did it under false pretenses."

Nate stepped forward. "Boss, give me a minute."

Travis pushed down his irritation. His foreman had proven his wisdom over the past few years, and he'd do well to listen. "All right. What?"

"The ranch is getting overrun with wolves, and Arizona spotted a mountain lion yesterday. We don't got a lot of choice at the moment."

"You're suggesting we hire this woman?"

Angel stiffened. "My name is Angel Ramirez, not 'this woman.'"

Travis gave a slow nod. "My apologies, ma'am."

Nate tipped his head to the side. "I do. Leastwise, for now. If she can track 'em, the boys can clean 'em out. Plus, we got some rank horses needing work."

"I don't like it. She might come recommended, but she's still a woman."

Angel took a step toward him. "And that's a problem—why?"

Travis whipped off his hat and slapped it against his leg. "You saw how the men reacted. It's different with Libby, her being my sister and newly widowed and all. You'll create all sorts of havoc among my cowboys. Besides, you can't sleep in the bunkhouse."

Angel shrugged. "I stay clear of the men. The job is all I care about. And I *never* stay in a bunkhouse. I live on the range."

"That may have worked before, but not now. I can't have the men sneaking out at night trying to find your camp so they can spark you."

She bristled. "No one gets close to my camp, day or night, without me knowing it. And I don't flirt with men."

Travis shook his head. "I won't have you sleeping out unless you're at least a half day's ride from the ranch. If I let you stay on, you'll have to take a room in the house."

Angel started to protest, but Travis stopped her. "That's my condition. My sister will act as chaperone when I'm at home. I'll give you the job until I find someone else, but you stay at the house. Agreed?"

Angel bit her lip. Her face reflected her struggle, and sympathy tugged at his heart, but he didn't relent. It was bad enough agreeing to let her stay on, but he'd be hog-tied if he'd allow her to sleep on the range with his men within easy riding distance.

"All right. But I don't cook or clean, and I don't aim to learn. I track critters and break horses. Period. You and your sister had best understand, or I'll move on."

Travis closed his eyes for a moment, then opened them and slowly nodded. "Understood. Now I just have to break the news to Libby."

* * * * *

Angel glared at Travis Morgan. The nerve of the man. If she'd be such a burden on his sister, why insist she live in the house? If she had another job lined up, she'd hit the saddle. But she didn't. A feeling of helplessness flooded Angel. She detested not having any options.

"Don't worry about it." Angel made a hasty decision and met

Travis's gaze. "I'll find something else. No need to upset your sister by asking a stranger to share her home."

Travis studied her. "That's not necessary. This is *my* home, and Libby will welcome anyone I choose to invite. Besides, it's not for long."

Angel's knuckles tingled. She was glad she'd punched him. He still didn't believe she could do the job. "Fine. I'm not happy about staying here, either. But I'll earn my keep. I'll not give you reason to regret you hired me, even if the job only lasts a few days."

"Could you"—he hesitated and glanced toward the ranch house—"wait here a few minutes?"

She shrugged. "I'm in no hurry."

He strode across the dirt clearing and didn't look back. He opened the front door of the house and closed it carefully behind him. Libby had seemed nice enough, but Angel wouldn't lay any bets on the woman welcoming her—even if the house belonged to her brother. The few women at the outlaw stronghold were jealous of the little they owned and guarded it closely. Some had shown her kindness when she was young but treated her differently when she showed signs of impending womanhood. No. She couldn't see this sister of Travis Morgan welcoming a strange woman into her domain, regardless of whose name appeared on the deed.

Chapter Five
....

A boot tramped on the packed ground behind her. She slipped her fingers around the butt of her gun and waited. No one spoke, but she sensed the person shifting his weight and edging closer. She whipped the revolver out of her holster and spun around, holding the weapon waist high. "What do you want?"

A wide-eyed boy gaped at her, and his hands slowly rose to chest height. "Please don't shoot, lady. I didn't mean any harm."

Angel stared for a moment, then holstered her gun. "It isn't a good idea to sneak up on a person. Who are you?"

The color slowly returned to the boy's face. "James. My uncle Travis owns this ranch." He straightened his shoulders. "I've never seen a woman in men's clothes before."

"Well, now you have. Didn't your mama teach you it's not polite to stare? You should close your mouth before something flies into it." The way the boy looked at her rankled. Were all the men on this ranch either rude or ignorant?

"Why are you dressed that way?" He ran his tongue over his lips. "Would you really have shot me?"

She tipped her head to the side. "I've never killed a little kid yet, and I don't aim to start now."

James's head jerked up. "I'm not a kid. I'm thirteen years old—almost a grown man. And you didn't answer my question."

"I track varmints and work horses. I can't very well do that in a dress, now can I?" She allowed a small smile to tilt up the corner of her lips.

"What kind of varmints? Wolves?" An eager light sprang to his eyes.

"Yes. Wolves, coyotes, cougars, bear—depending on what's killing the stock. I understand a couple of wolf packs are working this area."

"I shot at one a week ago. Uncle Travis lent me his rifle." The excited expression faded. "But I missed."

Angel glanced toward the door. Still no sign of anyone stirring. She could only imagine the conversation between Travis and his sister. She turned back to the boy. "We all miss sometimes. It takes practice to shoot well. I didn't hit the first target I shot at, either." No sense in telling him it was a cougar that had pulled down a colt the band acquired in the dead of the night.

"Would you teach me to shoot?" James took a step forward and eyed her gun.

Angel raised both hands and shook her head. "Not my job, boy. That's up to your uncle. I was hired to track varmints and break horses, not mollycoddle youngsters." His face fell, and Angel immediately regretted her words. She'd gotten along with most of the children raised in the band, so why be ornery with this one? "Of course, if I ever have time…"

James's mouth broke into a wide smile. "Golly, thanks! Are you sleeping in the bunkhouse?"

Angel stifled a chuckle. "No. That wouldn't be—appropriate. I'll be staying in a spare room in your uncle's house. And I don't know for how long. Until he finds someone else to do my job, I guess."

The hair on Angel's arms prickled. She whirled around just as someone cleared his throat. She stared into the eager faces of two of the cowboys who'd watched her earlier.

* * * * *

Libby stood with her arms folded. "That—girl—is going to live *where*?"

Travis sighed. "I can't let her stay in the bunkhouse with the men and it's not safe for her to sleep out on the range. That leaves one option—my house."

She sank onto the sofa in the large living area and drew a pillow onto her lap. "But she's been sleeping on the range for the past three years. What does it matter if she continues?" Her fingers tightened around the embroidered fabric, and she forced them to relax.

"Because she was masquerading as a man, but now everyone knows she's a woman. It wouldn't be safe for her to sleep outside."

"You don't trust your own men?"

A muscle in Travis's jaw clenched. "Yes. But she's an attractive woman—or would be if she dressed properly—and she might be a temptation for some of the men to—visit." He walked over to his favorite stuffed chair and sat. "It's not like she'll be here long, Libby. I don't see why it needs to be a problem."

She bit her lip. Sometimes her brother could be so thick-headed. "So you've decided to hire her?"

"For the time being—until someone qualified turns up."

"I find it hard to believe that a woman can do an adequate job." She wrinkled her nose. "Tracking and killing predators out on the range. It's such a horrible occupation, and so unladylike."

"I'm not hiring her to kill the varmints, Lib, just spot them. My cowboys will take care of cleaning them out, but I can't spare the men to track every wolf, bear, and cat threatening my herd."

A thought propelled her forward on her seat. "I have an idea, Travis." Real hope surged through her heart for the first time since she'd arrived at this lonely wasteland.

He raised one brow. "Go ahead."

"She can work in the house. I need someone to help with the cooking and cleaning, and this girl would be ideal."

Travis shook his head. "No. She has a job, and she'll be at it most of the day—sometimes well into the evening."

Libby pushed down a frown. "All of the men take two meals here, and Smokey can't keep up with all the work. I help clean up after we're finished, and do all the laundry, as well as changing the linens and trying to keep up with the dust that blows in, and the mud you track in. Think of the time I could give to the garden. We'd have fresh vegetables instead of relying on so many canned items from the store."

"I'm sorry, but I made a promise when I hired her. She said she won't do household chores and I agreed. I'm in a bind and don't have a choice."

Frustration rose in Libby's breast and she scowled, not caring if it made him angry. "You can pay for a woman to track down poor animals, but you can't hire any household help?" She jumped from her seat. "I'm sorry you think so little of your own family, Travis."

"That's enough, Lib. You know she's not tracking down 'poor animals,' but deadly wolves killing my stock. The very same stock whose sale puts food on the table and keeps this place going. Besides, she'll be busy riding some of the young horses, as well." He grasped the arms of the chair and pushed to his feet. "The time might come when we bring a woman in to help, but not now. I imagine Miss Ramirez will take care of her own laundry, although she doesn't appear to have an abundance of clothing. Any other household chores will continue to fall on you."

When he walked toward the door, hopelessness swamped Libby. This Western life was too hard, too demanding. Papa had catered to everything Mother wanted when Libby was growing up—but then after Mother's death, he'd changed too. As much as she loved Travis, she wouldn't have chosen to live here instead of with Papa, but Papa had grown so cold and demanding these past few years.

Loneliness had been her constant companion after her husband's death. She'd hoped to make a friend in the area, but the ranches were so far apart, and one church service per week didn't afford much time to get acquainted. Most of the women had their own households to look after and couldn't traipse around the country visiting heartsick widows.

She'd make the best of these circumstances with this new employee. Maybe the woman was lonely, as well, and in need of a friend. Surely when Miss Ramirez finished her outside chores, she'd understand the need to help inside—and work shared by a friend always seemed lighter. Yes. Her mood lifted, and hope surged into her mind. Living in this desolate wilderness might be endurable now. This new situation could easily be an answer to her prayers.

* * * * *

Angel rested her palm lightly on the butt of her revolver as the two cowboys edged closer. The tall, blond, handsome one covered the remaining few yards with a long stride while the short, bowlegged cowboy hobbled along beside him. Both wore horsehair chaps, dusty boots, and the tall one had a gun on his hip. A day's stubble edged the jaw of the shorter man, while the other's shone as though recently groomed. If it weren't for the gun, she'd think the man a dandy.

They halted a couple of yards away and stared, then leaned close together and whispered. The short one raised his hands, grinned, and backed off a step. The well-built cowpoke hooked his thumbs into the leather waistband of his chaps and sauntered forward. "Howdy, ma'am. Nice day, ain't it?" He grinned and waited for her reply.

Angel gawked at the man, then swung her gaze to his partner. What did they want? She relaxed her grip on her revolver.

As the silence stretched, the man's grin faded, and a red stain crept up his neck and into his cheeks. He dropped his head and scuffed his boot in the dust. "Guess I didn't learn the manners my mama tried to teach me." His shoulders squared, and he raised his chin. "I beg your pardon, ma'am, I shoulda introduced myself."

His friend grabbed his arm and hissed close to his ear, "Let's slope out of here. You done made an idj't of yerself." They took a step back, the shorter man still clutching the taller one's arm.

Angel broke from her stupor. "Wait. What *are* your names?"

The bowlegged cowboy's ears turned pink, and he yanked the hat from his head. "I'm Wren, and this here long drink of water is Arizona."

The cowboy in question withdrew his hat and bowed from the waist, leaning over until his sombrero almost swept the ground. He rose back up and laid his hat over his heart. "I am mighty pleased to meet you, ma'am. Sorry we got off on the wrong foot." Arizona shot a quick glance at Wren and took a step toward Angel. "You're some handy with that sidearm and rifle, and a purty woman to boot. Where'd you learn to shoot so good?"

Angel's smile faded. "My uncle taught me."

Wren edged closer. "He must be a fine man. Don't know too many uncles what would learn a girl to shoot."

She stiffened. "Yes." These two cowpokes were getting too personal. "I need to get my things." Angel turned on her heel and strode toward her horse. Time to put Bella up and find her a bait of grain.

"Aw, Wren, why'd you have to go and spook her? She was just warming up to us and you spoiled it." Arizona's drawl drifted after Angel as she sought refuge inside the barn.

* * * * *

Travis let the front door bang behind him. Maybe he should ease up on Libby and not expect so much. After all, she'd experienced a difficult loss a short time ago and was still adjusting to Western life. He settled his hat onto his head. Time to regain control of this day.

Heading toward the barn, he drew up short. James was standing at the nearly closed door of the barn, peeking inside. "James! What're you doing?"

The boy leapt as if shot. "Nothin', Uncle Travis. Honest."

"I hope you're not bothering Miss Ramirez."

"She's going to help me learn to shoot better."

Travis wagged his head and stifled a groan. "I didn't hire her to spend time with you."

The boy dropped his eyes but not before Travis saw a glint of something—anger…rebellion?

James spun away from Travis. "I'll go see if Ma needs me." He raced away from the barn.

It was bad enough that his cowboys were smitten with the woman, but James as well? He hoped the boy wasn't spying on Angelo. Angel. Miss Ramirez. He ground his teeth. What was he supposed to call the woman, anyway? Most of the men had nicknames, or went by their last name. No one stood on formality with a hand on a ranch, but he didn't see himself calling her Angel. What kind of name was that for a girl, anyway?

How did he get saddled with a female cowhand who was too

fetching for her own good? He hadn't been smitten with a woman since he was nineteen, and boy howdy, he'd guard his heart against this one if it was the last thing he did. Making the ranch a success must remain his top priority. He'd be hanged if he'd let his men forget it. First thing, he'd ask around about someone who could take her place. Trouble wearing britches didn't belong on his ranch.

Chapter Six

....

Angel swung her feet over the edge of the narrow mattress and stared around the room, prodding her memory like a rogue steer. She rubbed the small of her back and winced. After three years of bunking on the hard ground, this bed was a mite too soft.

It looked like the sun had risen at least a half hour ago, and sounds of breakfast preparations came from beyond her door. Angel's heart sank at the thought of sitting down to a meal with all those people. The boss had mentioned having his cowboys share the meals with his family. Social skills were *not* her strong suit.

A glance around her room revealed a tall bureau with a small oval mirror above it. An earthenware basin, pitcher, hairbrush, and comb set rested on top of a fancy bit of lace. She crossed the room and reached out a hesitant hand, touching the pitcher. What beautiful colors. A heart hunger rose inside her. She snatched back her hand and gripped it with her other one. How foolish. She was a tracker. Not a woman deserving of pretty things.

She started to turn away but paused when she glimpsed herself in the mirror. Black curls hung in disarray well past her shoulders, and touches of dust smudged her cheeks. Somehow she'd missed a few spots before falling into bed last night. Dare she use the hairbrush and comb? And maybe even the ribbon lying alongside? Braiding her hair would keep it out of her way, and surely Mrs. Waters—Libby, as she'd asked to be called—wouldn't have left the items if she wasn't to use them.

Five minutes later she stared with satisfaction at her image—neat and presentable, even if she did feel a little strange sporting a ribbon on the end of her braid. With her hair pulled back, maybe the men wouldn't be so apt to gawk. They might even forget she was a woman, when they saw her packing a rifle and wearing her denim trousers each day.

Angel cracked her door and peered out. Three men stood nearby, talking and laughing. Libby glided past, carrying a platter of fried potatoes. Angel's mouth watered, and her stomach growled. No more lollygagging in her room. She stepped out into the short hallway and in two quiet strides arrived at the dining area.

Silence fell over the group gathered near the long table. Arizona raised his head and stared. "Well, I'll be jigged. I wasn't dreaming yesterday, Wren. She's a looker, just like I said."

Wren elbowed his partner and scowled. "Shut yer trap, you dinged fool."

Angel swung her warm gaze away from the men, willing her color to return to normal. Men at the outlaw camp had bantered and tossed ribald comments at the women, and she'd hardly noticed.

If only she could resume her role as a man. She'd been stupid to reveal her womanhood, and now she'd pay, just like some of the women at her old camp. She hitched at her belt and raised her chin. Her gun. It would stand between her and these men, if need be. Arizona seemed harmless, but you never knew.

Arizona slapped his forehead. "Golly! I'm plumb sorry, Miss. Wren here is right. I'm a fool, no two ways about it." He bent pleading eyes on her and mustered a weak smile. "Can you forgive me. Agin?"

She opened her mouth to answer, but a young voice piped into the silence. "Where's your gun, Miss Angel? Are you going to shoot wolves today? Can I come with you?" The questions tumbled from James's lips, his voice breaking in a high note on the last words. He winced and cleared his throat. "If it's all right with Uncle Travis."

Libby plunked a platter of beefsteak on the table and turned with her hands on her hips. "It certainly is not all right with *me*, young man. I'm sure Miss Ramirez will have enough to do without you getting in her way. Besides, you know what I think about you shooting animals."

Resentment flashed across the boy's face. He hung his head and kicked his toe against the wood floor. "Yes, Ma."

Travis clapped James on the back and ushered him toward the table. "Enough talk. The food's getting cold." He turned toward Angel and nodded at the chair on the far side. "Why don't you sit there? Libby has the seat beside you."

Angel wasn't sure which was worse—trying to avoid the smitten cowboys or making conversation with Libby Waters. The woman was polite enough on the surface, but in her gut Angel knew Libby wasn't happy about her living here. She drew out the chair and sank onto its hard surface. Everything would look better when she was in the saddle and on her own.

* * * * *

Libby smoothed the napkin on her lap and chanced a peek at the strange woman sitting beside her. Angel Ramirez had been silent most of the meal, with only an occasional yes or no. Libby had tried to draw her out but got little return. She gave a mental shrug. The young woman wouldn't fit at any society party that she'd encountered—why, she didn't even seem comfortable in a roomful of men.

Part of her felt sorry for the girl. She seemed so alone—unsure of herself. Although that hadn't been the case when Miss Ramirez shot at the coins. Libby frowned. What made a woman want to dress like a man and hunt animals? Every woman she'd known enjoyed improving her feminine skills, eager to preside over her own home one day. All her life, she'd hungered for a family of her own—a husband who cherished her and a house full of happy children. George had loved her the best way he knew how, but she'd never known true contentment.

She shook off the troubling feelings. The last thing she wanted was a strange, taciturn woman underfoot. But she would be kind. Since early childhood she'd been taught to be polite. Not to be rude. Accept. Smile. Be gracious.

Her shoulders slumped. This was not her home. It belonged to her brother, and he set the rules. She *would* do this. She would tolerate this woman playing at being a man and even be courteous.

Maybe this Angel person might one day be a friend.

She almost laughed aloud at the thought and chanced another glance at the girl. No. She'd wager Angel wouldn't last long enough for that to happen. Travis wasn't happy about the arrangement, and from the stubborn set of the girl's face, neither was she.

* * * * *

Travis sat at the end of the table and kicked himself. Why had he put that woman so close? He could have placed Libby beside him, then his new hand, then James, and still protect her from the moonstruck cowboys. And why should he protect her, anyway? She'd posed as a man all this time and surely could take care of herself.

He twisted in his seat and raised his voice above the hubbub. "Smokey. Got any more of those flapjacks?"

The portly cook bustled out of the kitchen, wiping his hands on an apron and raising bushy brows. "More?" He eyed the empty platter and let out a guffaw, his breath wheezing between parted lips. "Wren, you hawg! How does a man your size put away so much food?"

Wren looked up from his plate piled six deep and grinned, the fork poised inches from his mouth. "I work circles around the rest of these geezers."

The room erupted in hoots and would have continued had Travis not lifted his hand. "All right, men, let's show a little respect for the ladies." He nodded toward Libby and Angel, and the room instantly quieted.

Bud plucked his napkin from his lap, swiped at his lips, and covered a belch. "Sorry, ma'am." Color rose in his cheeks.

"Ha! You blush better than any woman I ever did see, Bud." Arizona crowed the words. "Now your face matches your hair, jest fine and dandy."

Bud dropped his napkin and leaned forward, all sign of merriment gone. "Want to meet me outside and see who's a woman, cowpoke?"

Arizona pushed back his chair, the legs scraping the floor. "Sure thing, pard. Let's have at it."

Angel emitted a strangled sound and turned her head, but not before Travis saw amusement dance in her eyes.

Libby gasped, and her fingers flew to her lips. "Oh my. Travis, are you going to allow your men to fight?"

Travis wagged his head and sighed. "The next cowpoke who opens his mouth when he shouldn't stays here and builds the new branding pen."

Immediate silence fell, and all heads bent over their meal. Forks scraped across plates in the still room. Travis grunted with satisfaction and hazarded a look at his sister. Poor Libby. The past few months had been hard on her. She'd come from a genteel background and married a man who'd treated her like fine china. Had it not been for their mother insisting Libby learn to cook and clean while growing up, she'd be helpless. It hadn't been easy on her, moving so far from society. He needed to pray for his sister instead of allowing himself to get irritated.

A motion on his left pulled him that direction. Angel Ramirez carefully folded her napkin and placed it beside her plate. "I'd like to get to work now, if you don't mind?"

Her quiet voice surprised him. Why had he thought her rough and uncouth last night? She'd begged off having the evening meal with them, saying she wasn't hungry and needed to sleep. This was the first time he'd seen her up close with her hair braided and face scrubbed. Her sun-kissed skin was the color of a golden panther, and her dark eyes smoldered with an emotion he couldn't quite peg.

Trouble. Beautiful trouble, but nevertheless, still trouble. He'd better ride herd on his men for the next few days, or they'd stampede after this girl like wild buffalo in the middle of a lightning storm. He tossed his napkin on top of his plate, his appetite gone. "Sure thing. Come to my office, and I'll show you on the map where we've sighted the wolf packs over the past few weeks." He turned toward the kitchen again. "Smokey?"

The cook stepped back into view. "Yeah, Boss?"

"Pack a lunch for Miss Ramirez. She'll be out all day."

"Sure thing." The man grinned, exposing a gold tooth. "I'll whip you up something special for your first day, Miss."

Angel pushed back her chair and stood. "A couple of biscuits and a slice of leftover beef will do. I'll get my rifle and meet you in your office."

Travis nodded. "On the far side of the living room there's a door. The window in my office looks out over the barn and corrals."

Angel nodded and walked out with a confident stride.

A hush fell over the room.

A low whistle came from somewhere down the table and Travis turned his head, staring at each of his men in turn. Not one sheepish look graced the countenance of a single cowboy, but admiration appeared in nearly every set of eyes. Including James's. He might have more trouble than he'd bargained for.

He shoved his chair back and launched to his feet. "All right, you big-eyed calves. Get to work or find a new job."

All four men jumped to their feet and bolted for the door, barely looking back with a mumbled "ma'am" toward Libby. Of the cowboys, only his manager, Nate, remained, and he shook his head, not meeting Travis's gaze.

Travis glared at his foreman. "They're your responsibility today. I'm riding out with Miss Ramirez to show her some of the landmarks. Keep those boys close to the ranch, even if you put them to building fence. One of them shows up dogging our new hand, and he's done. Got it?"

Nate bit his lip and turned his head away, but from where Travis stood, he appeared to be struggling to hold back a smile. "Got it, Boss. Have yourself a good ride." The man walked quickly out of the room, but Travis could swear he heard a chuckle drift back.

Chapter Seven

....

Travis pushed open the door of his office and stepped inside. Angel stood with her back to him, gazing at the large wall map of the ranch and surrounding area. Her long black braid hung between her shoulder blades, and she must have stopped by her room, as her gun sat snug in its holster. He clenched his teeth, feeling as though a Texas tornado had slammed into his ranch and uprooted everything he held dear. Life hadn't been perfect, but it had been much less complicated a few short hours ago.

It wasn't fitting, a woman wearing a gun on her hip and toting a rifle. She should be wearing a dress and—he stopped, suddenly ashamed, as a memory returned. Travis had been teasing his sister because she was a girl. Mother had told him that, with God's help, he could be anything he wanted to be, but so could his sister.

He hadn't understood at the time, but a small patch of light shone into the darkness of his past prejudice. Could a person really become what he desired with God's help? Did God care about what he did with his life?

Angel whirled around and stared at him, her hand clenched. He took a step back and rubbed his jaw. "I apologize, Miss Ramirez. I didn't mean to startle you."

Her chin jutted out. "I wish everyone would quit calling me that. My name is Angel. Is that so difficult?"

Surprise coursed through him, and he raised his hands, palms out. "Hold on there, Miss…er…Angel. No need to get riled."

Her posture gradually relaxed. "Sorry. It's been—difficult—the past few hours."

"Difficult? How?" As soon as the words left his mouth, he wanted to jerk them back. Of course. Coming to a new place, being questioned and stared at.

"It probably doesn't matter, seeing I won't be here long. But if everyone would call me by my given name, it would help. I'm not used to such proper talk."

"Wait." He stopped her before a torrent of words could bury him. "I understand. Let's start over. Angel it is." He strode forward and pointed at the map. "You probably spotted the ranch house." He touched the lower left quadrant. "Did you come through Sundance?"

She nodded. "I skirted around the town, but yes, that's the trail I took."

Travis drew a large circle with his finger. "The ranch encompasses roughly two thousand acres. I homesteaded the first section and purchased land from ranchers wanting out." He touched three places on the map. "These are the main points where wolf packs have been sighted."

She kept her gaze fixed on the map.

He lightly touched her arm. "I've changed my mind about sending you out today."

Angel swung toward him. "You're making me stay here?"

"No. I'm just not sending you alone. I'll show you some of the landmarks. We can't cover half of the ranch today, but I can help you get the lay of the land."

Angel shook her head, and her braid flipped over her shoulder. "No need. I can find my way."

Travis stifled an irritated remark. "I'm sure you can, but my way will save time."

She tapped her toe. "I understand how to read a map. I've been working the range for years."

Travis wanted to snap at her stubbornness. "I'm sure you have, but I prefer to take you out the first day."

She hesitated, clearly torn. "All right. You're the boss. I'll meet you in the barn."

Travis stuffed down his impatience and grabbed his hat off the desk, slapping it on his head. Hopefully he'd made the right decision in hiring this woman. Why he thought he might be tempted to neglect his ranch work with this pretty employee around, he couldn't imagine. He just prayed he could keep from going loco until he found somebody else.

* * * * *

Angel slung her saddle onto Bella's back and stuffed her rifle in its sheath. The last thing she wanted was her new boss breathing down her neck. It would've been easier maintaining her old role, but she couldn't deny the feelings of rebellion at the lie she'd lived for so long. People needed to accept her for who she was, not for what they thought she should be.

Travis grasped his horse's reins. "Ready?"

"Yes."

They swung into the saddle and rode out of the barn at a hard trot, heading northeast. Neither spoke for the next twenty minutes or so, but Angel didn't mind. Getting a feel for this country was important— she was thankful Travis wasn't talkative. Her mind drifted to the cowboy called Arizona. Now *that* one would talk her ear off if given half a chance, and no doubt propose within a week if encouraged. She'd have to watch herself and not spend any time alone with the man.

Angel twisted in her saddle. She slowed Bella to a walk and pointed at a butte rising in the distance. "Is that peak on your land?"

Travis nodded. "Yes, and it's an excellent lookout. We keep part of the herd near the base, as there's a good spring and rich grass. That's where we're headed." He gathered his reins. "We've got a lot of ground to cover today. Let's pick up the pace." He grazed his gelding with a spur and the horse broke into a ground-eating canter.

A rush of warmth poured over Angel as she urged Bella to catch up. How wonderful to be in the saddle again, doing what she loved best. If only her parents or Uncle José could be here, life would be complete. That's what she missed the most—a sense of family. Since leaving José, she had no one to call her own. There'd been little interaction with any of the family members on the other ranches where she'd worked. Staying in Travis's home and sitting at the table had stirred a loneliness she'd thought buried. Angel pushed down the emotions, not wanting to dig too deep.

The cool wind nudged the rim of her sombrero, and the pounding of hoof beats filled the air. The sun-warmed needles on nearby pine trees emitted a fragrant odor and she inhaled deeply, thankful to be alive. No longer did she fear Bart Hinson finding her. Three years was more than enough; by now the man would have turned his attention elsewhere. She could relax, knowing the secret of her past would never be exposed.

The towering rock butte grew more distinct against the azure sky, and a long line of cattle spread along the base, contentedly grazing the knee-deep grass. Travis held up his hand and slowed his horse to a trot. Angel drew up alongside, letting Bella match her pace to the gelding. "Nice spot. How many cattle are you running in this location?"

Travis grinned, and the result surprised her. His normally somber expression relaxed, and smile lines creased the corners of his mouth. "About five hundred. This is one of my favorite places. Wait till you see the spring." He pointed toward a decidedly green patch near the foot of the butte. "Come on, I'll show you."

In another few minutes they reached the wide grassy patch where cattle grazed and calves dozed in the sun. There must be over three hundred head, and the herd extended out of sight around the far edge of the rock outcropping. The butte towered above them and encompassed an area of at least ten acres. Angel had noticed while still at a distance that the top was somewhat level and fell off sheer on the three sides visible.

Cows lumbered to their feet as the horses passed, and calves bucked and jumped across the grassy area. Water gushed nearby, but Travis said it was a spring, not a running stream. Most springs she'd encountered were pools, originating at a seep or trickle of water. Her eyes widened as they arrived at the source and swung down from their mounts.

The rock face split about two feet up from its base with bushes growing on each side. Water boiled from the narrow fissure as though anxious to reach its destination. The entire crack gushed with tumbling water that spilled into a basin below. The resulting pool measured as wide as a grown man could toss a rock, and two sides were ringed with boulders that must have tumbled down over the centuries. Grass grew on the shore, and one area that appeared shallow was trampled and churned by the hooves of thirsty cattle.

Angel walked around the edge, noting the imprints of elk and possibly deer. No wolf tracks that she could discern, but that wasn't surprising. She turned to Travis. "Amazing." She breathed the word reverently. "I've not seen the like of this anywhere in Wyoming—or on south to Texas, for that matter."

Travis's brows rose, and a curious light sparked in his eyes.

Angel winced. Most of her work had been done in Wyoming, at least over the past two years. The last thing she wanted was for anyone to know of her history in Texas.

"Sounds like you've done a lot of traveling. You track varmints down Texas way?"

She shook her head. "No. Wyoming and Colorado. That's all."

His mouth opened, then snapped shut. Good. She didn't intend to answer any more questions.

Angel turned toward the spring. "I'm surprised you didn't locate your house here."

He leaned his arm against his saddle. "I thought about it, but it's too far from town to bring in supplies. We have a good, year-round creek not far from the house, but this would've been nice. It's excellent grazing for the cattle, though."

"I can see that. You ever climb the bluff?"

"Yes. On the back side the slope is more gradual. Great view of the ranch from up there, and with a looking glass, you can see other locations where the cattle hole up."

"I'll try it. Might be a good place to spot predators."

"We haven't had much trouble with wolves over this way. At least not yet." He frowned. "But it couldn't hurt to keep watch." He gathered up his reins. "Let's head out. I want to reach the next grazing area before we eat."

They mounted and headed north. Angel looked back at the pool one more time. This was a place she'd return to—there was something about running water that soothed her soul—and right now, she could certainly use it. She chanced a look at Travis. Did he feel the same way, or was the man so focused on his ranch that he failed to notice the peace? She shrugged and pushed down the thought, irritated that she cared. He was her boss, not her friend, and his feelings weren't her concern.

* * * * *

Travis glanced back, wondering at the longing that flashed across Angel's face. What drove her to live this kind of life? Did she want a family, or did she have normal desires? He still had trouble using her given name, even in his mind. What was he thinking, giving this woman a man's job and asking her to spend long days alone roaming the range? Part of him longed to treat her like the lady she should be, not the man she pretended to be.

Disgust niggled at his heart. Not at this young woman riding beside him, but at himself for not having the strength to stick with his decision when he'd wanted to send her away. But something about the determined—no—*desperate* expression she'd worn when she thought he might turn her aside had gotten under his skin.

Another half hour of riding brought them within sight of a second herd. Distant bawling floated on the still air and small dust clouds rose. The grassy plain extended for as far as he could see, and he surveyed the area with satisfaction. More cattle grazed here than anywhere on the ranch. He leaned back in his saddle and relaxed. "Tell me about some of the places you've worked."

Angel didn't reply, and he stiffened. Surely she couldn't object to a casual question. A swift movement jerked him around—Angel had withdrawn her rifle.

"What do you see?" He rose in his stirrups but only saw calves butting heads and playing.

Angel leaned forward. Her rifle gripped in one hand and holding the reins with her other, she raked her horse with her spurs. The big mare nearly leapt from beneath her and sprang into a hard gallop. "Wolves!" Her voice carried back over the rapidly widening distance.

"Wolves?" Travis strained to see. He urged his gelding into a canter.

Angel leaned low over her horse's neck, seemingly part of the moving animal. Bella was running flat out now. Her long black mane streamed back as her extended stride covered the ground. The mare jumped over brush, kicking up clumps of sod in her wake. The young woman clinging to her back held her rifle balanced against her thigh, riding effortlessly. She lifted the gun to her shoulder but didn't slow the pace of her mount. A surge of reluctant admiration grew in Travis's chest. What a display of first-class horsemanship. She could ride as well as any man. The thought jarred him.

Travis turned his attention toward the cattle and removed his own rifle from its scabbard. The dust cloud intensified, and the bawling of the cattle increased. Suddenly, a young calf broke from the melee and streaked across the clearing. A gray, rangy form shot from the dust in long bounds, rapidly closing the distance. The calf's distraught mother followed, swinging her head back and forth and bellowing at the top of her lungs.

A loud crack echoed off the nearby hills. The wolf took one final, desperate leap and tumbled to the ground, rolling several times before crumpling. Travis drew back on his reins. But why wasn't Angel slowing?

He strained to see through the dusty haze. Angel headed for the middle of four wolves circling two mothers with their babies huddled alongside. The hairs on the back of his neck rose. One of the cows dropped her head and charged a wolf that edged closer, catching his chest with the tip of her horn. The animal yelped and sprang backward. Another beast closed on the empty spot in the circle and crouched low.

Travis shouted and spurred his horse forward. He'd nearly caught up with Angel now, as she slid her mare to a halt.

The young woman raised her rifle again. Holding his own weapon at the ready, Travis slowed to a trot and watched Angel's practiced movements. A series of shots rang out, and two wolves fell. A third yipped as he headed for the nearby trees. The fourth ran close on his heels, her tail tucked as she looked furtively toward the now silent gun.

Travis drew up alongside Angel, who sat reloading her rifle, a scowl marring her pretty face. "That was some shooting."

She raised her chin and stared at him. "I should have had those last two. My gun jammed." She flipped the chamber closed and shoved the rifle back in its sheath. "I'll check it when I get back to the ranch."

"I could have one of the men—" Travis nearly bit his tongue at the look she shot him. "I'm sure you're quite capable."

She nudged her horse forward. "We'd best check the herd. Make sure the wolves didn't injure any of the calves."

"Right." He followed her, suddenly at a loss for words. What was he supposed to do now? Angel had proven her worth as a hunter and horseman, but that didn't change how he felt. He still didn't believe she should be riding the range alone. Although she seemed capable of taking care of herself, there were more predators a woman had to worry about than wolves.

Chapter Eight

....

Angel drifted around the kitchen, feeling lost for the first time in years. Libby had taken the buggy to town and left instructions for Angel to help herself to whatever she could find for dinner. Shooting, riding, even brandings calves, were all easier than spending time in the kitchen. Of course, she'd fixed meals out on the range, but that was over an open campfire and with vittles the ranch cook supplied.

She could count on one hand the number of times she'd been alone in a house during a workday. Strange that Travis insisted she take the day off. Maybe he felt he owed her, even though she'd been on the job for only ten days.

This man was different from her past bosses. Of course, none of them had known she was a woman, so that could account. But Travis seemed gentler, even under his gruff, irritable exterior. She'd noticed the tender way he looked at Libby and how he ruffled James's hair. He even treated his cowboys with gratitude when they'd done a good job. Appreciation wasn't something she'd grown accustomed to, but it was nice, even if it meant a day away from the range.

She stepped into the pantry and surveyed the array of tinned goods, bags of sugar and flour, beans, rice, and other things she couldn't identify. Where to start? Maybe she'd just skip the noontime meal. One last look at the myriad of bags and tins on the shelves and she made her decision.

The air outside smelled fresh and clean after last night's shower.

What to do? Angel pondered her next step. Take a ride and pretend not to be working, but bring her rifle along just in case? She shook her head. Bella needed rest, and that wouldn't be fair.

Try to find a book to read? But Angel had never been a big hand at reading, and this day was too beautiful to sit indoors.

A boot crunched on the gravel, and Angel's hand flashed to her waist. Stupid! She'd left her gun in her room. A muscle twitched in her cheek, and she turned slowly.

Arizona stood there sporting a huge grin. "Sure glad you're not armed today, Miss Angel." He hooked his thumbs in his belt.

Angel squelched the smile threatening to slip out. "That can easily be remedied."

Arizona's grin faded, and he took a step back. "I didn't mean any harm. Jest wondered if maybe you was feeling lonesome, with Libby gone and Travis and James on the range."

"I enjoy being alone."

"I thought pretty girls always enjoyed company." He scratched his head.

Angel leaned against a post of the covered porch. "I'm not a pretty girl. I'm a ranch employee, the same as you."

Arizona hooted with laughter. "Sorry, Miss. But that you ain't. You and me, we're not a bit alike."

Angel straightened. It was time to take control of this situation. "Where's your sidekick?"

"You mean Wren? You ain't soft on *him*, are you?"

"Soft on him?" She wrinkled her nose. "Are women *all* you think about, Arizona?"

He stuffed his hands in his pockets and grinned. "Maybe, but I do have a few other interests. Nothing wrong with wanting to court a pretty woman, is there?"

"I guess that depends on the woman—and if she *wants* to be courted."

The cowboy leaned closer. "I'd be willing to show you around town if you'd have me."

Angel stared at the man. He was nice enough but seemed to have one thing on his mind—finding a sweetheart—and she didn't intend that to be her.

A buggy pulled into the lane and headed their way. Saved by Libby. "Sorry, cowboy, no can do." She wrinkled her nose and grinned. "I'm a working woman and don't have time to lollygag around town with lazy cowhands."

"Lazy?" He drew himself to his full height. "Why, I can work circles around the rest of the bozos on this spread."

"Arizona!" Libby called from the buggy as she drew her horse to a stop in front of the house. "I'm glad you're here. Help me unload the supplies?"

He pasted on a sweet smile and nodded. "Sure enough, Miss Libby. Glad to be of service. Idle hands are a tool of the devil, my pappy used to say, and I sure don't aim to be *lazy*." He shot a glance toward Angel, and a sly smirk peeked out.

Angel shook her head and stepped closer to the wagon. "Need my help?"

"Thank you. That would be nice."

The two women each took a box of foodstuffs and Arizona followed, his arms laden with full burlap bags. The next several minutes were spent unloading and shelving the items, then they shooed the cowboy back outside. Libby examined the kitchen. "You left things in perfect shape. Thank you, Angel."

"I, uh…" Angel avoided Libby's eyes. How could she admit she didn't know her way around a fancy kitchen? This pampered woman wouldn't understand. What would she know of outlaw camps and deprivation? Nothing. And Angel didn't care to educate her. "I wasn't hungry."

Libby planted her hands on her hips. "Not hungry? It's past two o'clock and breakfast was hours ago. Why didn't you cook something?"

Angel shrugged and started to turn away, but Libby touched her arm. "Angel. Do you know how to cook?"

Angel winced and pulled away. "I cook all the time."

"I'm sure you do. Over a campfire. But how about on a kitchen stove?" Libby softened her tone. "Come on, I'll help."

Angel shook her head and took a step back. "I'm fine, thanks."

"Pooh. You work hard every day, and I'm sure you have an appetite. I'll teach you to cook. It's not hard."

"I said I'm fine. Why does everyone want to change me?" Angel knew she was glaring but didn't care. "I've never liked girly things and have no desire to learn." She shook her head. "A woman like you wouldn't understand."

Libby crossed her arms. "And what kind of woman would that be?"

"You've had everything handed to you. You wear fine dresses, live in a nice house, and men probably fall over themselves in hopes of winning you. I'm guessing you've not had much hardship in your life. I wasn't that fortunate and, quite honestly, I wouldn't be any good at being a lady."

Libby gave a short laugh. "You know nothing about me. And I don't buy your nonsense about not wanting to be a lady, or you wouldn't feel so jealous over what you *think* I've had."

"I most certainly am *not* jealous." Angel gripped her hands in tight balls to keep from lashing out. She'd learned to fight at an early age, but this wasn't the time, as much as she'd like to put this woman in her place. How dare Libby think her jealous? Why, Angel had everything in life she wanted or needed. Everything...

Angel drew in a sharp breath. Except the one thing Libby seemed to take for granted—Lilly.

Libby tipped her head to the side. "You need to do some hard thinking about your life, Angel. Do you really want to dress like a man riding the range the rest of your life, or does some part of you want to settle down like other women?"

Angel tried not to wince. This conversation needed to end. She held up her hands. "I don't care to be lectured. Please let Travis know I'm headed out. I'll ask Smokey to put some grub together for me, and I'll be out of your way."

The hard set of Libby's mouth softened. "Wait, Angel. I'm sorry."

But Angel had heard enough. She spun on her heel and dashed from the room. No way could she let Libby see the tears threatening to spill over the rims of her eyes and down her cheeks. She'd head where she belonged—on the range tracking the varmints that were honest in what they did...unlike so many people she'd met over the years.

* * * * *

The next day, Angel pushed down her frustration and tightened her reins. Calves were still disappearing. Travis wouldn't keep her much longer if she couldn't prove her worth. She'd ridden over three hours this morning and had already seen two carcasses, but no sign of a wolf. In fact, there'd been no tracks near the kill, just churned-up grass where the mother must have fought for her baby. Poor mama. That's one of the reasons she hated these predators. They had to eat, but she'd found too many dying animals that suffered horribly from wolf attacks.

Strange. Typically a wolf pack dragged its prey a short distance from the herd and stayed till it was consumed, so there should've been tracks. She had to figure this out.

When she'd first arrived at Sundance Ranch nearly two weeks ago, her need for work had trumped everything else. But living in the ranch house had altered her view. Memories from her early childhood had started to return, when her parents were happy and no threats loomed. Laughter had been part of their life, and the cowboys' antics at meals occasionally brought a smile to her lips.

Something was missing—something important. Beyond being lonely, beyond the security of having parents. Bella stumbled and snorted. Angel tightened her legs. Getting thrown from her horse this far from the ranch wouldn't be smart, although she doubted Bella would leave her.

Something inside her felt empty. That's what she'd been struggling to get a handle on when she'd argued with Libby yesterday. Libby said she'd want a husband and family someday, and she'd denied it, but she'd not told the entire truth. She loved her life and was in no hurry to give it up, but part of her longed for something more.

Uncle José had tried to bring a sense of family to her life, and a couple of the women in the outlaw band had done so when she was young. But looking back now, Angel wondered if they'd been trying to shine up to her uncle. Had they cared about her? She'd never know, and maybe it didn't matter, but the thought stung. From the memories she had of her mother she knew she'd cared. She shrugged, trying to shake off the melancholy threatening to flood her.

Angel clucked to her mare, urging her into a canter. Time to check the butte with the gushing spring. She'd only been there once since her first day, and the place called to something deep in her spirit. Maybe she could find some answers there, and do her job at the same time.

A few minutes later Angel halted her horse close to a grove of trees ringing one side of the butte. Bella snorted and pranced—certainly not her normal steady behavior. An uneasy feeling niggled at Angel. She sensed someone—or something—watching her, but there'd been no sign of anyone. Could James have followed her without being seen? The boy had dogged her steps the first few days, but Travis had put a stop to that.

Angel urged her horse toward the trees and touched the butt of her rifle. No sense in taking any chances. Brush rustled on the far edge of the trees, and she turned her head. Nothing moved.

Silence lay over the grasslands and disquiet hovered over the wooded area nearby. Bella snorted again and shied sideways. Angel leaned down and stroked the mare's neck. "Easy, girl. What do you smell? Something I need to worry about?"

She slipped the rifle from its scabbard and rested it across her lap, comforted by the feel of the wood and steel beneath her fingers. "Come on, Bella. Let's get into the trees, and you can graze while I scout around." Angel pressed her legs against the mare's sides, and Bella bolted forward, breathing heavily. She plowed to a stop. Angel felt her stiffen. Bella reared, her front feet lifting high off the ground. The mare landed with a hard thump, her entire body quivering.

Angel spoke to her horse in a soothing tone, peering under the trees and into the brush. Nothing appeared amiss.

Suddenly a cow charged from the brush with a calf on her heels, racing away from the tree cover.

A blood-curdling scream rent the air.

Bella's body tensed. She lunged forward and kicked out sideways with her back legs. A tawny form leapt from a branch partway up the nearby tree. Angel saw the gleam of golden eyes locked on hers. The big cat extended his front paws and bared its teeth in a snarl. He came within inches of landing on Angel and swiped at her as he fell.

Pain tore through her arm as the cougar's claws shredded the sleeve of her jacket.

Angel lunged for her rifle but missed as it spun out of her reach, bouncing a few yards away.

The cat landed just beyond Bella and kept on running, its dark gold skin rippling over powerful muscles as it disappeared through the trees.

Bella charged across the clearing and headed for the butte, her neck stretched out and sides heaving. Angel held the reins with one hand and pressed her bleeding arm against her side, not trying to check the panicked horse.

She clung to the mare's back, biting her lip against the searing pain running through her arm.

She should have known sooner that something was wrong—should have checked the brush where the cow and calf hid. Her arrival had given the animals the chance they'd needed to escape. If only she hadn't been daydreaming about things that couldn't happen. This ranch wasn't her home and never would be. She'd best get her mind on business, or the next time she wouldn't be so lucky.

Her mare's frantic pace slowed, and Angel reined her to a stop, swinging down beside the water. Bella snorted and nudged her, then lowered her head to the grass and started to graze.

Angel stripped off her jacket, thankful for the heavy denim that helped protect her arm. She pushed up her sleeve and gazed at the pair of angry claw marks deep in her lower arm, extending from just below her elbow almost to her wrist. Blood ran in dark rivulets and dripped from her fingertips. The throbbing would intensify if she didn't clean it fast.

The cold water gushing out of the rock face soothed her arm. If only the water could wash away the remnants of her past the way it washed away the blood from her wound. She continued to bathe it, hoping the icy temperature would slow the bleeding. Angel took off her shirt and, using her teeth, tore a strip of cloth from the hem, then slipped the shirt back on. Three tight wraps around her arm and she tied the ends just below her elbow. She slung her tattered jacket in front of her saddle.

Time to retrieve her rifle and see if she could find that mountain lion. He'd been plenty mad that she'd interrupted his meal and he wouldn't give up stalking the herd. Funny she'd never seen his tracks before, but this big boy might be the mystery predator bringing down calves.

Her mare had edged away from the pool. It took three attempts before Angel grasped Bella's reins, and she gave a light jerk. "I don't need you running away on me, girl." She placed her foot in the stirrup, gripped the horn with her left hand, stretched up with her injured right arm, and winced. No strength remained to grasp the back of the saddle. She tucked her arm against her body and stepped up, carefully balancing as she settled onto the leather.

A short time later Angel trotted her mount to the edge of the trees and peered under the overhanging branches. The sun reflected off the barrel of her rifle resting on a bed of pine needles. She raised her head and listened. Nothing. Chances were the cat had slunk away, planning on following the mother and baby. Strange, the pair had moved away from the safety of the cattle grazing by the pool.

Bella stood quietly, ears pricked forward and body on alert, then she slowly relaxed. Angel clucked to the mare and she walked forward, hesitating every few feet and giving an occasional snort. She danced sideways at one point, lifting her head and gazing around. Angel ran her hand down the length of her neck. "It's all right. I think he's gone." Her horse quieted under her touch and dropped her head.

"Good girl. Let's go." They moved ahead until Bella stood within feet of the rifle.

Angel carefully swung from her horse, grasped the gun, and tucked it under her arm. She stood for a moment, watching and listening, but nothing moved. No sound touched her ears other than the chirp of a bird calling its mate. A slight shudder shook her body as she thought of her close call. If Bella hadn't bolted when she had, the cat would've landed square on Angel's back, knocking her from the saddle and bringing certain death. How wonderful to be alive.

She walked to her horse, slid her rifle back into its sheath, and carefully mounted, gritting her teeth. A searing pain ran from her fingers up her arm, and she leaned against her saddle horn. Blood oozed through the bandage and her head swam. She hoped Bella had been traveling this range long enough to get her back to the ranch if she passed out on the way.

Chapter Nine

....

A week and a half had dragged by since Angel's arrival, and Libby's work had only increased. On top of the extra laundry, cooking, and cleaning, James was acting peculiar. She'd called him for breakfast three days ago, and he'd not been in his room. On closer inspection, she'd sworn the bed hadn't been slept in, but that didn't make sense. He'd shown up ten minutes later, claiming he'd been in the barn with a new foal. No time to worry now, with the dishes needing to be done. What a blessing Smokey took care of cooking breakfast and supper.

Smokey walked into the kitchen, toting another load of dishes. "This is the last of it, Miz Waters."

She took the proffered stack and slid them into her dishpan. "Could you get me a little more hot water?"

"Sure." He grabbed a dishrag, slid the kettle from the top of the woodstove, and poured steaming water into the pan. "Want I should scrub the table, or dry them dishes?"

"Drying would be nice if you don't mind. I'd enjoy the company."

His cheeks took on a faint rosy tinge, and he smiled. "Not a'tall, ma'am." He swiped at a large platter and set it carefully aside. "You and that new gal gettin' along all right?"

Libby winced. The man had a way of going right to the heart of an issue. "She's—fine. Of course, I haven't seen much of her. She spends most of her time working."

"Ah-huh. I hear she's good with that long iron of hers. Brought down three wolves the first day she went out with the boss. The men are still talkin' about it." He scratched his chin. "Somethin' I been meanin' to talk to you about, Miz Waters."

She took another dish from the stack. "Please, Smokey. I've lived here almost four months. Can't you call me Libby like everyone else does?"

"Nate don't call you Libby."

This time it was her turn to blush. She'd noticed the deference Nate used and hadn't thought about it until she'd heard a couple of the cowboys whispering one morning. "Fine. If you insist." She waved a sudsy hand in the air. "What did you want to talk about?"

He cleared his throat and shot her a glance. "Your boy."

"James? Is something wrong?"

He shrugged. "Don't rightly know. Was hopin' you might tell me. I caught him crawlin' into his window one mornin'."

"*Into* his window? Not out?"

"Yes, ma'am."

"Did you ask him about it?"

"I did, but he said it wasn't none of my concern, so I didn't press him. Thought you should know."

"You didn't tell Travis?"

"No, ma'am. He's your son."

Libby nodded, more grateful than she could express. "Thank you. When did this happen?" Her heartbeat increasing, she wiped her hands and placed the towel on the counter. After the incident a few mornings ago when she'd worried he might not have slept in his bed, this didn't bode well.

"Yesterday. 'Bout eleven o'clock at night. I couldn't sleep and thought I'd take a stroll outside. Clear my head, know what I mean?"

She nodded, waiting for him to continue.

"I was headed back inside and heard a noise round the corner near the boy's bedroom window. He was standing on a big limb and steppin' across to the roof. Made me think maybe he'd come out that way, too. But 'course, I can't be sure."

Libby had seen James go out his window this way, just once. He'd been jubilant when they first moved here, and he'd seen the large oak tree with the limbs spreading so close to his window. It was natural a thirteen-year-old boy would pull a prank like this, but Travis had threatened to cut the limb. Her son had begged him to leave it, promising never to climb out again. Not that James could get seriously injured, as the limb was sturdy and only a foot or so above the gently sloping roof, but it wasn't something she cared to have him do.

"Thank you, Smokey. I'll talk to my son."

"No problem, ma'am. Hope I haven't stirred up too much trouble for the boy. I know youngsters like to play tricks, but I can't imagine James was doin' anything too terrible."

The next few minutes passed in silence as they worked side by side. Smokey hung his towel on a peg and grinned. "Guess I'd best be thinkin' on what to fix for supper."

Libby groaned. "Does it ever end?"

He wagged his head. "Not with this hungry crew of grub lovers. But I've got a few hours. Think I'll prop my feet up on the rail and take me a nap, if you don't need me?"

"Have a good rest, Smokey. I'm fine."

His boots clomped across the floor, and Libby heard the front door open and close. A few moments later the back door eased open, and Libby saw a flash of black hair. Why was Angel returning so early? Libby plucked a mug from a rack of shelves and poured it full of hot water. A cup of tea and a few minutes to rest would help put her world to rights—and maybe give her a chance to study on what James might be up to.

* * * * *

Angel tiptoed through the pantry and eased past the kitchen doorway, praying no one noticed.

"Angel?" Libby stepped toward the dining room. "Is that you?"

"Yes, ma'am."

"Is everything all right?"

A long pause ensued and Angel stepped closer to the hallway.

Libby came around the corner and halted. "Were you going to your room?" She stared at the bloody cloth wrapped around Angel's arm and rushed forward. "What happened?"

Angel stepped back. "I'm fine. No need to worry over a little cut."

"A *little* cut? With that much blood? Let me look." Libby held out her hand and waited.

Angel met Libby's gaze, unable to quell the pain she knew must shine from her eyes.

Libby gasped. "It's bad, isn't it? I'm going to find Travis."

Panic washed over Angel. "No. Please."

"But it needs to be looked at. What happened?"

"It doesn't matter. I can tend to it." She couldn't let Travis know. He'd think her incapable of caring for herself out on the range.

Libby narrowed her eyes. "Either you let me help, or I'll get Travis. He's in his office. Which one will it be?"

"Fine." Angel shrugged. "You can help."

Libby led the way into the kitchen and slid out a chair. "Sit. You're white and shaking."

Angel dropped onto the hard wooden seat with a low moan and rested her head in her hand. "You don't have to tell him about this, do you?"

"Travis? Why ever not?"

"He'll fire me if he knows I got attacked by a mountain lion."

Libby gasped and placed her hand over her heart. "What in the world? How can your job be more important than your safety?" She headed across the room and plucked a pot of salve from a shelf above the wash basin. "A mountain lion? How bad is it?"

"He was in a tree watching a cow and her calf, and I spoiled his dinner." Angel gave a guttural laugh. "Guess he figured I'd make a good substitute when the pair ran away, but Bella had other ideas." She looked up at Libby. "His claws raked my arm, that's all."

Libby gently touched the rough bandage. "We need to get this off." She hurried to the pantry and came back with a large, clean linen square. A quick pull at a drawer and she plucked out a pair of shears and cut the cloth in half. Folding one section into a pad, she smeared salve over the center and laid it aside. "I heated water for tea. It should still be warm enough to clean the wound."

Angel sat silently as Libby unwrapped her arm, wincing as the strip of cloth pulled away. The raw, double gash started to bleed again, and Libby gasped. "I think we need to get Doc Simmons out here, or take you to town. I don't know much about flesh wounds, but your arm may need stitches and could get infected."

Angel shook her head. No way would she visit a doctor and miss more work. "Just put something on it and wrap it for me. I'll be fine."

"Honestly, Angel, I think we need to have it looked at."

"Have what looked at?" Travis's voice filled the room and Angel wilted against the table, releasing a quiet moan.

* * * * *

Travis walked into the kitchen, wondering at the tense atmosphere hanging over the two women. Angel sat at the table with a cloth draped over her arm and Libby hovered nearby. "What's going on?" He peered more closely at Angel's arm and stopped. A hint of red showed in the center of the cloth. He took a long stride, drawing close to the two women. "Libby?"

His sister didn't reply, just looked at the top of Angel's bowed head. His new employee slowly peeled off the white linen. "It's a cut. Nothing to worry over." Two gashes ran along the inside of her arm and blood trickled from the wound.

He stepped closer when a loud rap at the door drew him up short. Now what? The men shouldn't be back from gathering the cattle yet. Travis spun around, frustrated at the interruption. How in the world had Angel gotten those cuts? "Libby. Please let me know if the doc needs to see her." The inflamed skin and jagged edges looked nasty, and he wanted to get to the bottom of this. He stalked to the door and yanked it open.

A tall, wiry man with his hat tucked under his arm stood outside. His sandy blond hair lay neatly against his head, and a matching mustache touched his top lip. "Howdy, Travis. Sorry to bother you."

"Sheriff Jensen. What brings you out?" Travis swung the door wide. "Come in and have a cup of coffee." He clenched his jaws. Right now he wanted to rush back and discover how Angel had been injured, but it was a rare event for the sheriff to visit. Libby had done volunteer nursing in San Francisco and she could tend to the wound—but that didn't stop the unease building in his chest.

"I'm here on business. I need to speak to your sister."

"What's the problem?"

Footsteps sounded on the floor of the sitting room, and Libby appeared in the open doorway. "I've finished wrapping Angel's arm..." She looked from Travis to the sheriff. "I'm sorry, gentlemen."

Sheriff Jensen took a step forward. "Mrs. Waters, I rode out to speak to you about your son."

Libby gasped, and her face blanched. "James? What's happened?" She gripped Travis's arm. "I thought he was riding with the men."

The sheriff held up his hand. "Whoa there, ma'am. Sorry I spooked you. James is fine, as far as I know."

"He's with Nate." Travis gestured toward a high-backed chair. "Why don't you have a seat?" He turned to Libby. "Angel's all right?"

She nodded. "I did the best I could for now, but I think a doctor needs to look at it."

Travis waited till the sheriff was seated and Libby sank onto a flowered divan, then Travis took his place in an upholstered chair. "Is my nephew in trouble?"

"I'm not sure, but I suspect he might be." Sheriff Jensen stroked his mustache. "I don't have any proof, just hearsay. I hadn't planned on coming out here, but one of the shopkeepers urged me to."

Libby gripped her hands in her lap. "I don't understand."

"Sorry, ma'am. I'd best start at the beginning." He sat up straight and cleared his throat. "There's been a group of three or four boys getting into mischief in town. They started innocent enough, just playing silly pranks. But they got bolder and tipped over a privy on the edge of town, back of the boardinghouse."

Travis pursed his lips and snorted. "That's not anything I approve of, but it's certainly not criminal. And I'm guessing more than one man in this town did something similar at that age."

The sheriff nodded. "I agree, if the pranks had stopped there."

"Ah-huh." Travis leaned back, dreading what might come. He

glanced at Libby, and a prickle of sympathy struck him. She looked so alone. Was she wishing for her husband to be sitting beside her, instead of lying in a cold grave in California? He shifted uncomfortably. Part of him wanted to slip over to the divan and place his arm around her shoulders and draw her close. Let her know she had his support. But maybe she'd push him away. He chanced another look and the stark fear showing in her face decided the matter for him. Travis wasn't his cold-hearted father. He rose from his chair and crossed to the sofa in two strides, sinking down beside his sister.

Libby turned wide eyes to his. "Travis?" The word came out in a whisper.

"I'm here, Sis." He gathered her small hand in his own and squeezed. She sighed and melted against him. "Go on, Sheriff."

"One of the townspeople was on his way home three nights ago and saw a couple of boys hanging around the back door of Copper's General Store. He thought he recognized your boy, Mrs. Waters."

Libby shook her head. "James wouldn't have gone into town. Why, it's almost a thirty-minute ride from the ranch."

The sheriff shrugged. "A healthy boy could easily walk there and back."

Travis nodded. "He could. But that's not a crime." He shot a glance at Libby. "Although I'm sure Libby would agree that if James were in town, he'd hear about it from her."

"And if they'd only been at the back door, I wouldn't be here today. Mr. Copper found damage inside his store, not far from the door, and there are a few things missing. Of course we can't be sure the boys did it, but it looks mighty suspicious."

Libby withdrew her hand from Travis's and frowned. "We've only lived here four months. Does this person who thought he saw James *know* my son well enough to identify him? In the dark?"

"I asked him that myself. The description he gave could have fit two or three boys your son's age, but it's my job to advise the parents, regardless. I'm stopping at all three homes."

Travis pushed himself up from the couch. "Thank you, Sheriff. We're beholden to you. I can't imagine my nephew would've walked to town. It's not like he's made friends with other boys in the area, having lived here such a short time, but we'll get to the bottom of it."

Sheriff Jensen picked up his hat from the sofa, rose, and extended his hand. "Thank you." His grip was firm as he shook Travis's hand. "I'm sorry to worry you, Mrs. Waters. It's very possible your boy isn't involved, but I thought you should know."

Libby stayed seated and made an effort to smile. "I understand. I appreciate you coming, and I agree with Travis. We'll talk to James."

A few minutes later Travis returned to the sitting room from seeing the sheriff out. Libby sat with her face in her hands. "Libby? You all right?" He sank onto the seat beside her and touched her shoulder.

A stifled sob came from between her fingers. "I'm not sure." She raised tearstained eyes. "Do you think James is involved?"

"I don't know. It's not like the boy, is it? Did you have trouble in San Francisco?"

Libby drew back but didn't reply.

"Libby?" Travis gripped her shoulders. "Did James have something similar happen?"

She shook her head. "Maybe. Just a little. But nothing like this."

"What, exactly, does that mean?"

"Well—" Libby fidgeted on the divan. "He had some friends his father and I didn't approve of. That's one reason—" She peeked at Travis and then dropped her gaze back to her hands twisting in her lap. "I decided to come here, instead of moving back with Papa. Since Papa lives in a city…"

"You thought there'd be less chance he'd get in trouble here."

"Yes."

Travis touched her trembling hands. "I'm not angry. We don't know for sure that James went to town."

She leaned against him and a sob slipped out. "You won't send us away?"

Travis drew her within the circle of his arm. "Of course not. You're my family. We'll talk to James together, if you'd like."

Libby nodded and sniffed. "Thank you, Travis. I'd like that."

Travis squeezed her shoulders and moved away, then froze. "We forgot about Angel! She might need a doctor." He jumped up and raced from the room, vaguely aware of Libby following.

They pulled up short and stared. Only a pan of bloody water and rags sat on the table. Angel was gone.

Chapter Ten

....

Angel slipped into her room, twisted the doorknob, and released it gently, her heart racing at what she'd just heard. She'd sat at the table for several minutes after Travis and Libby left the room—long enough to know who'd arrived. She'd nearly bolted, fearing the sheriff had come to take her away, but she'd forced herself to stay put. No one knew she'd ridden in that last cattle raid. She'd eased out of her chair and tiptoed to the edge of the door leading into the living room. It hadn't taken long to discover the man had come for another reason entirely.

She placed her hand over the bandage and lowered herself onto the edge of her bed. Libby had done a fine job of dressing it. She'd found some charcoal powder to draw out the poison and sprinkled it over the wounds before applying the bandage covered with salve.

Shame washed over her. She'd judged Libby, thinking her a spoiled woman who'd never known hardship, and here her boy had caused her grief for months—maybe even longer. Angel slipped away from the door when Libby started to cry, her sobs piercing the hard armor wrapped around Angel's heart.

But she couldn't let her guard down. If only she could find a place where she truly fit in, rather than just being tolerated. Travis kept her here out of desperation, not because he cared about her as a person. A rush of blood warmed her cheeks as the implication hit her. Of course he wouldn't care about her personally, and she didn't want that—did she? She tried to quench the longing that burned in her chest. It would be nice if Travis cared—and Libby too—but she wouldn't set herself up for disappointment by expecting that.

A soft knock sounded on her door, and she pushed to her feet. Libby probably wanted to make sure her arm was all right. The throbbing hadn't eased, and a terrible burning had started, running from the wound up past her elbow. She bit her lip and raised her chin. No need to be a baby. She'd been hurt before and hadn't complained.

She swung open her door and stood rooted to the spot. Travis had his hand raised, ready to knock again. "Travis. Is everything all right?"

He took a step back. "That's what I want to know. Are you up to talking?"

"Certainly." Angel drew the door shut behind her. Her bandaged arm brushed the door frame, and she winced.

Travis drew in a sharp breath. "You're in pain. I'll send for the doctor."

"No. I'm fine." She turned away and marched down the short hall to the dining room and slid out a chair. "Is that what you wanted to talk about? It's only a scratch."

His brow furrowed. "That's not what it looked like to me. Libby's afraid it might require stitches."

"She did a good job cleaning it. There's no need for worry."

Travis gripped the back of a chair. "You're my employee, so I need to concern myself. An injury like this could lay you up for days."

Angel's stomach clenched in a knot and she took a step back. Here she'd been hoping for a place where she'd fit, and Travis made it clear he only cared about her doing her job. Fine. She'd do it whether it pained her or not. "It won't. I'll be back to work tomorrow. Don't worry; you'll get your money's worth."

His mouth fell open and he snapped it shut, then started to open it again.

Someone pounded on the door.

Travis glared toward the front of the house and spun away from her. "What now?" He stalked out of the room.

"Boss. You'd better get out here and Miss Angel too, if she's inside." Wren's steely voice sent Angel racing out of the room. She hit the entryway and skidded to a stop in time to see James bolt in behind the cowboy.

The young man's hands shook. "Miss Angel, your horse— she's sick or something. She's thrashing all over."

Wren gripped the boy's arm and pushed him back. "I think it's colic. Looks bad."

Angel emitted a strangled cry and leapt through the opening and across the porch. José had given her the filly when Bella was born. He suggested the name, explaining it meant "my beautiful one" in her mother's language. Angel had taken one look at the long-legged foal and agreed. The baby had bonded with her quickly over the next few days. Bella couldn't die—she was Angel's last link to her family.

* * * * *

Travis raced around the corner of the barn in time to see Angel draw up near the corral. Colic could kill a horse. A deep groaning met his ears before he spotted Bella lying on her side in the dirt. The mare attempted to lunge to her feet but fell back with another loud groan. She lay panting for a moment, then jerked all four legs in the air and flopped over to the other side, repeating the movement several times. Angel leaned over the rail and spoke quietly to the horse, avoiding the flailing hooves.

Dismay hit Travis hard. Why had he been so harsh, allowing her to think he only cared about what she could do for him? He'd never been much good with women. Not with his mother in the past, or his sister—and apparently that carried over to female employees. He felt sick with worry about Angel's horse, but even more so about the injury she'd shrugged off. Infection could set in and cause gangrene. His throat ached at the thought of Angel suffering. When they got past this crisis, he'd talk to her again. Only this time he'd convince her she mattered to him as a person, not merely a hired hand.

Wren and James came from the barn, Wren gripping a rope halter. "You'll need to get her up and walking."

"I know." She took the halter and slipped it over her arm, tossing the long length of rope over her shoulder. "I'll wait till she's done thrashing so I don't get kicked."

James stopped beside her. "Why's she groaning? What's wrong with her?"

Angel leaned on the fence. "You ever have a bad bellyache? One that hurts so much you want to curl up and die?"

He nodded, his face solemn. "Yeah. One time when I was little Ma had to call the doctor, I was screaming so loud."

"That's how Bella feels—only she can't scream, she can only groan."

"Is she gonna die?"

Bella lay quiet, breathing hard.

"I sure hope not, but it's possible." Angel slipped between the wooden bars. "I'll get her on her feet and walk her for the next few hours. Rolling on the ground can twist her gut into a knot and then she'd die for sure."

"Can I help?" The boy hooked a leg over the rail, but Travis drew him back.

"Wait, son. You might spook her. She knows Angel, but she doesn't know us." Travis understood how the boy felt—he desperately wanted to lend a hand, as well. But the struggling mare would panic if too many strangers came close while she fought this pain. He'd never lost a horse to colic but had heard horrible stories about their suffering. He said a silent prayer for the animal, knowing Bella's future lay in God's capable and caring hands.

Angel inched her way closer. Bella lay on her side. A quick flick of her wrist and Angel slipped the halter over Bella's nose, securing it behind her ears. "You're going to be all right. Easy there." She knelt beside the mare's head, stroked the length of her neck, then gently rubbed behind her ears. "I need you to get up, Bella." She stood and took a step back, tightening the rope attached to the halter.

Travis gripped the rail and leaned forward. "Want any help?"

"No. If she can stand, she'll do it when I ask." Angel clucked to the horse and spoke again, too low for Travis to make out her words.

Wren moved close to Travis. "Since she don't want any help, I'm goin' to find Smokey. He's a wizard with sick horses."

"Good idea. Go." Travis kept his attention pinned on the girl as Wren's rapid footfalls grew fainter.

Travis clenched his jaw. He'd seen how attached she was to the mare. He'd never had a special relationship with an animal before. He'd always wanted a dog while growing up, but his father wouldn't allow it.

Maybe he'd see if Angel would accept another horse as a replacement, if anything happened to this one. She'd need a mount if she continued her work here. Shock hit him at the way his thoughts had turned. Did everything have to revolve around work? When had the feelings of others become less important? Was it so all-fired essential that he become a success and prove his worth to his father?

The sound of boots hitting the ground and loud puffing heralded the approach of Smokey. The stout man lumbered to a stop. "Wren says it's colic."

"From what we can tell. Bella's been thrashing and Angel's trying to get her on her feet."

Smokey leaned over and wiggled his way between the wood rails, grunting as he did so. "Need to quit cookin' so many blamed flapjacks." He crawled out and stood, brushing off his shirtfront. A few cautious steps brought him to Angel's side. "Little lady, I want you to pull on her head, and I'm going to stand by her hip. When you start heavin', I'll try to help her the rest of the way."

Angel nodded and waited for Smokey to step toward Bella's hindquarters. "All right, here goes." She gave the rope a long, steady pull. "Come on, Bella. You can do it, girl."

The mare extended her front hooves and struggled to rise, then fell back with a groan. Smokey shook his head. "Travis. Miss Angel's hurtin' too bad to pull hard. I need your help." He shot Angel a smile. "She'll make it this time, Miss Angel. We'll try 'er again."

Travis leapt over the bars, kicking himself as he thudded across the corral. In his worry over the mare getting spooked, he'd completely forgotten Angel's injury. He grabbed hold of the rope and Angel stepped to the side, staying close to Bella's neck and crooning encouragement.

Once again the mare fought to get on her feet. She pushed with her front hooves, and her back legs scrambled to get her body off the ground. Smokey stepped in as the mare half stood, half sat, and placed his bulk against her hip. As Travis tugged, Smokey wrapped his arms around the mare's rump and lifted. Bella gave one last heave and stood unsteadily, her sweaty body trembling with the effort. "Get her movin', Boss. Don't let her go down again." Smokey placed his open palm against her flank and urged her forward. "Got to keep walkin' her. Want me to do it?"

Angel turned anxious eyes toward the older man. "No. I need to." She reached for the lead rope and clucked to the horse.

"Could be hours. Got to get her gut working again—need her to pass whatever's causin' the problem." He turned away. "Boss?"

"Yes, Smokey. What do you need?"

"Send the boy in to get some of that oil in the kitchen. We need to get it into this mare to lubricate her insides."

Travis jogged over to James. "Run quick and bring the cod-liver oil."

"Yes, sir!" The boy bolted from the corral without looking back.

Angel walked beside her horse, keeping one hand on the rope and stroking the mare's neck with the other. "Do you think she'll make it, Smokey?"

"Have to wait and see. Any idea what she got into?"

"No. I fed her this morning and turned her out. I gave her the normal amount of grain and a couple of carrots, but that's all."

Bella jerked at the rope and twisted her neck, nipping at her flank and snorting. Angel patted the satiny coat. "I know it hurts, girl, but you've got to keep walking." She led the mare in a wide circle around the inside of the fence. Her arm ached and her head hurt, but she wasn't about to give up on the last thing on earth that she loved. She'd stay up all night if she had to. Bella was not going to die.

Chapter Eleven

....

Smokey and Travis took turns walking Bella, insisting Angel rest—
but sleep wasn't an option until her mare had passed the crisis point.
The men stayed till well after midnight when Bella's distress had less-
ened and she'd been taken to her stall. They headed to bed and, while
Angel assured them she'd do the same, she sat in the corner of the
stall, hating to leave.

She'd wanted nothing more than to find a blanket and curl up in
the hay. Finally, Angel summoned the energy to stand. Seven hours
after the ordeal started, she stumbled to her room, almost too tired to
undress and crawl under the covers.

She fell into a restless slumber, waking every hour or so burning
with thirst. One time she crawled out of bed and poured herself a
glass of water. Thirsty. So hot and thirsty. Her arm throbbed under-
neath the bandage and moisture saturated the cloth.

Angel vaguely remembered bumping her arm when she'd
crawled through the rails on the corral but brushed the pain aside
in her worry over Bella. Sleep. It sounded so good. She slipped back
under the covers, then tossed them aside. Too hot. Mustn't sleep long.
She'd promised Travis she'd be on the job.

Travis. She frowned, her hazy mind drifting in and out, trying
to focus. Why didn't he like her? Was she such a terrible person? She
knew she wasn't pretty. The women at the outlaw camp had told her

that often enough, but she didn't think she was ugly. Angel twisted onto her side and buried her face into her pillow and groaned.

If Travis thought of her as a woman, could he ever love her? Her body jerked, and her eyes flew open. Where had that come from? Not out of any rational part of her brain. Pain induced, that was the problem. She didn't need Travis to love her. Did she? *Stop it, Angel. He's your boss.*

Her head swam and her arm throbbed. Work. She'd prove herself by what she could do. Find the mountain lion before it brought down any more calves. Tomorrow. Blackness swirled around her and she sank into a pit of heat and pain.

* * * * *

Travis walked into the kitchen, grabbed an earthenware mug, and poured himself a cup of steaming coffee. "Angel up yet?" Thoughts of her had haunted him through the wee hours of the morning. He couldn't get the picture out of his head—her gentle hands stroking her sick horse or the crooning words of encouragement as she helped Bella to stand.

Libby shook her head. "No. Is the mare going to be all right?" She set a basket of fresh eggs by the washbasin, pumped the water handle, and rinsed her hands.

Travis took a long drink of the strong brew. "She should be fine. Smokey and I turned in well after midnight when Bella showed signs of recovery. Angel promised she'd head to bed shortly after."

"I didn't hear her come in, but with my room upstairs I'm not surprised." Libby topped off her own cup. "Smokey's not here yet."

The back door banged and boots clomped across the floor of the pantry. Smokey rushed into the room as fast as his bulk would allow and hung his hat on a peg just inside the door. "Sorry, Boss. I checked on Bella. I'll have breakfast goin' in a jiffy."

"That's fine, Smokey. How's the mare?"

"She's hungry and lookin' fit this mornin'."

"Good. The men should be hitting the door soon."

Smokey grunted and reached for a cast-iron skillet. "Those men are like hogs at a trough. I swear, you'd think they'd never been fed."

Libby laughed. "That's a compliment to your excellent cooking." She dipped an egg in the bucket of water, rinsed it, then placed it in a wire basket nearby. "Do we let Angel sleep?"

Travis scratched his head. "I'm sure she could use it, but I'd like to talk to her before I head out for the day. Maybe you'd best see how her arm is."

"All right." Libby wiped her hands on a towel and then hung it on a hook above the washbasin. She glanced around the room. "James isn't up either. Can you check on him?"

"Sure thing." Travis headed for the stairs as Libby walked down the hall toward Angel's room. He started up, wishing he could check on Angel, but that wouldn't be appropriate. He probably should've forced her to see the doctor, but Bella's injury swept aside everything in its path.

"Travis! Come quick!" Libby's stricken cry rang through the house.

Travis pivoted on his toe, launched himself down the three steps to the landing, and bolted across the living area and down the hall.

He stopped short at Angel's open door. He heard the thudding of boots on the floor behind him and sensed at least one person peering over his shoulder. Libby sat on the edge of Angel's bed, stroking her hair.

"What's wrong?"

Libby raised a troubled face. "Get the water pitcher. She's burning up. Send someone for clean rags."

"Got it, Boss." Smokey dashed toward the kitchen.

Angel's bedcovers were tangled around her body and one bare foot stuck out. She rolled her head on the pillow. Beads of sweat dotted her skin, and her hands plucked at the covers. "Bella. Can't lose… Bella. All I have left." A sob slipped past her parted lips.

"What's the problem, Miss Libby?" Arizona's drawl was missing, and his sharp words conveyed his concern. He peered in the door and Wren crowded in behind him. "Miss Angel sick?"

Travis lifted the heavy earthenware pitcher and poured water into the ivory bowl. "Wren, would you go upstairs and wake James? Arizona, throw some feed to the horses and check Bella again."

"I did, Boss, afore I came in. She's munching her hay like nobody's business. Don't appear to be any worse for what she went through."

"Good." Travis gave a grim smile. "Head back to the kitchen, and we'll let you know what we find."

"Sure, Boss. I'll check on the boy." Wren twisted his hat in his hands and turned away. They clomped off, their worried voices drifting back until they passed out of earshot.

Smokey appeared at the door with his arms full of rags and stepped inside, laying them on a chair near the bed. "Here you go, Miz Waters. I'll be in the kitchen fixin' breakfast. If you need anything more, jest holler."

"Thank you, Smokey. I will." Libby dipped a rag in the water, wrung it out, and tenderly wiped Angel's cheeks. "Shh, it's going to be all right, Angel. Bella's fine."

Travis dampened another rag and passed it to his sister. "Libby? You think it's her arm?"

"Yes. I checked, and it's oozing through her bandage. I'm going to change it. You wait in the other room."

He straightened and frowned. "I hate leaving. What if you need help? What if she gets worse?"

"You can't be in here, Travis. I can take care of it. Go." Her compressed lips and firm glance decided him, and he took a step toward the door. A smile softened her grim features. "I'll call if I need you."

Travis paused. "Think I should send for the doc?"

"More than likely, but let me take a look first, then decide."

* * * * *

Angel tried to open her eyes, but they felt so heavy. She had to check on Bella. What if she hadn't made it through the night? A couple of hours ago she'd tried to get out of bed but got tangled in the blankets and couldn't fight free. She must have fallen back asleep. She pushed at the covers, desperate to cool off. Couldn't let her horse die.

"Shh—it's okay, Angel." A soothing hand stroked her hair, and something wet and cool touched her forehead. "Arizona checked on Bella, and she's fine. You need to hold still. You're ill."

"Arizona?" She shook her head, trying to clear the darkness. "Bella—" She managed to pry open her eyes this time, blinking against the strong light coming in the window. The door latch clicked and boots thumped down the hall. Had someone else been here while she slept? One of the cowboys? Travis? Her already warm face grew warmer at the thought of the men seeing her. "Why am I so hot?" She pushed at the blanket and tried to moisten her dry lips. "Thirsty. So thirsty."

Libby hurried to the bureau, poured water into a glass, and brought it to the bed. She slipped her hand under Angel's neck. "Let me help you sit up a bit." She lifted her head a few inches and placed the glass to her lips. "Here you go. Nice and slow."

Angel took several long drinks and lay back with a sigh. "Thanks. Need to work. I promised Travis."

Libby placed her hands against Angel's shoulders and shook her head. "Lay back. Travis knows you're not feeling well. May I look at your arm?"

"Travis knows? How—?" She closed her eyes, trying to take in the disturbing thought. "Don't want anyone in here." She tried to sit up but a flash of pain sent her reeling against her pillow. "Oh. It hurts. Like fire."

"Let me see." Libby pulled back the top blanket and sheet to Angel's waist and picked up the bandaged arm. "I'm going to remove part of the wrapping, but I'll need to soak it to get it all off. When did it start bleeding again, Angel? You should have told me."

"I couldn't lose my best friend, could I?" She tried to muster a laugh, but it turned into a sob. "Bella mattered, not me."

* * * * *

Libby worked silently, unwinding the cloth until she reached the pad pressed against the raw flesh. It appeared to be glued to the wound and a red stain showed around the edges. She suppressed a shudder as her mind went back to the long days she'd tended her husband, George, as he lay dying. Infection had set in, then gangrene. The doctor did all he could to save him, but it was too late. George's delirium turned from thrashing to a deep sleep that he never woke from. *Please, God, don't let that happen to Angel.*

From what she could tell, the young woman had no family, no friends, and very possibly no relationship with the Almighty. Remorse struck Libby as she realized she'd never spoken to her about the Lord. She'd allowed Angel to go her own way, working, riding, and mostly keeping to herself without a thought to what the girl might need.

"I'll be right back, Angel. I'll get clean water so I can soak this bandage." She rose from the edge of the bed and walked to the door with the bowl, balancing it on one hip as she grasped the knob and drew the door open. Her brother stood in the hallway. "Travis?"

She heard a soft gasp and turned. Angel's eyes were wide open and staring. "I don't want him in here, please!"

"Don't worry, dear, he won't come in." Libby slipped out into the hall, drawing the door closed behind her.

Travis's face was drawn. "Can I help?"

"No. Angel doesn't want anyone else in her room. If I'd been thinking clearly before, I'd not have allowed you or Smokey to enter."

"All right." Travis ran his hand over his chin. "She's awake."

"Yes. She's feverish but coherent, and the arm doesn't look good. It started bleeding again, probably when she was caring for Bella. I need you to toss this water and rinse out the bowl. Send someone to the door to fill the pitcher."

"Sure, Sis, will do." He gave her a warm smile. "I'm thankful you're here. Not sure what I'd do without you."

Something resembling joy surged through her breast and almost left her trembling. George had loved her in his own way, but he'd rarely shown appreciation. Even if it was her brother instead of her husband, it was still nice to know someone cared. "Thanks. Did Wren wake James?"

Wren entered the hall. He scratched his ear and wrinkled his forehead. "Miss Libby, your boy weren't in his room. I reckoned he musta been plumb worried about Miss Angel's horse, so I hightailed it to the barn to check on him, and haul him back inside." He expelled a loud breath. "But he don't seem to be in the barn, either. I told Nate, and he set Bud and Charlie to lookin' for him. He cain't have gone far."

Travis's head came up. "Any ideas where he might be, Lib?"

"I'm sure Wren's right. The men will find him." Libby felt amazement at her casual attitude. A few weeks ago she'd have been frantic with worry, but right now she couldn't muster more than mild concern. James wouldn't ride off alone, and he didn't enjoy walking enough to have gone far. He was probably at the privy and would come in for breakfast any moment.

The next half hour or so passed swiftly, with the cowboys tiptoeing down the hall to stand outside Angel's door, only to scurry away at Libby's stern reprimand. The wound beneath the crusted bandage was inflamed and hot to the touch. Libby applied a liberal amount of salve and wrapped it again. She dipped a cloth in the water, wiped Angel's cheeks, and pulled the sheet up around her shoulders. "There you go, my dear. I'll bring you a cup of tea and then I want you to rest."

Angel shook her head, her black, tangled curls moving against her pillow. "Need to get to work. Don't want to disappoint Travis." Her husky voice rasped out the words.

"Travis's orders. Now please get some sleep."

"Bella?" Angel drew in a ragged breath. "You're sure she's all right?"

"I'm sure." Libby smoothed Angel's hair away from her forehead. "Rest until I bring your tea." She waited until the girl's eyes closed and slipped from the room.

Travis stopped pacing when she entered the kitchen. "Do you want me to send someone for the doctor?"

"Yes. I'd suggest putting her in the wagon and taking her to town, but I'm not sure she's up to the trip."

Nate stepped forward, his forehead creased with worry. "We could make a mighty comfortable bed in the back, ma'am. Pile in all our bedding and take the trip slow and easy."

She cast him a soft smile and shook her head. "Just send one of the men into town and ask the doctor to come straight out. I think it's best to let her rest, but thank you for offering."

He turned sharply around. "Bud."

"Yes, sir!" The slender young man jerked upright and almost saluted.

"Take our fastest horse and ride to town. Tell Doc Simmons we need him out here, pronto."

Bud bolted for the door and didn't look back.

Travis gripped Libby's arm and drew her aside. "You're sure she'll be all right until Doc gets here?"

"I can't be sure, Travis, but it won't do her any good to jostle her in the wagon. She's awake and seems to be in her right mind, and that's a good sign. We need to pray she doesn't get worse."

"Of course. Pray." He rammed his hands into his jeans pockets and began to pace the floor, his head bowed and lips moving.

Libby turned back toward Nate, sudden concern for her son hitting her hard. She hadn't seen James yet, and the boy surely couldn't still be out at the privy. "Nate?"

He swung around with a smile. "Ma'am?"

"Did Bud or Charlie find James?"

"I forgot to ask Bud. Charlie!" He lifted his voice and the cowhand came running from the dining room.

"Yes, Boss?"

"You find James yet?"

"No, sir. Bud was supposed to tell you." He cast a look around the room.

"I sent him after Doc Simmons. What was he supposed to tell me?"

"James ain't nowhere around, and his horse is gone."

Chapter Twelve
....

Travis stalked to the corral, Libby's horrified voice ringing in his ears. He'd see for himself if James's horse was gone, but his gut told him Charlie had made a mistake. Maybe the boy had returned by now—no sense in worrying until he'd checked it out.

"Hey, Boss. Want some help?" Wren hoofed it across the yard on bowed legs more suited to riding than walking. "I done looked in the corral."

Travis slowed his pace and waited for the cowboy. "How about the hayloft?"

Wren tugged at his collar and panted but swung in beside Travis. "We hollered all over in the barn, and he didn't answer. But why would his hoss be gone?"

Travis shoved open the door of the drafty barn and peered into the dark interior.

"James. You in here, boy?" His voice echoed from the rafters and bounced around the open space. "James!" No one answered his call. "Where'd that kid go? He's going to get a serious talking-to when I find him."

"Ah, wasn't you ever adventurous? Seems you're bein' a mite hard on the youngster." Wren plucked a piece of hay and stuck it between his teeth.

Travis's thoughts drifted back to the sheriff's visit, and he scowled.

Was it possible that James had snuck to town without their knowledge? It didn't seem likely, as they'd surely notice his absence. Just one more thing to take up with the boy.

"Travis?" Libby's distressed voice penetrated the wood of the barn walls. She stepped through the open door and glanced around. "It's dark in here. Where are you?"

"Here, Lib. Leave the door open wide so more light will come in." Travis hurried forward and stopped a couple of yards from his sister. "Any sign of James?"

"No, and I'm getting worried. It's not like him to miss a meal. I'm not sure how much more I can take. First Angel and now James."

"What's wrong with Miss Angel?" A sleepy voice sounded from the top of the ladder ending in the loft. Bits of hay drifted down. Dust particles glimmered in a lone shaft of light coming through the open door.

"James?" Travis bolted for the base of the ladder and looked up. "What are you doing up there, boy?" At this point he didn't care if his relief at finding his nephew released itself in a bellow. Even better if it scared the boy, like he'd scared the rest of them.

Libby stopped beside Travis and clutched his arm. "Is he all right?"

Wren sidled up to the pair and choked back a laugh. "The rascal sounds like he's been sleepin' whilst we've all been scamperin' around huntin' for him. Ha!"

Libby planted her fists on her hips and glared up at her son. "You get down here this instant, James Tyrone Waters. You've got some explaining to do."

"Aw, Ma. I wasn't doing nothin' wrong." James swung a leg over the edge of the upper floor and placed his foot on the top rung.

"Anything, James. You weren't doing *anything* wrong." Libby's voice cracked with irritation.

James plodded down the ladder and jumped the last two rungs, landing a few feet away from his mother. "That's right, Ma, not a thing."

She sighed in exasperation and gripped his arm, drawing him close. "Do you have any idea how worried I was? We've been looking everywhere for you."

He rubbed his knuckles against his eyes and yawned. "I woke up early, just before the sun came up, and couldn't get back to sleep. I remembered Wren telling me about some kittens up in the loft and I wanted to find them. I played with them for a while, and I guess I fell asleep." He shrugged. "Don't know why everybody's all in a stew about it. I wasn't doin' nothin' wrong."

"Anything, James."

He shrugged. "I'm hungry. Can we eat now?" A quick twist and he'd jerked his arm out of her grasp.

Travis stepped forward. "Where's your horse, boy? We didn't find him in the corral."

"I took Jasper down to the creek for water and found a nice patch of grass and staked him out. Figured I could go get him after breakfast." He started to walk away, then turned around. "You said something about worrying over Miss Angel. What's wrong?"

"Oh my goodness!" Libby gasped and placed her palms against her cheeks. "I've been so busy fretting about James I forgot about Angel." She picked up her skirts and dashed out the door but called over her shoulder. "Travis, make sure that son of mine makes it to the house this time."

"Yes, ma'am." Travis strangled a chuckle and placed his arm across James's shoulders. "Come on, son. I'll tell you about Miss Angel on the way."

* * * * *

Travis sent his cowboys to work despite their protests. They wanted to hang around outside Angel's door and wait for the doctor to arrive, but the ranch wouldn't run itself. He'd put the talk with James on hold till things settled down and they determined Angel's condition. At least the boy was safe and hadn't gotten into trouble. A couple hours later Travis stepped outside and walked to the edge of the porch. The midday sun felt good.

The doctor's buggy pulled into the yard, and he drew his mare to a halt at the hitching rail. "Whoa there, Maggie. Time to rest now." He wrapped the reins around the brake handle and clambered down from the padded seat, dropping onto the hard-packed ground. The horse snorted and dropped her head, bobbing it a couple of times.

Travis walked across the porch and down the steps to meet the older man. Doc Simmons leaned into his buggy for his medical bag. He placed the bag on the ground, removed his hat, and wiped his forehead with the back of his sleeve, revealing wavy brown hair in need of a cut. "Tolerable warm today, Travis. Bud says you've got a woman here who got clawed by a cougar?" He hoisted his bag and headed for the steps.

"Thanks for coming, Doc. We'd have brought Miss Ramirez to you, but Libby was worried it might not be good for her, since she's a mite feverish."

"No problem. Your cowboy caught me at a good time. Just got back from delivering another healthy baby for Mrs. Sorenson early this morning."

"What's that make, six?" Travis pushed open the door and ushered the older man in first.

"Seven. Two girls and five boys. Says she's done having children, but we'll see. Said that two babies ago." He sighed. "Sure would help if her husband got off his lazy backside and found a job."

Travis nodded, unsure of the proper reply. "Miss Ramirez is in a room behind the kitchen. Libby's with her."

"Sounds good, son." The doctor followed Travis with a brisk step to Angel's room.

Travis rapped on the door and stepped aside, expecting Libby's immediate response, but none came. He lifted his hand again. A sharp cry from inside the room froze him in his tracks.

Chapter Thirteen
....

"I told you, I don't want a doctor!" Angel's voice rose an octave. Libby laid a gentle hand on hers, but the girl pushed her away. "Travis will send me packing if I can't work. I need this job!" She struggled to rise but fell back against the bed, unshed tears glistening.

Libby's mouth parted but no words came. Travis was as worried about Angel as she, and she'd heard no talk of hiring someone else.

"Angel, it's all right. Shh…" She tucked a strand of black hair behind the young woman's ear. "No one's going to send you away because you're hurt."

Another knock sounded at the door, and it opened softly. "Everything all right?" Travis spoke through the crack. "The doctor is here."

"Yes. Have him come in, please."

Travis opened the door and then stepped back into the hall. His hurried footsteps disappeared in the distance as the doctor walked into the room.

* * * * *

Travis balled his fingers into fists and stared out the window of the front room overlooking the barn. He hadn't felt this helpless since his mother took sick. Father had been stoic, seemingly emotionless, while he'd been trapped in worry. But no amount of worry had saved Mother. He dropped his head. Why was prayer almost always the last thing he thought of? *God forgive me, and please take care of Angel.*

A wave of peace washed over his heart, and he straightened. God was in charge, not him.

When had he started to care about the woman lying in the other room? Compassion he could understand, but true caring? He didn't even know her. But he'd seen her plucky spirit, determination, and honesty. She'd chosen to reveal her identity rather than live a lie. And the words he'd overheard made him wince. Did Angel honestly think he'd send her away because she was unable to do her job? She must see him as hard and unyielding—that would *have* to change.

Travis valued honesty and courage, and he saw those in abundance in this young woman. Only one thing surpassed those qualities in his mind—faith. He drew in a sharp breath. Not once had he heard Angel express a belief in God. But in all fairness, they'd never discussed the subject. Surely she'd been raised in a household where faith was part of her life.

He wrinkled his brow and turned away from the window, staring at the massive set of antlers over the fireplace. What did he know of her family, or the home where she'd been raised, or anything else, for that matter? Absolutely nothing. Unease sent fingers of doubt into his mind. Who was this woman who'd ridden into his life two short weeks ago? Where did she come from, and who were her people? He thought back over the couple of times he'd broached the topic only to have her change the subject. At the time he hadn't thought much of it. Now it gave rise to curiosity—and caution.

Libby stepped into the room. "Doc Simmons will spend the night and keep an eye on her. We'll know more in the morning."

* * * * *

Travis paced the floor in the living room early the next morning, anxious for an update on Angel. Libby had helped through the night and come out once with an encouraging report. The fever had broken, and she believed the worst had passed.

Boots thudded on the front porch. Something warned him to keep quiet and stay out of sight, and he stepped behind a corner cabinet.

The door creaked open, and Wren poked his head in. "All clear." He hissed the words over his shoulder and shoved it open a little further. "Come on, you lovesick bozos. I ain't waitin' around forever."

Charlie, Arizona, and Bud crept in behind him, each clutching something in their fists. Arizona held a bouquet of wildflowers that he must have ridden far and wide to find, based on the variety and colors. Bright yellow arnica, deep red Indian paintbrush, and purple lupine, all vied for attention. Charlie and Bud each grasped a small paper bag, and Wren sported a length of ribbon wrapped around his gnarled fingers.

Travis stifled a laugh and nearly choked. Of all the infatuated pups, this took the prize. He purposely dropped his voice to a low growl and stepped out from behind the cabinet, his arms crossed over his chest. "What do you men think you're doing?"

Arizona jumped and grabbed at his flowers, and Charlie's sack hit the floor, spilling a few pieces of hard candy. "Aw, Boss. Now see what you made me do!" Charlie dropped to his knees and scrambled after the sweets.

Wren tucked his hand behind his back and glared. "What you sneakin' up on us for?"

"Yeah." Arizona raised the bouquet to his chin. "We're bringing Miss Angel some posies and candy. That ain't no reason for you to shout at us."

"Sorry, men." Travis relaxed his stance and grinned. "You all looked so funny that I couldn't help joshing you. Sorry I ruined your surprise, Charlie."

The cowboy snatched at the final piece, stuffed it back into his bag, and straightened to his full height. "Bud's got more. Guess we'll have to share."

Bud's eyes narrowed. "Not on your life. These sweets are mine, paid for with my own money."

"Aw, Bud, that's not fair!" Charlie's voice rose to almost a wail.

"Cut it, you two." Arizona stepped forward and grabbed the bag from Bud's grip. "Miss Angel's sick, and you're out here caterwaulin' like a couple of new pups."

Travis wagged his head and turned a stern gaze on Charlie. "Arizona's right. While I'm sure Miss Ramirez will appreciate your gifts, I don't think she should be disturbed. Doc Simmons is with her right now and—"

"Travis?" The doctor's voice brought a halt to the conversation.

The men froze, then slowly turned toward the hallway.

"Yes, sir." Travis stepped away from the cluster of cowboys and raised his hand. "How's Angel?"

"Better. Your sister missed her calling. Miss Ramirez's temperature is down, and the young lady appears to be improving. One of the gashes in her arm wasn't deep, but I put a few stitches in the other one. If I'd been called sooner—" He tipped his head and glared over the edge of his spectacles. "Well, let's just say she'll probably have a scar. Not a lot I could do with a wound that was over a day old."

Travis felt like he had as a schoolboy when the teacher rapped his knuckles. "I should have insisted she come to town right after she was injured, but her horse took sick with colic."

"People are more important than horses, son, or didn't your

pappy teach you that?" The doctor set his bag on a chair and adjusted the spectacles perched on his nose.

"He did, and I agree." Travis heard the hint of a snicker coming from the cowboys. "She'll recover?"

"Yes. She's a strong young woman." The stern look gave way to a twinkle. "And a pretty one, at that."

"Yes, sir." Travis ran a hand through his hair. Another snicker broke out, and he swung around and glared. "Don't you men have work to do?"

The merriment died from their faces. "Gee-willikers, Boss." Bud took off his hat and slapped it against his leg. "We was all kinda hopin' to see Miss Angel first."

"Not going to happen, boys." Travis softened at their agony-filled faces. "Unless Doc thinks it's wise."

"Her fever broke, and she needs her rest." Doc Simmons's voice was firm. He glanced from one cowboy to the next and released a sigh. "All right. But you can't go in the room. Stand at her door and give the things to Mrs. Waters."

"Thanks, Doc!" Arizona sprang for the hall and the other three raced after him.

"Men!" Travis barked the single word and the four cowboys tumbled into each other. "You aren't cattle stampeding to water. Act like gentlemen. Five minutes—that's it."

"Yes, Boss."

Travis couldn't tell which humble voice offered the words, but the small group crept forward barely making a sound. As soon as they were out of sight, he sobered and swung back to the doctor. "What if the fever returns?"

"Not likely. Besides, Mrs. Waters can care for her. Too bad there isn't another woman living close by, though. Hate to see your sister up too many nights and wearing herself out." He scratched the light stubble on his chin. "I'll come back in the morning."

"Could I sit with her for a spell tonight, and let Libby rest?" Eagerness rushed into his heart like a colt racing for a green pasture. The thought brought an unexpected pleasure that he didn't care to examine right now.

"Should be fine. By the way, I didn't ask Mrs. Waters—this girl a relative or...sweetheart, maybe? And how come you're keeping her hid and not brought her to church?"

Travis tugged at his collar. "Uh—no, she's neither one. She works for me."

"Ah. Housekeeper then?" The doctor turned a penetrating gaze on Travis and waited.

"Varmint tracker." Travis winced at the harsh sound of the words and hurried to soften the impression. "I hired her to help until I can find someone else. She came highly recommended."

The doctor's brows rose to the bushy brown fringe dangling over his forehead. "What kind of job is that for a woman? Tarnation! No wonder she got clawed by a lion. What are you thinking letting a young gal traipse around the hills shooting wolves and cougars and such?"

Travis squared his shoulders, ready to end this discussion. "She asked for the job, she was qualified, and I hired her." He didn't want to offend the only doctor within a hundred miles, but sometimes Doc Simmons didn't know when to quit. "I'm grateful you took the time to drive all the way out here. We'll take good care of her and see you in the morning."

The doctor slid a pocket watch from his vest and held it up. "By jiminy, it's getting late. I'd best be heading along. Sorry for biting your head off, Travis. I need to get some sleep."

Travis relaxed and smiled. "We appreciate you coming."

Several pairs of boots clomped on the hardwood floor and the four cowboys appeared, their faces shining like they'd seen a glimpse of glory. The doctor hustled across the room and out the front door. Travis signaled for the men to stop. "You stayed more than a couple of minutes. The doctor told you not to tire her."

Arizona threw his hands in a wide gesture and shook his head. "We didn't do any such thing, Boss. Miss Libby, she took the presents we brought to Miss Angel and she perked right up. We got to see her through the open door. She loved the flowers I gave her." He preened like a peacock strutting in front of its mate.

Travis shook his head. Sometimes he wondered why he kept the cocky, good-looking cowboy, the way he went on about women. But Arizona had a good heart and was one of the best hands he'd ever hired. Too bad his curly blond hair and square-jawed good looks had drawn so much attention from the fair sex over the years. He needed to settle down and get married. The thought jolted him. What if Arizona were interested in Angel and she in him? They'd make a handsome pair. But Angel? He shook his head, not liking the direction his thoughts had taken him.

"Something wrong, Boss?" Wren stuffed his hands into his pockets and rocked on his heels. "If you don't need nothin' else, I reckon we'd best get to work."

"Yeah, I agree." Arizona sauntered toward the door. "I want to rustle and finish up. Miss Angel said I could come back and visit her later." He grinned and headed for the door, whistling a jaunty tune.

"Hold it, men." Travis stepped toward them. "No one visits Angel today. The doctor said she needs quiet and sleep. He's coming back in the morning, but until then, she's off limits."

Arizona let out a loud groan. "But I promised her I'd come. What's she gonna think of me?"

Travis smiled and clapped Arizona on the shoulder. "I'll be sure and tell her you wanted to come, when I sit with her later tonight."

Wren elbowed Arizona and whispered something too low to hear. Arizona growled in return, scowled, and stalked out the door.

Chapter Fourteen

....

Later that evening Travis knocked gently on Angel's door and waited. He'd seen her anxiety when he'd escorted the doctor here yesterday, and he didn't want to upset her if she were awake.

The door eased open, and Libby beckoned him inside. "She's sleeping. I hate leaving her, but I'm having trouble staying awake."

Travis slipped his arm around her shoulder and squeezed. "I'm sorry. Guess I should've come sooner."

"No." She shook her head. "Angel only fell asleep less than an hour ago. It's better this way."

"Anything I need to know?"

"She's past the point of danger, but watch for signs of restlessness. If her face is flushed or her skin warm to the touch, you'll need to bathe her forehead with cool water."

"All right. Have a good night, Lib." Travis patted her arm and smiled. "Doc Simmons says you're a first-rate nurse and missed your calling."

Libby shrugged. "It's nice feeling useful, besides just cooking and cleaning." She slipped out the door and eased it shut behind her.

Travis made his way to the chair near the edge of Angel's bed and sank into it with a quiet grunt. Libby must still be struggling with living here and he couldn't blame her. Nothing but rough men surrounded her most of the time, and more work than she was accustomed to. Maybe he *should* try to find a woman to move in and help. That would give Libby more time with James. He'd meant to talk to the boy regarding the sheriff's concerns. He and Libby would have to tackle that issue soon.

His gaze rested on the still form burrowed under the covers, her face and hair peeking out from the blanket. How small she appeared. Warmth crept up into his cheeks and he averted his gaze. What would Angel think if she knew he was sitting beside her bed? Under normal circumstances, it wouldn't be seemly, but what else could he do? Libby shouldn't be expected to care for her alone, and he certainly wouldn't send one of his cowboys in here.

The memory of Arizona's request smote him hard. The man seemed infatuated with Angel, and according to him, she'd welcomed his attention. He should be happy for Arizona, as his cowboy seemed lonely since arriving at the ranch. But the picture of Arizona and Angel making a life together left a sour taste in his mouth.

He looked around the room, which was dimly lit by a lantern perched on the bureau. Its glow cast fingers of light in a shallow circle. He'd planned this room for guests, with the hope that someday his father might visit. But Father's presence had never graced his home.

A barely audible moan came from a few feet away. "Thirsty." Her slender hand escaped from the covers and stretched toward him.

Travis nearly toppled the chair in his haste to get the water. He'd not expected her to wake. Maybe she'd drink and slip back into sleep, never realizing who'd sat beside her. His hand trembled as he lifted the pitcher and tipped it over the glass. He then stepped across to Angel's bedside and offered the drink without a word, holding his breath and praying she'd take it without noting his presence.

Her fingers twitched, and her arm dropped to the top of the quilt. "Help me, Libby? Don't think I can sit up alone."

Travis stifled a groan. Now what? Should he call Libby or urge Angel to try? Surely it wouldn't be proper to help Angel sit up. He'd have to touch her to do that.

He wrestled with the dilemma for nearly a minute, hating himself for the battle raging inside. On the range he had no problem making a quick and accurate judgment, even when danger lurked. But he'd never felt as great a danger as he sensed now, with this black-haired beauty lying so close. What was he afraid of? Sure she was a beautiful woman, but she was his employee, not his sweetheart.

"Libby?" Angel struggled to sit on her own, then fell back with a whimper.

He stepped closer and leaned over the bed, praying he wouldn't startle her. "It's not Libby. It's me. Travis."

She gasped, but Travis couldn't see her face with his body blocking the lantern's light.

"Shh, it's all right. I'll help you sit if you need me to."

"What—are you—doing here?" She forced the words through clenched teeth. "Where's Libby?"

He sank back into the chair. "She needed sleep, and I sent her to bed."

"But why you?"

"There's no one else I trust to care for you." The words startled him with the starkness of their truth. "Smokey might have been all right, but he has to be up early to fix breakfast."

"Arizona or Wren?" The whisper was almost too low to hear.

"Didn't seem like a good idea." He lifted the glass and rose to his feet again. "Let me help you."

"No!" She braced one elbow under herself and pushed, grunting with the exertion. "I—can—do it."

Travis reached out his free hand to help, but she shook her head and glared. "No." Angel struggled to rise, and beads of sweat popped out on her forehead. When she achieved the halfway point she paused, her arm shaking, then fell back against the pillow. "Go. Please. I'll just sleep."

"I'm afraid not, young lady." Travis had had enough. It was a good thing his father switched him hard the one time he'd let loose with a curse word, or he'd surely be using one now. What a stubborn, mule-headed woman. "You need water, and I'm going to help you, like it or not. We can't have your fever returning." He leaned over the bed and started to slip his hand under her neck when a lone tear trickled down her cheek.

She turned her head away.

Travis nearly buckled. That tear was like a kick in the gut by a wild steer. What was he doing in this woman's room, forcing his presence on her? He'd made her cry, and he doubted that Angel Ramirez cried easily. He steeled himself and carefully slid his hand under her neck and lifted, then placed the glass to her lips.

She raised her good arm and grasped the glass with strong fingers, drinking eagerly. Travis waited until she'd almost drained it and gently laid her back down. His hand tingled, and a tremor ran up his arm. He must be getting weak. Angel didn't weigh a thing, and it had been no effort at all to hold her, but here he was, shaking like a boy battling his first crush. "Did you get enough?"

"Yes, thank you." Her normally firm voice was hesitant. "I'd like to go back to sleep, if you don't mind."

"Certainly. I'll just sit quietly and try not to bother you. Would you like me to douse the lantern?"

"No. Leave it. I don't want…" She bit her lip.

"Want what?" He leaned forward, afraid he'd miss the answer, but none came. "Angel?" Travis longed to comfort her but knew his touch wouldn't be welcomed.

"Nothing. I'm fine." She turned her head away.

* * * * *

Angel fought to open her heavy eyelids. She'd gone to sleep and dreamed of the room being black as sin and a stranger slipping in through the door. He'd walked to her bed and bent over, his leering smile sending a sliver of fear into her heart. Had something like that happened in her past? Why was her blood pounding through her veins like a runaway horse? Surely no man would enter her room without her permission.

A vague image stirred. Uncle José's voice growling low and the click of a gun. Heavy footsteps leaving her room and a savage curse drifting back on the night air. Had it been a dream, or was her mind trying to tell her something?

She rolled over onto her side facing the door, and her body jerked. A man sat slumped in the chair nearby, his head lolling to the side. Had the man she'd dreamt about come back? Where was her gun? Her numbed brain couldn't remember. She'd put it under the edge of her bed, instead of her pillow.

A whiffling snore broke from his lips. Travis.

Angel scooted a couple of inches closer to the wall and relaxed. But Libby had been here when she drifted off to sleep, hadn't she? The afternoon and evening blurred together in her mind, and she worked to separate reality from the dreamlike state she'd fallen into the past few hours. A hazy memory returned of a hand slipping under her neck and someone lifting a glass to her lips. She'd been so very thirsty, but not too long ago the consuming thirst had abated. Had Travis talked to her and given her a drink before she fell back into a troubled sleep? How long had he been here, and why?

She remembered the four cowboys coming to see her earlier with an assortment of gifts. Arizona had actually blushed when he'd offered his bouquet of wildflowers drooping over his clasped fist. She sensed that the cowboy was sweet on her, and it gave her a strange feeling inside. More than once in the past she'd had a low-down outlaw look at her in a way that made her cringe, but not once had a decent young man showered her with gifts or kind words. She'd longed for somewhere to fit in, and often wondered if she'd ever have a home of her own. Might Arizona—?

Travis shifted, grunted, and eased upright, shaking his head. He mumbled something Angel couldn't understand and slowly slid back into the chair.

Angel wished she could reach the glass of water on her own, but her arm throbbed and she doubted she could creep out of bed without waking her boss. "Are you awake, Travis?"

He straightened so quickly the chair rocked. "Huh? What?" He turned his head back and forth, then fixed his bleary eyes on her. "Angel? How come…?"

"You're in my room? I was hoping you could tell me." She paused. "After you give me a drink of water."

"Water?" He ran his hand over his head, making the dark brown locks stick out several different directions. "Oh. I'll get it." The glass sat on a small, round table close to his elbow, and he passed it over to her outstretched hand. "Need some help?"

"No. I'm better. Thanks." Angel put her feet flat against the mattress, pushed herself higher on her pillow, then drew the blanket up under her chin. A long, slow drink moistened her dry mouth. She sighed and handed the glass back to him. "Sorry to wake you."

Travis set it carefully on the table and grunted. "I'm the one who should apologize. I can't believe I fell asleep." He grimaced, looking like a little boy who'd been caught doing something naughty. "You go back to sleep, and I'll stay awake in case you need anything."

Angel slid back against her pillow. "I don't think I'll be able to now. Seems like all I've done lately is sleep."

"How do you feel?" He extended his hand toward her and hesitated. "I'm supposed to keep an eye on you, in case you have a fever again. Do you mind if I touch your forehead?"

She squirmed and tried not to shrink back. How silly to mind Travis's touch. José placed a cool cloth on her head when she had a fever one time and smoothed his hand over her hair. His touch soothed her thrashing and calmed her so she could sleep. But Travis *wasn't* her uncle. "Sure. I guess it's all right."

Travis placed gentle fingers against her skin and let them rest there for several moments. Angel felt as though her skin were on fire.

"You feel cool. No sign of a fever that I can tell." He sat back in his chair and grinned. "The doctor will be back this morning." He glanced out the window at the lightening sky. "Hopefully you'll be back on your feet in no time."

Angel winced. "Don't worry. I'll be able to ride in another day or so. A couple of scratches aren't going to keep me down." Weariness pulled at her. "I think I'll rest now. I guess I'm tired, after all."

* * * * *

Travis sat frozen, unsure whether to speak or allow Angel to sleep. She needed her rest, but he hated the impression he'd once again planted in her mind. "Angel?" She lay silent, unmoving, but he couldn't let this go. "I'd like to talk to you for another minute." He waited, his gut tense and his mouth dry.

She didn't turn her head. "I need to sleep."

"I know." He leaned forward, his hands clasped between his knees. "I apologize for how that sounded. I keep putting my foot in my mouth, and I'm sorry. Take as long as you need to, before you go back to work." Travis sat up and squared his shoulders. "In fact, I insist that you listen to the doctor and don't overdo. You mustn't have a setback."

He sighed. "And not because of your job. I care about you. As a person, not just as an employee." He felt like he was stumbling over his words.

She didn't appear convinced. She kept her gaze averted, and her teeth worried her lower lip.

"Angel? Would you look at me? Please?"

Her lovely face swiveled his direction, but no smile softened her features. "You don't have to worry. I'll be fine and back to work soon."

He blew his breath out hard between his lips. "I meant what I said." He struggled to push out the words. "When I hired you, I had serious doubts about you doing the job, but I've changed my mind." The air around them grew still. He was intent on continuing his explanation, when a gentle knock sounded at the door.

"Travis?" The door opened a few inches, and Libby peeked around the edge. "I thought I heard voices. Is Angel awake?"

Travis leaned back hard against the chair, not knowing whether to feel irritated or relieved. Had Angel even heard the last thing he'd said? Her gaze was trained on Libby, and he pushed to his feet, frustrated at the interruption. "Yes, and she's all yours, Libby. I'll get to my chores and see you at breakfast."

Travis chanced a quick look at Angel before leaving the room, but she'd already closed her eyes. So much for trying to explain. He shoved his hands in his pockets and walked to the door. There was work to do, and plenty of it—and no time to stand around regretting what hadn't been said.

Chapter Fifteen

....

Travis tossed back his blanket and swung his feet to the floor, grimacing as his bare skin made contact with the cold wood. Early June mornings in Wyoming still had a bite. He passed his knuckles over his eyes. What he'd give for a couple more hours of sleep. He'd spelled Libby again last night, but she'd come in the wee hours and insisted he rest for a while. He didn't know whether he was thankful or disappointed that Angel had slept the entire time he'd sat beside her.

During the day yesterday there'd been no opportunity to talk about the misunderstanding of the night before. He'd make a point of speaking to her today. Doc Simmons had seemed satisfied with her progress when he'd stopped by yesterday, insisting she was on the mend.

A yawn slipped out. He stifled it and grabbed his jeans. Slipping into his cotton shirt and splashing water on his face, he forced himself to take his time and not rush out the door. No sense in accosting Angel this early in the morning.

Travis rolled his shoulders, hoping to ease the tension. Why in the world was he tense over talking to one of his employees? He snatched at the towel hanging on a hook next to the bureau. After all, he was the boss and Angel—well, Angel was...

His thoughts stalled. He shoved his hat onto his head and bolted for the door.

At the top of the stairs he slowed his pace, keenly aware of the hush lying over the house. James would still be rolled in his blankets and Angel undoubtedly slept. Clomping down the stairs with his hard-heeled boots beating a tattoo might wake his family, so he eased down the staircase, gripping the oak handrail.

A soft metal thump in the kitchen made him pick up the pace. Libby stood, frowning at the stove.

"Libby? I didn't expect to see you in here yet. Is Angel sleeping?"

Libby swung away from the stove and brushed a lock of hair off her forehead. "Yes. And I don't understand this cookstove. The cantankerous thing won't light, and I want a pot of coffee."

Travis opened the cast-iron door of the stove. He peered inside and chuckled. "You can't start a fire with just a log and paper, Lib. You've got to use kindling." He withdrew the chunk of split wood, set it on the hearth, and reached into the bin next to the stove for a handful of kindling. The small box of matches lay within easy reach on a shelf, and he struck one against the side of the oven. A few moments later he dusted off his hands and shut the door. "The draft needs to be open. If it doesn't get air, the wood won't burn."

"Thank you. I think I can get it next time, but I like it better when Smokey beats me to the kitchen." She slid the coffeepot to the front of the stove and removed two mugs from the shelf. "Why didn't you stay in bed longer?"

"Couldn't sleep. Too much on my mind, I guess."

"Want to talk about it? I used to be a pretty good listener when we were kids." She opened a bin built into the outside wall and removed a few plump russet potatoes, placing them in the washbasin. "I can peel potatoes and talk, if you want to keep me company."

Travis leaned his shoulder against the wall. "First, how's Angel? Any change?"

"She woke up once, a few minutes after you left the room. Said she wants to talk to you today and seemed more like her old self. I assured her you'd make time, and she slipped back into a peaceful sleep." Libby lifted a jug of water and poured it over the potatoes. She picked up a rag and scrubbed each one in turn, placing them to the side when finished. When that task was complete, she pulled open a drawer and withdrew a sharp knife. "I know Smokey likes to cook these with the skins on, but that feels so uncivilized to me. I told him when he's cooking, that's fine, but when I beat him to the kitchen, I'm peeling them." She tossed him a cocky grin and lifted the knife, pointing it at him. "Now talk."

"Yes, ma'am." Travis hefted the bubbling coffeepot and poured the steaming liquid into his mug. "Want yours now or later?" He raised the second cup.

"Later is fine. I'll finish these, then come sit with you." She wagged a potato at him. "Don't try stalling, little brother. I could tell yesterday that something was bothering you. Is it the ranch?"

Travis sank into a nearby chair and took a sip of the strong brew. Libby made true cowboy coffee, none of the weak belly wash you'd find back East. "The ranch is fine. I guess it's more than one thing. Part of it is Father, part of it Angel."

"Father?" She turned toward him and raised her brows. "What does he have to do with Angel?"

"Nothing." He shook his head. "Sorry. I just meant they've both been on my mind the past couple of days. When's the last time you heard from him, Lib?"

Her hands stilled. "I'm not sure. I guess just after George died. I sent a telegram from San Francisco letting him know about George's death, and he responded fairly quickly."

"You told him you were coming here, I assume?"

"Yes. He asked if I wanted to come home. I thanked him but explained I planned to visit you for a while." She dropped her gaze.

"You didn't tell him you were moving here?"

She shrugged. "I guess I didn't say much about it, either way."

"Why not? You think he'd care that you're with me?"

Libby raised her chin. "I'm not sure, Trav. He's—prickly—where you're concerned."

"I know. He's angry with me again. In his last letter he almost demanded I give up ranching and return to take up law. Said I needed to 'grow up and quit playing at being a cowboy' and come back East where I belong."

Libby winced. "I'm sorry. He's been difficult since Mother died."

"Is that one of the reasons you didn't want to go home when George died?"

"Yes." She put the last potato in a pan of clean water and wiped her hands. "I can't take her place." She wrapped a cloth around the handle of the coffeepot and tipped it over her mug, filling it close to the brim. "I'm sorry Father won't accept what you've chosen to do with your life."

Travis stood and pulled out a chair, waiting till she sat before returning to his own. "I'm trying to make peace with it." He was quiet for a minute, then asked, "Do you think Angel knows the Lord?"

She turned a startled face toward him. "I beg your pardon?"

"I've never heard her talk about God, and she's never asked to attend church with us."

Libby raised her brows. "I've never thought about it. She's only been here two weeks, and she's been busy. Plus, this injury hasn't helped."

Travis took another slow sip of his coffee. "Angel is such a loner. The times we've talked, I've tried to broach the subject but hit a wall.

Maybe we need to ask her to go with us this Sunday. It's still four days away, and she should be well enough by then, don't you think?"

"From what the doctor said yesterday, I'd agree. Angel hasn't shown a sign of fever for two days, and her strength is returning. I wouldn't be surprised if she'll be fighting to get out of that room soon."

"Good. So will you ask her?"

Libby sat back and narrowed her eyes. "No. It was your idea. You should ask her."

Travis rubbed his neck with the palm of his hand. "I don't think she likes me, Lib."

"What in the world makes you say that?"

"Just a hunch."

"I don't believe that for a minute. You said Angel was on your mind, and now I understand why—and it's not simply due to her not attending church. So talk. What's going on between you two?"

"Nothing. Everything." He thunked his coffee cup back onto the table. "I don't know. I make a hash of things whenever I talk to her. She believes the only thing I care about is the ranch."

"Is it?" Libby crossed her arms over her chest.

"What's *that* supposed to mean?"

"You must have given her a reason to think that or it wouldn't worry you. Besides, I've noticed you tend to get rather—shall we say—*focused*, when it comes to your work." She took a sip of her drink. "So what did you say to make Angel think you don't care about her?"

"I've spoken without thinking more than once. Nothing specific about her, but she's gotten the impression I want her to get well quickly so she can tend to her job."

Libby pursed her lips. "So, what will you do to make things right?"

"I was hoping you could help me with that. Maybe—talk to her for me?"

"That is not my place, Travis, and you know it. I've certainly never thought of you as a coward, not even where women are concerned."

Travis groaned. "Angel isn't just any woman."

"No." Libby met his eyes. "She isn't, at that. Do I detect a hint of interest in our new employee, little brother?"

Travis jerked upright, slopping coffee from his cup. "I don't care to be misunderstood, that's all."

"I see." Libby gave a secretive smile and tipped her head to the side. "Then I guess you'd best march in there after breakfast and get the issue settled." She held up a hand when he started to protest. "She's not going to shoot you. In fact, I'm quite certain her gun is out of reach in her present condition."

"Thanks. That sets my mind at ease." Travis turned his head at the sound of footsteps crossing the pantry and heading toward the kitchen. "Smokey's here. I'll consider your suggestion."

* * * * *

Angel woke from a deep sleep—the kind that passes without dream, thought, or memory, leaving one refreshed and ready to tackle the day. How many days had she spent in this bed? Her bones ached and muscles screamed in protest at the forced inactivity. She gingerly sat up and pushed back the covers. Shame rolled over her as she thought of the wasted hours she'd been laid up in this room—and Libby waiting on her like a common housemaid when Angel was the hired hand.

Could she wash up and pull on her pants, boots, and a shirt without help? Yes. The intense throbbing had eased in her arm. She raised it a few inches and straightened it, locking her elbow. The swelling had gone down, as well. Her fingers worked fine, and pain had never stopped her before. Good thing she didn't wear fancy dresses like

Libby with dozens of tiny buttons. She'd have a hard enough time managing the few on the front of her shirt.

The rumble of men's voices faded on the other side of her door as she tugged on her boots and stood. A glance out the window confirmed her guess—the cowboys were sauntering off the front porch and heading toward the barn. Breakfast was over. Her stomach growled, and she clapped her good hand over her middle. Hopefully Smokey had saved her a plate.

Angel cracked open the door and listened. Dishes and pans rattled in the kitchen. She'd wanted to talk to Travis, but right now she'd as soon avoid him. Eating a hearty meal after days of picking at food sounded like just the thing—but she didn't care to be distracted by his handsome face.

She winced. That wasn't the first time she'd thought of Travis in that light, and she needed to stop. It wasn't fitting. It was no secret he hoped to find another tracker. But a vision of the man lifting her shoulders off the pillow to give her a drink haunted her thoughts. She could still smell his masculine scent—wood smoke mixed with some kind of cologne. He must have shaved before coming to her room and stopped to stoke the fire in the potbellied stove. She'd wanted to close her eyes and breathe in the fragrance, but she'd steeled herself against it. It was hard enough maintaining an aloof attitude with him hovering so close.

Angel walked down the hall and entered the kitchen, pausing to make sure no one but Smokey was there. A cheerful whistle broke from the man's lips as he scraped a dish into a pan on the sideboard. "Smokey?"

"Huh?" The heavyset man moved fast for his size and whirled around, nearly dropping the plate. "Angel. You liked to scare me out of seven-years' growth." He patted his bulging belly and laughed.

"Not that I need to do any more growin', mind you." He peered at her under lowered brows. "What you doin' out of bed? Ain't you supposed to stay put till the doc says you can get up?"

She shook her head and smiled. "Nope. Doc said yesterday that I was mending real well. Besides, my body aches from lying abed so long. And I'm hungry. I can't have people waiting on me any longer, so I aim to fend for myself."

Smokey hurried across the kitchen and pulled out a chair at the small table near the stove. "You sit yourself down this minute. Someone ought to knock me upside the head with a good stout branch for not bringin' you a plate a'whilst ago. Libby's gonna scold me when she finds out yer not in bed."

"No, she won't. I'll tell her it was my idea, and I'm feeling fine. In fact, I'm ready to go back to work."

"I don't think so, young lady." Travis's gentle rebuke sent a shiver up Angel's spine and she spun around in her chair.

He leaned against the doorjamb wearing a serious expression. "When you're finished eating, you should head back to your room. No work until Doc Simmons says, and even then I might want you to wait another day just to be sure."

Angel pushed back her chair and stood, uncertainty nearly making her mute. Hadn't Travis implied that he was anxious for her to get back to work? She frowned. "I'm tired of lying around."

"Doesn't matter. I'm your boss, and you won't go back to work till I say."

She gritted her teeth and restrained a sharp retort. Why was this man so difficult? "Fine. I won't work today, but I'm not staying in that room another minute."

Travis straightened and the corner of his mouth lifted in a half smile. "Good." His lips continued their upward tilt until a full-blown grin broke free. "I'm glad we got that settled. And I don't expect you to stay in your room—just off your horse."

Angel wanted to throw something at him. He was her boss, but that didn't give him the right to—to—boss her around. Her thoughts ground to a halt, and she slumped back into her chair. Last night she'd lain awake worrying she'd lose this job, and now she wanted nothing more than to challenge the man who had it in his power to take it away. What was wrong with her, anyway?

"All right." She dropped her gaze to the table as Smokey slid a plate of bread, eggs, and applesauce under her nose. "Thanks, Smokey." She smiled. "What a treat! Where did you get applesauce?"

His face turned a rosy hue, and he twisted his apron in work-roughened hands. "I had a few jars put away for a special occasion, and the boss suggested you might like some. 'Sides, I figured you gettin' well qualifies as a special occasion."

Tears sprang to her eyes, and she turned away. "I don't know what to say."

Travis had told Smokey to fix her something special? The thought nearly choked her. No one but José had ever looked out for her that way since her parents died.

"Don't need to say nothin'; just eat up and enjoy." He backed away and scurried to the wash pan, plunging a dish into the water and rattling it energetically.

Angel dipped her spoon into the golden concoction and lifted it to her mouth, savoring the flavor as it lingered on her tongue. She hadn't had anything this wonderful since she was a youngster. Her uncle once brought home canned peaches after a trip to town. They'd tasted better than any candy she'd ever had, and she'd cried when she'd eaten the last bite. What had prompted Travis to part with such a precious gift?

Travis cleared his throat, and she raised her chin. Her fingers trembled. She placed the spoon carefully next to her bowl and dropped her hands into her lap. "Thank you for thinking of me. This was lovely."

"You're welcome. I'm glad you're enjoying it." He pushed himself away from the doorjamb. "Libby said you wanted to talk to me."

Angel glanced at Smokey and shook her head. "It's not important."

Travis followed her gaze and seemed to understand. "Why don't you stop by my office a little later?"

She shrugged. "Like I said, it's nothing."

Travis turned his head and took a step toward the next room. "I hear a buggy. Doc Simmons must be here. You finish your breakfast, and I'll see him in."

Angel waited till he'd left the room, then picked up her spoon and devoured the last of the applesauce. "That was wonderful, Smokey. Thank you so much." She took a mouthful of her bread and stabbed at the eggs with her fork. "I guess I worked up an appetite lying in that room the past few days."

Smokey's laugh rumbled across the room. "Glad to hear it. I like to see people enjoy my food."

"Is Libby here?" Angel lifted the bread to her mouth and chewed slowly.

"Yeah. I think she's upstairs havin' a little chat with James. It's been so busy around here lately, she's been neglectin' the lad." His eyes suddenly widened, and his lips parted. "I'm sorry. That was a blamed thing to say. I didn't mean it the way it sounded."

Angel pasted on a smile. "It's all right. I'm sorry I've been such a bother." She laid her fork next to her plate and pushed it away.

"You ain't been, Miss Angel. Honest." He heaved a big sigh and twisted his towel into a knot. "Between Libby, Travis, and me—why, we've been plumb honored to care for you. Glad you're up and around for your own sake, but you weren't no bother a'tall."

Smokey swiveled toward the footfalls coming down the staircase, along with louder ones following. Libby walked into the kitchen, her amber skirt swishing around her ankles, and James appeared close behind. He skidded to a halt and stared at Angel. "You're up! Boy howdy, I thought you'd never come out of that room. When can you take me shooting?"

Libby pivoted and glared at her son. "James. She's barely out of bed and probably needs to head straight back now that she's eaten. Besides, no one said you could go shooting."

James's lips drooped in a pout. "Miss Angel said she'd take me."

Angel blinked a few times, surprised at the declaration. "No, James, I didn't. I said I'd consider it. But if your mother doesn't approve, I won't."

"Not fair." James kicked at an imaginary object on the floor. "Nobody lets me do anything fun around this place. I want to go back to San Francisco." He bolted from the room and raced back up the stairs.

Angel dropped her head and pushed a strand of hair from her face, wishing she'd braided it before coming to breakfast. Why had James lied? Of course, the boy was probably merely excited about the prospect of doing something new and hadn't thought of it as anything more. Too bad Libby didn't seem inclined to let him spread his wings and learn more about ranch life.

Libby stepped forward and touched Angel's shoulder. "I'm sorry about that. James doesn't always think before he speaks."

"It's all right. And I'd be happy to take him with me sometime, if you agree."

"I'm not sure that's a good idea." Libby sank into a chair across from Angel. "It's not that I don't approve of what you do for a living, it's just that—" She seemed to search for the right words. "This is such a harsh, unforgiving land. My brother has changed so much since coming here, and sometimes I'm afraid for my son."

"Of what? You're right, it's a rugged land, but it makes men stronger. I'd imagine your brother is an example of how this country helps mold a man into someone more than he was."

"And sometimes it breaks them, or turns them toward things better left alone." Libby expelled a sigh. "I know it means a lot to James, and I *have* allowed him to ride with both Travis and Nate. I'll think about it."

Angel opened her mouth to reply, but an unfamiliar woman's voice stilled her words. That surely wasn't the doctor. Could he have brought his wife on his rounds, possibly to visit with Libby? She turned her gaze toward the doorway leading into the living room.

Travis entered with a petite, dark-haired woman who appeared to be in her early sixties. Her small hand rested within the crook of Travis's elbow, and her free hand adjusted the black velvet hat perched on her salt-and-pepper curls. A black satin dress hugged her slender form and was amazingly free from the dust that typically accompanied travelers. Her sparkling, dark brown eyes darted from Angel to Libby and back again, settling with shimmering warmth on Angel. With a quick movement she released her grip on Travis's arm and raised her hands in the air. "This is her, Signor? This is *la mia nipotina*, my granddaughter? The child of my beloved Maria?"

Travis glanced across the room at Angel and nodded. "If Angel Ramirez is your granddaughter, then yes, Signora de Luca, that's her."

Chapter Sixteen

....

Angel stared at the diminutive woman who beamed at her like she'd found something precious and didn't want to let go. Her grandmother? She'd never seen this person before. She shook her head, hoping to dislodge the confusion. "I'm sorry. What makes you think I'm your granddaughter?"

Before the woman could answer, Travis looked her way and raised his brows. "You're welcome to use my office if you'd like."

"No, thank you." Angel shook her head decisively. The woman looked harmless enough, but she didn't care to be alone with her until she understood the claim she'd presented. "Maybe we could move to the living room and sit? I'd like you and Libby to come, if you don't mind."

Libby moved to stand beside Angel. "Certainly, we'd be happy to. Travis, why don't you show Signora de Luca to a seat and we'll be right along."

Travis offered his arm to the matron, and she walked regally beside him into the adjoining room.

Libby leaned close and dropped her voice. "You don't know her?"

"No." Angel hated whispering in front of someone, but she didn't care for this woman to hear. "My parents died when I was young. I don't know much about my mother's family except she migrated to this country from Italy with her older brother when she was seventeen." She rose from her chair. "I guess we should join them."

"Yes, that would be sensible." Libby moved out of the way and allowed Angel to precede her into the next room. Signora de Luca sat like a delicate queen on Travis's easy chair, and Travis stood nearby.

While Angel had been in this room before, she'd never spent any real time here. She stopped for a moment, taking in her surroundings. Definitely a man's domain, it boasted an elk's rack above the river-rock fireplace and a bear skin on the wall next to the chimney. Colorful rugs graced the floors. Comfortable sofas and sturdy tables were positioned in a half circle facing the fire. It radiated a feeling of peace and contentment like nothing she'd ever felt. She longed to curl up in a chair, lean her head back, and rest. Instead, she perched on the corner of a dark-brown leather chair with a blanket draped across its back.

Travis sat beside Libby on a sofa across the room from Angel and nodded toward Signora de Luca. "We're happy to have you here, Signora, but I think I speak for all of us when I say we're curious how you happened to come, since Angel doesn't seem to know you."

The matron bowed her head in a grave nod. "I would be most honored if you would call me by my given name, Maria."

Angel gave a small start. Her mother's name had been Maria.

"Of course. Now please, tell us what brought you here and how you found us so far out in the wilderness."

Maria sat ramrod straight in her chair. "It is a long story, but I will try not to take too much of your time. And please"—she glanced at Angel—"do not hesitate to ask me questions."

Angel gave a brief nod. This tiny woman held a certain fascination. The thought that she might be family was enough to ignite a spark of longing in her heart. She'd felt alone for so long.

Maria laced her fingers in her lap. "My husband and I were heartbroken when our two eldest children decided to venture to America. They hoped to escape the confines of the life we lived in Italy. Gino, my husband, had a successful watchmaking business and did not want to leave our homeland for a new country, as our children urged us to do. We begged them to stay, but no. So they sailed away and never returned."

Libby leaned forward, her gaze reflecting sympathy for this woman's loss. "Did you ever hear from them again?"

"Maria wrote frequently at first." She nodded at Angel. "After she married your papa, la mia nipotina, her letters grew scarce. They traveled far away from the cities and were living in the West. Stagecoaches did not travel to their area often, and it was difficult to send mail. They moved frequently, as your papa's work was unpredictable."

Angel gripped her hands together, trying to still their shaking. Had Papa been involved with shady men like his older brother, José, had? Best not to think about it now—just listen and hope to understand the new revelations about her parents that this woman shared—if indeed she spoke of her parents, and not someone else.

Maria pressed on, her lined face intent and her dark eyes moving from person to person, lingering at last on Angel. "We learned of your birth and rejoiced. My husband and I hoped to visit you in America, but Guido, our youngest, took sick. He lingered for ten years before he finally went to heaven. The letters stopped coming, and many years passed. We never knew what happened to our daughter and her baby, or the man that Maria married." She peered at Angel, her mouth drawn in a pain-filled line. "Are your parents living?"

Angel bit her lip. "No. They died of the fever when I was eight. Papa's older brother, José, raised me."

"Ah. That is as we feared. That would explain why the letters ceased." Maria nodded as a shadow of sadness cloaked her face. "Gino and I determined to close the business and come to America. The last time we heard from your mama, she wrote to us from Wyoming. We sent out letters, hoping to find her. We spent three years searching and had nearly given up, when word came from a town marshal saying he had heard of an Angelo de Luca working on a nearby ranch."

Angel's heart contracted, and she felt as though she'd been cow-kicked. If a marshal had heard of her, what more might he know? Letters sent to law officers could stir up questions into a past best left alone.

Maria leaned forward. "We felt hope for the first time and made plans to sail on the next ship." Her voice faltered, and she sniffed.

Travis withdrew a handkerchief from his pocket and leaned across to press it into her hand. "What of your husband, Maria?"

The older woman dabbed at her eyes. "His heart was weak and could not stand the excitement. I buried him two months before leaving my Italy. My only hope lay in this Wyoming, where I was told my Maria and her baby lived."

A flower of hope blossomed in Angel's heart, as the light of Maria's words poured into her spirit. She'd never known Mama and Papa had lived in Wyoming before moving to Texas. Maybe the God she remembered her mother talking about had cared enough to bring her back to the place where her grandmother could find her.

Grandmother. She shivered at the word, her thoughts in turmoil. What would it mean, having someone who belonged to her? Would this woman love and understand her, accept her for all that she was and all this country had helped her become? Or would she strive to change her and scorn the work she did? Maria must never know of Angel's past. The woman sitting across the room had endured much already—this would be more than anyone should have to bear.

"Angel? Are you feeling all right?" Libby's words roused Angel from her deep reflection. "Maybe you need to lie down. You shouldn't tax yourself on your first day out of bed."

A gasp left Maria's lips, and she pushed from her chair. "Child, you have been ill? Forgive me for my thoughtless chatter."

"I'm all right, just tired." Angel smiled at Maria and rose from the couch, uncomfortable at the attention. "I think I'll go to my room, if you don't mind?"

Maria took a step toward her and lifted her arms. "Do you believe me, child of my heart? That I am your grandmother come to find you at last? Can you forgive an old woman for taking so long to come?"

Angel shook her head. "There's nothing to forgive. It's all come as such a surprise. Will you be here when I get up?"

Travis cleared his throat and smiled. "I hope I can answer that. Signora, my sister and I would like to extend an invitation for you to stay as long as you'd like. We have a room upstairs and would be honored to have you here."

A tiny tremor of surprise shook Angel. Travis's offer indicated a willingness to believe Maria's story.

Maria dipped her head and turned to Libby. "You are sure it will not be an imposition? I am certain you have much to do without adding another burden to your day."

Libby reached out her hand and took the older woman's, giving it a squeeze. "No imposition at all. It will be our pleasure."

"Then it is settled. I thank you both." Maria looked from one to the other and turned her gaze on Angel. "I understand your confusion, little one. Go. Sleep well. We will speak again when you are rested. I want to know everything about you, your parents, and how you were raised."

* * * * *

Angel spent much of the next two days in her room. The lack of exercise chafed at her, but she didn't care to chance a private meeting with Maria. She could deal with having a relative, even anticipated the prospect of getting acquainted with a grandmother she'd never known. Her heart told her the older woman spoke the truth, but Maria's final statement shot fear into Angel's mind.

She woke the next morning determined to take a ride and get away from the house. If nothing else, she'd make sure any time spent with Maria was in someone else's company, where she could draw Libby, Travis, or James into the conversation. Better yet, the cowboys might offer a welcome diversion. Relief flooded her as men's jovial voices drifted toward her from the dining area. She slipped out her bedroom door and down the hall.

Angel slid into her seat just as Travis quieted the table for prayer. Maria sat on Travis's left and Libby graced her normal place to his right. Angel's seat next to Libby remained open, and she heaved a sigh of relief. At least Libby hadn't decided to place her next to Maria, where the older woman could pester her with questions. Having James to Angel's right would give her someone to visit with. Bless Libby for coming up with the new seating arrangement.

The sudden hush and the quiet words to the Almighty brought an unexpected sense of peace to Angel's spirit. She remembered the gushing spring at the plateau and how the water called to her—Travis's prayer tugged at her heart in the same way, although she wasn't sure why. Was it the man, and the words he spoke, or something that went deeper?

Angel met Maria's tranquil, warm gaze. The message came through. "I'm here. I care." And it scared Angel a little. She ducked her head and turned toward James, dropping her voice. "I think your mother might allow you to go riding with me, but you'll need to ask her to be sure."

James's freckled face lit with joy. "Ah, golly, Angel, thank you. Uh—I mean, Miss Angel." A blush crept into his cheeks. "Can I bring a rifle?"

"Not this time." She placed a finger against her lips. "Let's not push your mother, all right? I think it's enough if she lets you come along this first time." She dipped the large serving spoon into the pot of oatmeal sitting near her plate, filled her bowl, and topped it off with a helping of sugar. Not one of her favorite dishes, but the hot bread smothered in some of Smokey's apple jam would help it go down.

Libby touched Angel's forearm. "How are you feeling? Did your rest yesterday help?"

"Yes. My arm is much better, and my strength is back. I thought I might take a short ride today."

Libby's forehead scrunched and her lips puckered. "Are you sure it's wise to go back to work so soon? Shouldn't you ask the doctor first?"

"I'm not going to work, just take a ride, and I promise it won't be more than couple of hours. I need to get out of the house and back on my horse. Being cooped up is difficult for me."

"I understand." Libby took the plate of bread that Travis handed her, took a slice, and passed it along to Angel.

Angel helped herself and turned back to Libby. "I have a favor to ask. Would it be all right if James comes along? I won't let him take a gun, or shoot mine."

Libby sat for a moment, her gaze moving from Angel to James and back again. "Yes, I think that would be fine. I appreciate your thoughtfulness in not allowing him to shoot. At least, this time." She finished with a small smile.

James let out a whoop, then covered his mouth with his hand. "Sorry." He whispered the word.

Travis broke off his conversation with Maria and stared at the boy. "James? What was that for?"

"Sorry, Uncle Travis. Mom said I can go riding with Angel—Miss Angel—today."

Travis glanced from James to Libby, then stared directly at Angel. "You're riding?"

Maria raised her brows but didn't speak. Angel could tell the woman appeared worried. No doubt she'd hoped to spend time together today.

Angel held up her hand and smiled. "Not working, don't worry. Merely going for a short ride before I go crazy." Something fluttered inside. Libby had expressed concern for her well-being, but something in Travis's voice denoted more than simple worry over a new employee. She stuffed down the thought before it could surge too far to the fore.

"Sounds like a good plan. I think I'll tag along."

Her arm froze partway to her mouth. "Why?"

He shrugged. "I'd like to keep you company on your first ride after your accident, if you don't mind."

"James is coming with me."

"Good. Should make an enjoyable ride." He gave her a cocky grin.

Her heart rate increased and she took several shallow breaths, hoping to calm herself. Did he think her incompetent to ride alone, even with James along? Or didn't he trust she'd keep her word about not going back to work? She shook off the thought and glanced at Maria. Even if Travis came along, that would be preferable to staying. Yes, riding with Travis might not be such a bad thing, after all.

* * * * *

Travis whistled as he walked to the barn a couple of hours later. It had been a long time since he'd gone out on a ride just for pleasure. The sun shone bright, a light breeze blew across his skin, and the fragrance of baking donuts drifted from the house. His mouth watered thinking of the special treats Libby was making in honor of their guest. They'd be sprinkled with sugar and waiting when he returned. He grinned and jerked open the barn door.

Angel collided with his chest. She stumbled, and Travis gripped her upper arms. She flinched and took a step back.

Travis dropped his hands to his side. An empty feeling washed over him as she retreated yet another step. "I barreled through the door without looking. You all right?" He glanced at her still bandaged arm.

"Yes. Fine." She turned and headed back into the barn, but the wince of pain belied her words.

"I can catch Bella and saddle her for you. I don't want you lifting anything heavy."

"No need, Boss." Arizona poked his head around the stall partition. "I moseyed out here when I seen her heading to the corral. Got Bella all tacked up and ready to go." A smile lit his handsome face. "Want I should come along?"

Irritation shot through Travis, and he nearly bit off his tongue to keep from shouting. "No. You've got work to tend to, and you'd best get to it." Arizona's lips drooped, and Travis felt a pang of remorse. "Sorry, Arizona. But there's a lot of work waiting, and I can't spare you now."

"Right. I get it, Boss." The cowboy swung toward Angel, turning his back on Travis. "Maybe next time, Miss Angel?"

Angel glanced from one man to the other and shrugged. "Sure. And thanks for saddling Bella."

"Anytime." Arizona shot a hard glance toward Travis and stalked from the barn.

Travis stared at the retreating man. That hadn't gone well. His best hand was smitten with Angel. The surge of jealousy shocked Travis. Had Angel invited Arizona along? He felt a twinge of shame—

ever since Arizona arrived on the ranch Travis had attempted to talk to him about the Lord, to no avail. The cowboy didn't see his own need. Travis had hoped his life would serve as an example. From Arizona's scowl of disgust before he walked out the door, he'd botched things good.

"Am I late?" James bolted through the open doorway and skidded to a stop a few feet from Travis, his chest heaving. "Ma made me stay and help clear the table." Loathing laced the words, and he kicked at a clod of dirt. "That's women's work."

Angel drew herself upright. "My uncle helped me with the dishes every night he was home, and he was more of a man than most I've met." She reached for Bella's bridle. "You should be thankful you have a mother, and not complain."

"Sorry." James hung his head. "Didn't mean nothing bad by it."

Travis tousled the boy's hair. "Miss Angel is right, but you've apologized, so catch your horse and let's head out."

James brightened and grabbed a rope. "Thanks, Uncle Travis. I'll be right back."

Travis leaned his arms against the wooden rail where Bella was tied, avoiding Angel's gaze. He sure hoped the last few minutes would be the end of the irritations between them.

Angel turned a somber expression his way. "It's none of my business how you treat your cowhands, but I appreciated what Arizona did for me."

He clamped his jaw shut. She'd probably asked Arizona to go along, and now she'd be mad that he'd killed the idea. And that got under his skin more than it had any right to.

Travis brushed away the feelings of jealousy and reminded himself Angel was his employee, nothing more. And he intended to keep it that way.

Chapter Seventeen

....

Angel rode in silence, barely registering James's prattling voice as he bounced along beside her. She glanced over her shoulder. Travis brought up the rear. Right now the last thing she wanted was conversation with the man. What was riding him, anyway? He'd been rude to Arizona when the cowboy had done nothing to provoke him. Travis's expression when he poked his head around the stall was—what? Angry? No. More like frustrated. Could he be irritated that someone needed to saddle her horse? She scowled.

"You say something, Miss Angel?" James turned in his saddle and squinted against the sunlight.

Angel straightened and picked up her reins. No sense in allowing the boy to see her exasperation. She turned toward Travis. "Mind if James and I lope the horses a bit?"

"Sure. I'll mosey along and catch up if you don't go too far."

"We'll stay within sight." She turned to James and grinned. "No running your horse or racing, but we can let them out a mite, if you want to."

"Whoopee!" James kicked his buckskin gelding in the sides, and the big animal lunged forward, nearly unseating the boy.

"James!" Travis raised his voice, but the boy didn't slow Jasper's pace.

Angel sat for a moment in stunned silence as Travis clucked to his horse, then urged him into a gallop. She leaned forward in her saddle, driving Bella into a fast lope, her gaze trained on James as his mount flew across the level ground, his long stride extending as he gained momentum with each advancing moment.

"Pull your horse in, James." Travis's voice thundered across the open prairie.

Angel could see James's arms extended in front of him; he appeared unwilling to slow Jasper. She urged Bella on and loosened the mare's reins, letting her have her head. She was sure-footed and steady, having been raised on badlands worse than what she ran across now. Bella veered around a boulder and jumped a shallow wash. Her black mane blew in the wind and tendrils slapped Angel's face. Puffs of dust from Travis's horse running just ahead clogged her nostrils.

What was that boy thinking, putting his horse to this kind of pace? From what she'd heard, he wasn't an experienced horseman. Had the idea of galloping gone to his head, or had the gelding's response to being booted taken James by surprise? She peered ahead, hoping to see James slowing his foolhardy race, but she was met with disappointment.

The horse that Travis rode was a big-boned, long-limbed bay with four white stockings that flashed as his stride ate up the ground. He'd gotten a headstart, but Bella was gaining. The steady rhythm of hoof-beats filled her ears—no labored breathing and the mare hadn't so much as broken a sweat. Angel stroked Bella's neck, satisfaction swelling inside. She winced at the ache running up her arm but pushed it aside.

Travis turned his head for a moment, determination hardening his features, then faced forward and grazed his gelding with his spurs. No words passed between them, but Angel felt the mix of the man's driving anxiety and anger. His nephew could be in mortal danger and was too naïve to realize it. One misstep by his horse into a groundhog hole, or a hoof landing wrong on a round rock, and it would all be over. James could fly over the buckskin's head as the horse went down, and at this speed, the least he'd get would be broken bones. She shuddered to think of Libby's agony if they were forced to pack the body of her son back to the ranch.

"James!" Travis bellowed again. "Pull that horse in *now*."

Angel watched with her heart in her throat, praying he'd respond. They had gained on the pair and ran fifty feet or so behind. The boy suddenly sat back in his saddle and his elbows drew to his sides, the reins taut in his hands. The buckskin snorted, shook his head, and stretched his neck out, continuing to run. Angel's heart sank. Jasper had the bit between his teeth and James wasn't strong enough to stop him. James sawed on the reins to no avail. The animal dug in his haunches, dropped his head, and plowed forward.

"Uncle Travis. Make him stop!" The panic in the boy's voice was apparent, even at this distance. "I'm scared!"

"Hold on, James. We're coming." Travis seemed to will his horse to go faster. His mount's sides heaved and his neck stretched.

The horse moved at a full run, and his dark sides glistened with sweat. Angel hadn't believed it possible, but Travis gained a few more yards on the runaway. She urged Bella forward, keeping only a stride or two behind the gelding.

Travis was magnificent in the saddle, sitting the running horse like someone born to ride. The fabric of his shirt stretched tight against his muscled shoulders as he extended his arms and called for more speed. His long, lean legs remained steady and firm against his horse's sides, and his clenched jaw showed his dogged determination to save his nephew. But what could he do, even if he caught up with Jasper? Angel shot up a prayer, hoping God would listen.

James hunkered over the saddle horn, his hands gripping the reins but no longer putting out an effort to stop his speed-crazed mount. The horse jumped a small bush, nearly unseating the boy a second time. Angel watched in horror as James slipped to the side. He dropped the knotted reins and clutched the horn.

"Hold on, boy. I'm almost there." Travis yelled the words, although Angel doubted James could hear. She drew further to the side, running almost parallel to the two riders. James's pallor and grip on the saddle screamed out his fear. He slipped a little more and fought to keep his balance. His foot shoved hard in the stirrup and he righted himself, then he slumped over his horse's neck, his head bowed.

Bushes passed in a blur, and Bella continued to dodge and jump small obstructions, but Angel kept her gaze trained on Travis. A few more long strides brought him abreast of the runaway gelding. He leaned away from his saddle and reached for the rein closest to him, but James's horse snorted and jerked away.

"Please, God," Angel mumbled.

Travis urged his bay closer and tried again. Angel could see his long bronzed fingers just inches from the rein. Suddenly, his arm snaked out and he snagged the leather strip. The knot at the end of the reins kept him from pulling it all the way toward him. "James. James!"

The boy's head bobbed, and he turned frightened eyes on his uncle, but his mouth seemed frozen and no words tumbled out.

"Untie the reins." Travis kept his horse moving at the same speed as the buckskin, but Angel could tell the effort of balancing in the saddle and holding the reins was wearing on him. "Hurry, boy. Untie them."

James came to life at his uncle's words, and his fingers fumbled with the knot. Long moments passed as he struggled to keep his balance in the seat and loosen the leather, but it finally broke free. Angel slowed Bella's gallop to a fast trot, understanding dawning at what course Travis planned to take.

Travis drew the strip toward him and sat upright in his saddle, then slowly directed his mount in a wide circle. Jasper seemed almost relieved to follow along, his frantic pace slackening as the circle tightened. Finally, the two heaving, sweat-soaked geldings drew to a stop.

Travis jumped from his saddle, his entire body shaking—with what? Fear, anger, or a little of both? He took two strides to James's side and plucked the trembling boy from his seat. "If you ever do that again—" He gripped James as though he'd shake him, but he simply stared at the boy for a moment, then snatched James to his chest.

The scared young man emitted a sob. Then a wail tore from his lips, and he threw his arms around his uncle's neck. "I'm sorry, Uncle Travis. I'm sorry. I—didn't—know he'd—run. Honest—I didn't." Tears coursed down his cheeks, and he hiccupped between the words.

Angel sat her horse watching the two—so different, yet so alike. She'd been afraid Travis might be harsh, and now admiration flooded her. Travis reminded her of Papa when she'd done something naughty as a small child, and he'd disciplined her with tenderness and love.

Travis drew back, still gripping his nephew's shoulders. "I understand, but you didn't think before you acted. I've told you numerous times that the decisions you make out here can have life-and-death consequences. I hope you learned that today."

James swiped at his tearstained cheeks. "Yes, sir. I won't do anything like that again. Ever." He struggled to smile. "Thank you for stopping my horse. I thought he'd run forever."

"My biggest concern wasn't his running, but what would happen if he stepped in a hole and sent you flying. When he jumped that bush you lost your balance, and if you'd fallen, you could've been killed."

Angel winced but she understood the need to be brutally honest with James. If the boy thought the danger was in the horse running away until he tired and eventually stopped, it might not make a deep enough impression. She nudged her horse forward. "James?"

He turned toward her. "Miss Angel?" His eyes widened. "I forgot you were here."

She nodded. "Your uncle is right. This is rough ground, and I expected to see your horse go down any second. Bella is sure-footed, but even she was picking her way. All I can figure is that God must be watching over you today, or we'd be packing you home across your saddle, and your mama would be grieving another loss."

James's face sagged, and it looked like he might burst into tears again. "I don't want Ma to cry over me like she did my pa. I promise I'll be careful."

Travis retrieved his horse's reins that dragged on the ground. "Good. Now let's head back to the house. Nice and slow." He swung into the saddle and motioned for James to do the same.

Angel turned her horse the direction they'd come. She was content to let the two men ride together. The memory of Travis's courage would stay with her for a long time. A sense of deep gratitude to God hit her. It might not be so bad attending church with Libby and Travis.

Then a thought froze her in her saddle, and she nearly dropped her reins. All she owned was men's clothes and boots. What in the world would she wear?

* * * * *

Travis shot a look at Angel sitting relaxed in her saddle and frowned. He'd had high hopes for what should have been a leisurely ride, and it had turned into a nightmare instead. Since Angel's accident, he'd had little time to talk to her, and now with her grandmother visiting he doubted that would improve. Her arm was well on the way to mending, although she still needed to be careful. Thank the good Lord he'd come on this ride and James was all right. Not that Angel's riding skills weren't up to muster, but with her injury it could've been difficult for her to catch the reins and turn the runaway horse.

Maria de Luca posed another interesting problem—one he needed to give further thought to. She seemed genuine enough, and he had no reason to doubt her identity, but Angel hadn't warmed up to the woman and seemed to avoid her. Travis brushed at a pesky fly buzzing around his head. Raven swished his tail as the fly moved back to his hindquarters.

James rode quietly beside him, seeming content to rest and, for once, not chattering. The thirteen-year-old generally had more comments and questions than three grown men strung together in a week, but that was part of growing up. Travis remembered his own childhood and the times he'd pestered his father. He'd quickly learned to keep his thoughts to himself, or get snapped at for his pains.

His gaze once again strayed to the lovely, raven-haired woman ahead of him. What would it be like, having a wife who understood ranch life and supported him in what he hoped to accomplish? A slight smile tipped up the corners of his lips. He'd always wanted children. Would they have dark hair and eyes, or—he pulled up short and nearly yanked his horse's head off. What in tarnation was he doing, daydreaming about a woman who didn't know he existed other than to receive her orders and get a paycheck? Besides, he had no indication she knew the Lord, and he wouldn't waffle in that area.

James reined in and turned in his saddle. "Uncle Travis. You okay?" His brows crinkled.

"Yeah. Sorry, James. Guess I was thinking and forgot where I was."

"That's not safe. You have to be aware of your surroundings all the time in this country. Isn't that what you told me?" There was no censure in the boy's tone, but Travis detected a hint of a smile behind the words.

Angel swung Bella around toward them. "You're right, James. This is a hard land that can take a bite out of you quicker than a bear takes a chunk out of a honeycomb." She tossed a smile at Travis, and her voice gentled. "But sometimes it's all right to daydream when your horse is tired and you're on the way home." She raised her brows and grinned. "As long as you don't overdo it, that is."

Travis felt warmth stealing up his neck and ducked his head, letting his hat cast a shadow over his face. He knew it was nonsense, but it felt like she'd been poking around in his mind. He nudged his horse forward and grunted. "Yeah. I don't know about you two, but those donuts are sounding mighty fine."

James brightened, and he clucked to his gelding but kept constant pressure on the reins. "Yum! Ma makes the best bear sign in the West."

Travis let loose a guffaw. "When did you start using cowboy talk?"

"Arizona and Wren been teaching me. They said if'n I'm gonna be a proper cowpoke someday, I got to know how to talk right."

Angel's laugh was pure poetry, and the sound made Travis mute. It was the first time she'd laughed that he could remember, and he prayed it wouldn't be the last. He'd be jiggered if he wouldn't find a way to get her to do it again.

She shook her head and her smile faded, but her eyes still sparkled. "Do you think your uncle is a good cowboy?"

"Sure. He's the best! Otherwise, he never would've caught my horse and saved me today." James's head bobbed up and down, making his hat jiggle.

"Does he talk like Arizona and Wren?"

The boy grew thoughtful. "Uh. I guess not. But why can't I talk like the cowboys?"

Travis sent a grateful smile toward Angel and stepped in. "It's fine to use words like *bear sign* for donuts, but it's not all right to use coarse words. Besides, you know your mother likes you to use good English."

"I know." James sighed and flicked the end of his reins against his thigh. "I don't like disappointing Ma."

"Good boy. Now if you think we can hold to a nice, slow lope, let's get back to the ranch for some of that bear sign!" Travis grazed his horse's side with his spur, and they moved into a controlled gait. It looked like talking to Angel would have to wait. But hearing her laugh and seeing the light in her eyes had made his entire day worthwhile.

Chapter Eighteen

. . . .

A week later Angel slipped out of her room and headed for the barn, thankful she'd successfully avoided time alone with Maria. A couple of times the older woman came close to cornering her, but James or one of the cowboys had appeared in the nick of time. She had to admit that Maria was growing on her, and the sense of dread she'd experienced had retreated somewhat since her arrival, but she still didn't care to be interrogated about her childhood or parents. Calling her "grandmother" as Maria had requested still didn't sit well, so she simply steered clear of calling her anything at all.

Her foot hit the bottom step when the front door of the house opened. Angel swung around, hoping no one was looking for her.

"Angel?" Maria stepped out of the front door and walked to the edge of the covered porch. She clasped her hands in front of her waist and her fingers alternately tightened and loosened. "May I speak to you for a moment?"

Angel glanced around but saw no one who might come to her rescue. She shrugged. "If it won't take too long. I really need to brush my horse and give her some grain."

"*Grazie.* I mean, thank you. I forget that your mother did not teach you our native tongue. I'm so thankful I learned English in my country." She waved her fingertips toward the bench to the left of the door and the chair nearby. "Would you care to sit?"

169

Angel hesitated, then headed for the porch. "Sure." She sank onto the chair, scooted it several more inches away from the bench, and leaned back, crossing her arms over her middle.

Maria heaved a deep sigh as she seated herself on the wooden surface. "Why are you afraid of me, Granddaughter?"

Angel lurched upright and stared. "Afraid? I'm not in the least frightened of you."

The older woman's face reflected a sad smile. "You avoid me each day, you smile but it does not reach your eyes, you say the right words when you speak, but they do not come from your heart." She pointed her finger. "And you make sure you do not sit close enough for me to touch you. All signs you are afraid of me, sí?"

Angel's thoughts raced. The woman saw through her attempts to evade. How could she be honest and not hurt Maria? At times like this she wished she'd just kept riding and never answered Travis's telegram. She'd be on another ranch somewhere, living a simple life, and not faced with her past and all that entailed. A tiny voice of reason nudged at her heart. If she hadn't come, she wouldn't have met Travis and she'd still be living a lie. She forced a smile. "No, Signora. I just don't know you, and your claims make me—uncomfortable."

Maria's eyebrows rose. "My claims? You mean that I am your grandmother?"

"Yes."

"You do not believe me?"

"I guess I'm not sure. I was young when my parents died, and my uncle never spoke of you or your husband. Why wouldn't he have told me about my mother's people if they were still alive?"

"I cannot say, *Cara*."

Angel bristled. "I'm not your darling."

"Ah. You know that word?"

"I'm—not sure. Maybe I heard my parents use it—" Angel dropped her hands into her lap. "I'm sorry I snapped at you."

Maria gave an airy wave with her fingertips. "No matter. My late husband, he could growl like a giant bear. I think you call them grizzly bears in this country, sí?"

"Sí." Angel smiled at the picture the comparison created. "Your husband was an unhappy man?"

"No. He was quite happy most of his days. But when he did not get his sleep or someone disturbed him while he read his paper—" A tinkling laugh escaped her lips. "You understand? He was a man who valued his privacy, but oh, how he loved those he gave his heart to." Her face took on a faraway expression momentarily before she turned her attention back to Angel. "Pardon. I drift away on the clouds of memory. We were talking of your happiness and fear, not my husband's. What has been wrong, *piccolina*? I hope you do not mind me calling you that. It was my husband's name for your mother when she was a girl."

"Little one." Angel nearly whispered the words. "Piccolina— pequeña." She'd heard both growing up. Mama had called Papa *darling* and Papa had called her *little one*. Even when she grew up, José insisted on using it. Could he have gotten it from her parents? She had a vague recollection of Papa doing so when she was a child.

"Ah. I see that means something." Maria leaned forward, her face aglow. "Did your mother…?"

"No. My papa and then my uncle." Angel made her decision. "Tell me about her, please. I remember Mama, but only bits and pieces. I want to know everything."

* * * * *

Over an hour later Angel headed to the barn, her mind reeling. The stories, the family memories, and the very mannerisms Maria used brought back glimpses of her mother—and it all shouted the truth. Maria was her grandmother. She even knew the story of why her mother named her Angel—Mama had written Maria a letter shortly after her birth, telling her about the little angel that God sent to live at their house. It was hard to take in, but part of her spun in circles with joy as she had when just a small girl. Family. She had her own family now. There were older relatives still in Italy, but she was the youngest of their line. What would this mean to her future?

Maria—Angel shook her head—*Grandmother* hadn't asked her to return with her to the old country, but she'd not indicated she planned to stay here, either.

Angel stepped inside the barn and inhaled the sweet fragrance of hay piled near the door. Bella would be impatient for her feed by now, but Angel wanted nothing more than to race like the wind across the Wyoming sod. If only she could run away from the questions assaulting her mind.

But no. She squared her shoulders and lifted her chin. José always said, "We tackle our troubles and deal with them." Except that one time. The time he'd urged her to leave her life in the camp so she wouldn't have to confront Bart Hinson. New hatred for the outlaw welled up inside and for once she didn't try to push it away. He'd killed a Texas Ranger and had designs on her, as well. She should have drawn her gun and shot Hinson when she had the chance, but she'd done as Uncle asked and disappeared.

Could God have stopped her parents' death if He'd wanted? Why would He allow them to die when she still needed them in her life? So many questions she didn't have answers for. She hadn't kept her promise to God last Sunday when Grandmother had gone to church with Travis and his family. It was still hard thinking of Maria as her grandmother, but Angel needed to try. They'd all begged her to come, but the thought of riding all that way in the wagon, trapped and vulnerable to Grandmother's questions, had kept her at home.

Maybe tomorrow she'd think about going. But did she need to? What had God done for her? She picked up a crop someone had dropped on the floor of the barn and slapped the side of her leg. Nothing. He'd let Mama and Papa die, and Uncle send her away.

Then shame swamped her as she remembered her frantic plea as James's horse raced across the grasslands. God had answered when Travis caught the runaway. She'd never broken a promise in the past, and it might not be a good idea for her first broken one to be with the Almighty.

* * * * *

Travis swung down and patted his stallion's neck. He'd been breaking in the big black for the past couple of weeks. This horse had heart and stamina, both qualities needed on this range. He'd give him a rubdown and turn him out for a roll in the pasture. Travis pushed open the door and walked in, tugging at his horse's reins.

Someone or something moved in the shadows and Travis paused, waiting for his eyes to adjust. "Nate, that you?" His foreman had planned on doing some saddle repair this afternoon.

"No. It's Angel. I'm graining Bella and rubbing her down." She stepped around the divider and smiled.

Travis's heart somersaulted all the way to his toes. "You just get back from a ride?"

"No. I spent some time—with Grandmother." She said the final two words in a rush.

"So you've decided she's telling the truth?" He slipped off Raven's bridle and placed a rope halter on his head.

Angel shrugged and avoided his gaze. "I guess so. Yes." She fiddled with the curry brush. "You noticed?"

"That you were avoiding her for the past few days? Yep." Travis slung the rope around a nearby post and reached for the cinch strap on his saddle, loosening it as he talked. "What changed your mind?"

"Some of the things she said about my mother." Angel's voice trailed off. She turned away and scrubbed Bella's back with the brush.

"Want to talk?" Travis slid his saddle off and hefted it over a low crossbeam.

"No."

"Ah-huh."

Silence settled over the barn as both worked on their horses, but Travis's mind raced faster than the dust raised by his brush. He knew little more about this woman today than he had when she rode onto his ranch. Why was she so reluctant to talk about herself or even what her grandmother had shared? Of course, it was none of his business. He tossed the brush into a bucket and extracted a hoof pick. "Sorry if I asked something I shouldn't."

"Hmm?" Angel lifted a puzzled face and stared. "About what?"

"The talk you had with your grandmother."

"What about it?"

He tried not to smirk. "Are you intentionally being obtuse?"

"I beg your pardon?"

"You don't seem like someone who's slow-witted, but I must say you're acting a bit strange right now."

Angel pointed a finger at his chest. "I am not slow-witted, and I'll thank you to keep your opinions to yourself."

Travis dropped the hoof pick. "So I'm not allowed to speak my mind, is that it?"

"Not if you're going to call me names." She stepped close to him and jabbed him on the shoulder with her finger. "I don't have to work here, you know. I can find something else."

Travis refrained from saying something more, but he wanted to crow with laughter. He'd finally gotten a reaction from his normally reserved employee, and her beautiful eyes shot sparks that nearly singed him. His hand snaked out and grasped her wrist. "I'm not calling you names, Miss Ramirez, but you *are* mighty frustrating at times."

She jerked her good arm, but he held on tight, pulling her closer. "And you aren't going to ride away and find another job. We have an agreement that you'll work for me until I find someone to replace you, remember?"

"Let go of me." Angel scowled.

Travis gazed down at the upturned face only a few inches from his own and broke out in a sweat. Her full lower lip trembled in anger, and her cheeks flushed with color. Her gaze bored into his, but his eyes kept wandering to that enticing mouth. He ran his tongue over his dry lips and slowly dipped his head, the temptation to kiss her almost more than he could resist.

Her arm relaxed in his grip. No longer did she pull away but stood quietly, a quizzical expression softening her features.

Travis lowered his head another inch, his mind pulsing with the need to see what those lips would taste like. Suddenly, his stallion stamped and snorted, destroying the spell.

Angel gasped and lunged backward, breaking free of his grasp. Her hands flew up to cover her blazing cheeks. She shot him a wild glance, then turned without a word and fled from the stall.

* * * * *

Angel raced through the barn, her pounding heart almost choking the breath from her body. What had just happened? Better yet, what had Travis been thinking? She should've laughed it off, but she'd been mesmerized by the sight of his lips moving close to hers and hadn't been able to move. Her palms hit the door, slamming it open, and she catapulted through and into the light. Three more long strides across the barnyard brought her smack into a hard object.

"Oof." Arizona reached out to steady himself and gripped her shoulders with iron fingers. "You 'bout knocked me six ways to Sunday, little lady. What's the hurry?"

Angel stiffened in his grip. The last thing she needed right now was another encounter with a man, no matter how friendly. "Nothing. Just need some air."

"Something stink in the barn?" He removed his hat, scratched his scalp, and plunked it back on.

She could have shrieked with laughter at the ludicrous question, but her emotions were giving her fits. She didn't trust herself to speak, so she simply shook her head.

"Just felt like runnin', did ya? Well now, I guess a man can't figure out the strange ways of a woman, no matter how hard he tries." His dark brown eyes twinkled and he grinned. "I don't mind, though. You can run into me anytime you want to."

Angel gasped and shook herself free, realizing he still held her arms. "I need to get to the house and..." She searched her mind for something plausible. "Talk to Libby about going to church."

Arizona scowled. "Thought you didn't go in for that type of thing. You been staying home on Sundays since you got here. I was hoping you might take a ride with me tomorrow."

"Sorry, Arizona, but I made a promise that I'd go to church, and I need to keep it."

He jerked his head toward the emerging figure of Travis stalking out of the barn. "To him?"

Angel felt heat creep up her neck and ducked her head. "No. I need to go." She chanced a peek at Travis, then swung on her heel and dashed for the house, feeling like a thousand imps pursued her. First Travis and now Arizona. Next thing she knew James would try to corner her. A small, wild laugh flitted from her lips. The boy was only thirteen, but he'd been shooting her looks that bespoke of young love. Had someone poured a potion into the well water?

She slowed as she mounted the steps to the porch, suddenly aware of what she'd told Arizona. It was out in the open now, and she'd made a commitment. What would Travis think of her attending church with the family? She could wear her trousers, take Bella, and slip into the back of the building after they'd arrived, then head home a few minutes before the service ended.

A tug at the door and she stepped inside. This was ridiculous. She'd come to this ranch because she wanted to start over, not continue the charade of being a man. At some point she had to start acting like a woman, but she didn't know how. A couple steps took her through the front of the house and into the living room. Libby sat in a wingback chair with an embroidery hoop in her hand, and Grandmother lay with her head on a pillow propped on the arm of the nearby sofa, a soft snore coming from her lips.

Angel tiptoed into the room and whispered, "I'd like to talk to you, but I don't want to wake her."

Libby looked up and smiled. "I don't think you will. James blasted into the room talking a blue streak not long ago, and she slept through it all." She waved at a chair not far from her own. "Did you have a nice time?"

Angel's thoughts flew to the episode in the barn. "What do you mean?"

Libby nodded toward the sleeping woman. "I saw you sitting on the porch with Maria, and you seemed to be having a good chat."

"Oh. Yes, it was nice. But I need to ask you something."

Libby lay the needlework down in her lap and turned her full attention on Angel. "Of course."

"I thought. That is, I wondered…" Angel was unsure how to go on.

"What is it, Angel?" Libby leaned forward with an encouraging smile.

"I'd like to attend church with you tomorrow, if that's all right?" There. She'd said it and couldn't take it back. After this one time, she wouldn't have to return. She'd keep her promise to God and then go back to her regular life.

Libby beamed. "That would be lovely!" She sat back, studying Angel for several moments in silence. "Do you own a dress, or a skirt and shirtwaist? How about shoes and a hat?"

Angel shrank back against her chair and shook her head. "Uh—no. None of those things."

"You only have men's clothing?" Libby's brows knit together.

"Yes. That's all I've needed for the past few years."

"I see." Libby set her sewing aside, rose, and held out her hand to Angel. "Come, dear. We're going to get you all fixed up."

"Fixed up?" Angel felt like the slow-witted person Travis had chided her about earlier.

"Yes." Libby scanned Angel's body from head to toe and back again. "I saw the perfect thing for you at Steven's Dry Goods store in town."

"But—but—" Angel stammered.

"No argument, young lady. Why, by the time we get done with you, the men on this ranch won't know what hit them." She released a chiming laugh.

Angel gasped and drew back, her heart hammering at the picture presented. "I've changed my mind. I probably need to work tomorrow anyway. I've been off far too long and need to make up some of the time I've been lying around since my injury."

"Piffle. No such thing. Come on now, we're going to Sundance so you can see the outfit I have in mind." Libby smiled smugly. "My, won't it be fun to see their expressions when you come in to breakfast tomorrow."

* * * * *

Angel felt strange riding in the buggy instead of on her horse, but she took the opportunity to gaze up the dusty street of Sundance as Libby drove toward the dry goods store. Ponderosa pines dotted the foothills, but very few remained within the confines of the town. Angel's gaze was drawn to a massive building. "Libby, look at that beautiful brick building. What is it?"

Libby leaned forward and peered past her. "That contains the courthouse, the jail, and the sheriff's office. It was built four years ago and is the pride of the county. That's where they kept Harry Longabough after he was arrested."

"I heard something about that. Aren't they calling him 'The Sundance Kid' now?"

Libby laughed. "I think so, and it started because he spent so much time in jail here in Sundance."

Angel's curiosity died. The courthouse, the jail, and the sheriff's office were the last places she cared to visit. "This is the first time I've been in town since I came to the ranch. It's bigger than I expected."

They turned a corner onto the main street and Angel noted the businesses with keen interest. Nettlehorst and Irvin Drug store, a doctor's office, Nelson's Shoe store, and The Tiny Barber shop were all just beyond the Zane Hotel, along with Robert's hardware store.

Libby pointed her whip at the Barber shop and grinned. "See that sign, The Tiny Barber Shop?"

Angel nodded.

"A man named Tiny is the barber, and he's one of the biggest men you'll ever meet. I guess someone gave him the nickname years ago, and it stuck. He's a good barber, even if he does take up a lot of room in his small shop." She drew the horse to a stop in front of Frank and Co., General Merchandise Store. "Here we are. Abe Frank carries some of the best goods in the county."

They tied the horse, stepped onto the boardwalk, and made their way into the store. Angel paused, amazed at the display of merchandise. Bolts of cloth lay spread out on counters, pots and pans, dishes, and other sundry kitchen goods lined several shelves, food stuffs took up a large portion of one corner, and she caught a glimpse of tools down one aisle. "Why, this store has everything!"

Libby nodded and slipped her arm through Angel's. "Just about. Come on, the dress I want to show you is back here. You're going to love it."

A middle-aged man wearing a white apron stepped around the corner and pushed a pair of spectacles up on his nose. "Can I help you ladies?" He glanced from one to the other, his gaze resting for several moments on Angel's trousers and boot-clad feet.

Libby tipped her head toward the dry goods section. "Yes. You had a deep green dress here a week or so ago."

"Ah yes. That's a lovely garment. Just a moment, please." He hurried between two tables of fabric to the back wall and reached up, lifting down a wooden hanger from a pole and draping the gown over his arm. A couple long strides brought him back to the front of the store. He held it toward Libby and smiled. "For you, madam?"

She shook her head. "No, it's for Angel. Miss Ramirez. Could you hold it up for us, please?"

The fabric unfurled as the clerk held it up for their inspection. Angel gasped. A lace collar set off the rounded neckline and tapered bodice, touches of lace edged the cuffs of the sleeves, and folds of rich emerald green cascaded to the floor.

He swung it around and pointed to the pearl buttons running from the neck to the waist. "Real mother of pearl. Not something you see every day."

Angel gripped Libby's arm and drew her close, whispering in her ear, "I can't wear something like this, and I certainly can't afford it. We need to find a skirt and blouse, or maybe just a new pair of trousers."

Libby plucked the dress out of the clerk's hand and held it up in front of Angel. "It looks like it was made for you. It's going to fit perfectly."

"Libby, I can't…"

"Of course you can. You haven't spent a cent since you arrived. You can't wear trousers to church, and you need a dress. This one is perfect." She turned back to the clerk. "We'll take it. Would you wrap it for us, please?"

"Certainly." He beamed his pleasure and took the dress carefully, disappearing into a room behind the high counter. Minutes later he returned, bearing a paper-wrapped parcel and holding it out to Angel. "Here you go, Miss. How did you want to pay for that?"

Libby waved her gloved hand in the air. "Put it on my brother's account. Travis Morgan, out at Sundance Ranch."

"Libby!" Angel gasped and drew back from the proffered parcel. "Did you ask Travis? What will he think?"

"Don't worry so much. I'll let him know, and he can take it out of your wages. Come on, we need to find shoes and stockings and a hat."

Angel planted her hands on her hips. "I am not spending any more money, and that's final."

Libby chewed her bottom lip for a moment. "All right. I'll loan you a pair of shoes and stockings, and you don't really need a hat. I tend to forget sometimes that we're not in the city. I'm sure the people at the Methodist Church won't mind if you attend without one."

Angel tried to relax, but she still felt as though a tornado had swept her along for a dizzying ride. "They'd better not, because I have no intention of wearing one, unless it's my sombrero."

A chuckle broke from the clerk's lips, but he quickly stifled it. "Sorry, Miss. Was there anything else?"

Angel answered before Libby had the chance to open her lips. "No. Thank you. This will be just fine." She snatched the package from his hands and headed for the door. "I think we've done enough damage for one day."

Chapter Nineteen

....

The next morning Libby finished buttoning the emerald-green dress for Angel and gently pushed her into a chair. "Do you mind if I fix your hair?"

Angel touched her plait. "Not at all, but what's wrong with it?"

Libby bit her lip to keep a smile from peeking out. Angel didn't have a vain bone in her body. The longer she knew this young woman, the more she liked her—and to think she hadn't wanted Travis to hire her when she'd first arrived. "Your hair is lovely, but I thought we might do something a bit different."

Angel shrugged. "If you want to." She fingered the lace at her throat and raised a quizzical face.

"As soon as I finish, I'll turn you around so you can take a look." The mirror hanging above her vanity covered nearly half of the wall and was the one thing she'd insisted on bringing with her. Mama had surprised her with it before her coming-out party, and she wouldn't leave it behind.

"I feel funny having you do so much for me. I could have worn my best pants and shirt."

"It's no bother. I loved playing dress-up with my friends when I was little, and while you aren't young enough to be my daughter, I can still have fun if you'll allow me to." Libby loosened the ends of the braid and unwound the tresses, running her fingers through the black hair and marveling at the thickness. She'd never met a woman before who truly didn't know her own beauty. The women she knew in San Francisco would've jumped at the chance to wear this satin gown trimmed in lace. Not Angel.

Silence reigned while Libby brushed Angel's hair. She'd never had a daughter, and she'd always wanted a sister. She could only hope the bride Travis chose would be as unassuming as Angel.

Her hand froze as the idea penetrated deeper. What a grand notion! Angel had agreed to attend church with them, so surely she was open and interested in the gospel. Her eyes narrowed. Had Travis shown any interest in Angel since she'd arrived? Libby thought back over the past weeks and began to smile. When Angel was injured, her brother had insisted he care for her when Libby needed sleep.

Then her shoulders slumped. Who else would he have asked? She'd need to study on this when she had a bit more time.

Libby plucked a large ivory comb from the top of the vanity behind her. It would've been much easier to have Angel turned around, but she didn't want her looking in the mirror until she'd finished. A couple of deft twists and she'd secured a portion of hair from both sides of Angel's face and pulled it to the back of her head. She left one tiny ringlet in front of each ear.

"There. All done. Look in the mirror and tell me what you think." Libby held her breath while Angel stood and hesitated a moment before turning. "Angel?"

Angel bit her bottom lip. "I'm nervous. I haven't worn a dress since before Mama died."

"You haven't worn a dress? I had no idea…"

Before she could comment further Angel swung around, her hands clasped in front of her waist. She peered into the mirror. "Oh my. Is that really me?" She touched her curls. "I look—like a lady."

Libby released a peal of laughter, her heart swelling with pleasure. "You do at that, my dear. A real, true lady. In fact, you're beautiful. The lace collar and pearl buttons give the right feminine touch. I don't think I could've done better, if I do say so myself." She grasped Angel's hand and tugged. "Now we'd better get out there before breakfast is over."

"Breakfast?" Angel shrank back. "I have to wear this getup to breakfast? In front of all the cowboys, and Travis and everybody?"

"Why of course, silly girl. You have to eat. Besides, you're going to church and a lot of people will be there."

Angel shook her head. "I can't do it. I won't do it." She fumbled behind her neck and started to unbutton the gown.

Libby sprang forward and wrapped her hand around Angel's fingers. "Hush, now. Of course you can. I'll walk out with you, and we'll sit together at the table. The men are there to eat breakfast, not you."

Angel's cheeks flamed bright red at her words. "They might."

* * * * *

Angel's heart pounded, and her hands shook. Why hadn't she thought this through? How foolish to think she could step into a frilly gown and become something she wasn't. She'd been raised like a boy and trained to think like a man. Right now all she wanted was to slip back into her jeans and hide in a corner. Libby meant well, but this new look didn't suit her.

She peeked in the mirror one more time and caught her breath. Was that really her wearing the green creation that clung to every curve and shouted her femininity? The braid that usually hung down her back had been replaced with soft curls piled high on her head. Angel raised her hand and touched a strand. She'd had no idea it could look like this. "It is kind of nice, isn't it?"

"It's beautiful. *You* are beautiful. Accept that, and don't let it scare you."

"I never thought—" She sighed. "Thank you, Libby. For everything."

Libby's eyes misted with tears and she shook her head. "I'm the one who should thank you."

Angel raised her brows. "For what?"

"I was so lonely before you arrived. I'll admit I didn't think we'd have anything in common when we met, but I'm so glad you came. I'd like to think we might become friends."

Joy surged through Angel's heart and a newfound confidence filled her. "I'd like that."

Libby slipped her arm around Angel's waist. "Come on. It's time to show those men what a real woman looks like."

Angel swallowed. She could do this, with Libby beside her. Nothing was too hard when you had a friend who believed in you.

* * * * *

Travis glanced around the table. The men were restless. What was taking Libby and Angel so long? Libby had never been late to breakfast on a Sunday morning, and she typically helped Smokey. If they waited much longer he'd have to lasso and hogtie a few of his cowboys to keep them from rushing the food.

Charlie took a swig of his coffee, the only thing Smokey allowed them to touch, then thumped his cup on the table. "I'm starving, Boss. When do we eat?"

Nate elbowed the man. "Pipe down. Miss Angel and Libby will be here soon enough. You aren't going to die."

Wren growled low in his throat. "Don't bet on it. My stomach thinks my throat's been cut and ain't never gettin' food again."

Arizona glared at his partner. "Ah, shut your big bazoo. Miss Angel and the boss's sister are worth waiting for. It's not gonna help to keep bellyaching."

Travis grunted. "I agree." A door shut upstairs and he heard two sets of shoes walking down the steps. "Here they come now. Mind your manners, men. No more grousing."

He wondered if Libby lent Angel a skirt of some sort, or maybe a blouse to go with her trousers. From what he'd seen, the girl was only comfortable in men's garb, and he doubted she could be convinced to wear anything else.

Libby stepped into the room and Angel hovered behind her. Travis caught a flash of deep green color and dark curls peeking from behind Libby. Finally, his sister stepped to the side and all movement at the table halted. A spell seemed to weave itself over the men and turned them into carved statues rather than ravenous cowboys.

Every eye focused on the lovely vision standing a few feet away. Travis gulped a mouthful of coffee and tried not to choke. Could this possibly be the dusty, boot-clad woman he'd mistaken for a boy? The rich green of her dress set off her dusky skin and black hair to perfection. His gaze strayed to the fitted bodice hugging her tiny waist, and he had to quell the urge to tear at the collar tightening around his throat. The word *beautiful* didn't do her justice. *Breathtaking* came closer.

Arizona pushed away from the table and stood, giving a gallant bow. "Good morning, lovely lady." He gripped the back of her chair and slid it out. "Allow me?" He waited until she was seated and gently moved it forward until she was perfectly positioned at her place. Turning, he did the same for Libby.

Travis ground his teeth, chastising himself for sitting like a dolt and allowing his cowboy to do the honors. By Arizona's smug expression the cowboy believed he'd scored a win.

"Thank you, Arizona, you're very kind." Angel's lilting voice broke the cowboys' restraint.

Wren sat up straight and grinned. "I never seen nothin' as bee-oo-tiful as you, Miss Angel." His smile suddenly faded. He flushed and turned to Libby. "Exceptin' present company, of course, ma'am."

Libby gave a solemn nod. "Thank you, Wren, but you're quite right. Angel is exquisite."

Charlie leaned forward, his homely face alight. "Purty as a picture, I declare."

Each of the cowboys added their consensus until Travis wanted to shout at them to stop. Did they have to slobber all over the woman?

He raised his voice above the hubbub. "All right, men. We'd better eat before the food gets cold, and some of us are late for church." He reached for the platter of fried potatoes.

Nate cleared his throat and gave him a look, but Travis had no idea what he was trying to convey. He scooped up a serving, and Nate coughed. Travis glared. "What is it, man? I'd have thought you were as hungry as the rest of these geezers."

"Just had a notion you'd want to bless the food like you usually do, Boss. Unless you're too hungry to wait."

Travis's hand halted in midair. "Yeah. Right. Sorry." He felt too flustered to pray. When had he ever forgotten to say a blessing before a meal? "Nate, maybe you'd do the honors?"

He tried to calm his mind while Nate uttered a short prayer. Afterward, the clanking of glasses and silverware filled the room. Travis noticed more than one man stealing a glance at Angel, but she didn't seem to notice. If he thought his ranch was in the midst of upheaval since this woman arrived, what in the world would it be after today?

* * * * *

Angel stood beside the family buggy, hesitant about where she should sit. The elegant carriage had a covered top with a roomy front and back seat; each could comfortably fit two people, and three in a pinch. She grasped the handle and lifted her foot, thankful for the black laced-up shoes Libby lent her. Someone touched her arm.

Libby stood beside her. "Would you mind sitting with Travis on the way to church?"

Angel frowned, not sure how to respond. Sit next to Travis? He was *Libby's* brother. "Why? I can ride in the back with James."

"I'd like to, if you don't mind. I haven't had much time with my son the past few days, and I'd appreciate being able to chat with him."

"How about Grandmother? She should sit up front, not me. I can stay home and go in a couple of weeks when the reverend comes back to town—" Her voice broke on the last note.

"Maria told me she's tired and decided to spend the morning resting."

"Tired?" Alarm surged through Angel's heart. "Is she ill?"

Libby shook her head. "She's fine. She didn't sleep well last night. Even if you stayed home, she'd probably doze for the next couple of hours. Smokey will keep an eye on her." She gripped Angel's arm and urged her forward. "Come now, climb up. Travis will be out any minute."

At that moment James and Travis exited the house, their boots clomping on the wood planks as they made their way toward the steps. "Hey, Ma!" James waved at his mother and grinned. "Can I sit with Miss Angel?"

Libby waited until they approached before she answered. "No, Son. You can sit in the back and visit with your mother. Miss Angel is sitting up front with your uncle."

Angel glanced at Travis, wondering what he might think, but only a brief flash of surprise crossed his features. He quickly masked the emotion and nodded, reached out a hand, and took her arm. "Here, let me help you up."

Angel felt a rush of relief. She'd never tried to navigate in a skirt with so much material before—or any type of dress, for that matter—and had no idea how she'd keep from stepping on the hem and falling. She settled onto the padded cushion with a sigh. "What a nice buggy."

Libby answered from her place in the back where she'd climbed without assistance. "Yes. Travis purchased it right after I arrived at the ranch. All he had before was a rickety buckboard that jarred your teeth on every little bump in the road. And this isn't a bit hard to drive, either."

James piped up from beside his mother. "Yeah. Uncle Travis is going to teach me to drive soon. Can I ride up front with you on the way back and try?"

Travis picked up the reins and glanced over his shoulder. "We'll see how it goes, but I'm not sure it's a good idea to have your first lesson with other people onboard."

"Ah, tarnation. I gotta learn sometime!"

"James!" Libby's tone was shocked. "I will not have you using that kind of language. Do I need to send you to your room without supper when we return home?"

"No."

"No, what?"

"No, ma'am. I'm sorry." James's words barely connected with Angel's ears.

The next mile or so rolled by in silence. Occasionally Travis's arm brushed hers as he tugged on the reins, creating a deep sense of awareness in Angel. He looked handsome in his gray trousers and white shirt partly covered by a buttoned-up vest. The light scent of cologne wafted from his clean-shaven face. He gazed straight ahead and the muscles in his forearms rippled beneath the fabric of his shirt. Her hands grew moist. She rubbed them on her skirt, then yanked them away, realizing what she'd done. Why hadn't she insisted on sitting in the back with Libby? The nearness of this man disturbed her more than she could account for.

She turned her attention to her surroundings, working to rein in her physical response to Travis. The vast grassy fields disappeared, and they entered a more rugged, heavily treed area. Ridges and rock outcroppings grew more frequent as they drove parallel to a line of mountains.

"How long since you've been to a church service?" Travis asked, then clucked to his team as they entered a straight stretch of road.

Angel tipped her head toward him. "I've never been to church before. Or I guess I should say, not that I can remember. I think my parents took me when I was very young."

Travis cocked his head toward her. "I had no idea. I just assumed—"

She shrugged. "We lived a long ways from town, and there was no church nearby." Angel bit her lip—that much was true. He didn't need to know that church wasn't something anyone in the outlaw camp thought of. A couple of the Mexican women had a Catholic background, but they weren't devout. No one else had seemed to care.

"So, where exactly did you grow up?" His tone was curious.

Angel hesitated, gripping the side rail as the buggy rattled over a rough patch of ground. A hard jolt threw her against Travis and he reached out to steady her, clasping her arm. A pleasant shock traveled through her body. She liked the feel of his strong grip, and she stifled disappointment when he moved away.

Travis slowed the team from a trot back to a walk. "Sorry. I don't usually rush through here. Guess I wasn't paying enough attention."

Angel nodded. "Speaking of growing up, have you lived in the West all your life? I know your sister is from San Francisco." She spoke in a rush, hoping he'd forget his own question and move on to hers.

He opened his mouth, then scowled. They traveled a few minutes without speaking. "I was raised in St. Louis, as was Libby. She moved to San Francisco after she married. I left home when I was seventeen."

"Do you still have family there?"

"Yes. My father." His answer was curt and didn't invite anything more.

Angel settled against the seat, wishing she were sitting in the back with Libby. This man disturbed her too much. She'd make sure James got his wish to ride up front on the way home, whatever it took.

* * * * *

Travis gripped the reins and mentally kicked himself. Sure he'd been a little miffed when Angel evaded his question and pointed it back at him, but that was no reason to be short. He'd felt her stiffen and withdraw, and he couldn't say he blamed her. Why was it that the very thought of his father set his teeth on edge? It shouldn't bother him so much. He was a grown man with his own life now, and if Father wouldn't acknowledge that fact, there was nothing Travis could do.

He'd hoped to draw Angel out about her past—find a clue as to why she had no religious background. How could she grow up and never attend church? For that matter, why hadn't she known her grandparents were living? If Maria and her husband hadn't sent letters to practically every sheriff from Texas to Wyoming asking for word of a woman named Maria de Luca or her husband, Carlo Ramirez, Angel still wouldn't know her grandmother existed. It was a good thing Angel had chosen to use her mother's last name while riding as a man.

Libby's soft voice caught his ear, but he couldn't decipher the words. Hopefully she was discussing the sheriff's concerns with James, since Travis hadn't made time to follow through on that chore. He heaved a sigh. There was so much that he didn't seem to get right in this life. He'd have to apologize to Libby for not spending more time with James and setting a better example. The boy needed a strong man to shape his life now that his father was dead. Not that Travis had a lot of positive input in his life from his own father.

Angel shifted her position beside him, and he turned his head. "Comfortable? We're almost to town."

"I'm fine. Thank you." Her tone didn't invite conversation.

If the return trip was anything like this, it would be a long ride home. Maybe he'd allow James a few minutes at the reins, after all.

* * * * *

Angel stood beside the buggy after the church service, gazing at the beautiful Church of the Good Shepherd. Faint memories of attending a Catholic church with her parents niggled her mind, and gratitude flooded her that this Episcopal service hadn't been too far different from what she recalled. She tipped her head back, noting the beauty of multiple windows above the peaked front entrance to the soaring, steepled bell tower above.

She glanced back at the crowd gathering outside the building, grateful Travis had invited James to sit beside him on the way home. She wondered if it had anything to do with not answering his question about where she grew up. He'd been none too forthcoming about his childhood, either, and *she* hadn't gotten angry. The last thing she wanted was anyone prying into her background and uncovering her secrets. If they discovered she'd ridden on that last cattle drive where a Texas Ranger and posse were killed, she'd have to disappear. Fast.

Libby stood chatting with an older woman in the churchyard, and James was laughing with a boy who appeared close to his age. She'd liked the service well enough, although she didn't know any of the songs and couldn't make sense of much of what the pastor said. But the music was nice and the preacher didn't shout. Some of the men back at the camp made jokes about the hellfire-and-brimstone preachers who did nothing but scream at their flock, and she'd shuddered at the picture that painted in her mind. She'd been tense when the man stepped behind his big wooden stand, but he'd started out by greeting the people and praying in a gentle voice.

She headed for the buggy as soon as the service ended. She didn't know these people and had no desire to get acquainted. It was doubtful she'd come again anyway before she hit the trail for a new job.

A stab of pain sharp enough to make her wince hit her at the thought. A few weeks ago losing her job created concern, but now it was so much more. Now it hurt. And what of Grandmother, if Travis found someone to take her place? Would Maria return to Italy, or go with Angel? Angel shook her head. Too many unknowns.

A hand touched her arm, and she jumped. Libby smiled. "I'm sorry I startled you. I called James and told Travis we're ready to go. James is so excited his uncle is allowing him to ride up front, and I'll admit, I'm looking forward to sitting by someone who's not sulking all the way home." She grasped the handle on the outside of the buggy, picked up her skirt with her other hand, and swung aboard.

Angel clambered in after her, struggling to avoid getting tangled in her skirt as she moved from the step to the seat.

James bounded up to the buggy, his face alight. "Where's Uncle Travis? I want to get going so I can drive."

Libby leaned forward and shook her head. "He didn't say you could drive, James. Just that he'd show you the proper way to hold the reins. You mustn't pester him."

The boy's shoulders slumped and his expression turned sullen. "Yes, Ma." He perked up. "But maybe he'll let me for a few minutes." James scrambled onto the seat and twisted around to face the two women. "Don't worry, I won't beg him—too much." He grinned and turned back to the front, his hands hovering over the reins wound around the brake.

"Don't touch that brake, James." Travis stepped into view alongside the boy. "Scoot over. I've got a lot of explaining to do before I let you handle the team."

He settled into his seat, picked up the buggy whip, and pulled out of the churchyard. Libby patted Angel's arm and whispered, "So nice to have another woman to chat with."

Angel's heart swelled with gratitude. When had she ever had someone she could think of as a friend? "Yes. You're much easier to talk to than Travis." She nearly bit off the tip of her tongue after the words left her mouth. This was Travis's sister. "I'm sorry. I didn't mean…"

Libby chuckled. "Not to worry, my dear. Men are strange creatures. They think *we're* hard to understand, but we're easy in comparison. And *believe me*, I know Travis isn't always the best communicator in the world."

"Thank you for understanding. I haven't met many men like your brother, so I'm not always sure what to think."

"In what way?"

"Most of the time he's kind and courteous, but other times he snaps at me, or seems worried I'm doing something wrong." She shrugged. "Maybe I irritate him. I'm not sure."

"I wouldn't fret about it. What did you think of the service?"

The sudden change in topic caught Angel off guard. "Excuse me?"

"Church. Was it similar to other services you've attended?"

Angel stifled a groan. She didn't care to go through this again. Travis would probably tell Libby later what a sinner she was, never having attended church. Seeing disappointment or censure on Libby's face didn't appeal. "It was fine. I liked the singing."

Libby beamed. "The music is one of my favorite things. Our pastor has taught us several new hymns lately, and I'm glad. Our church in San Francisco stayed up to date on things like that."

James turned in his seat, his eyes wide and sparkling. "Ma—Miss Angel. I get to hold the reins, but don't worry, I won't wreck the buggy. I promised Uncle Travis I'd do everything he tells me."

Angel snatched at the chance to move the subject away from church. "That's wonderful, James. I'm sure you'll do a fine job."

The boy beamed and turned back around. He held out both hands, and Travis placed the reins in them as the horses moved at a lazy walk. It might take some time to get home at this pace, but she didn't care. She had a lot to think about, and Libby's attention would be on her son's new experience. Angel settled into her seat, her mind on Travis. Why did the man go from genial, to snapping, to worried in a short space of time? Whatever the reason, she'd make sure another episode like the one in the barn didn't occur again. For several seconds she'd been sure he intended to kiss her. The look in his eyes as he'd bent over her had held something she couldn't define—and aroused feelings she didn't understand—and wasn't sure she dared repeat.

Chapter Twenty

....

Bart Hinson let loose a string of oaths and kicked the feet of the man wrapped in a bedroll a couple of yards from the fire. "Get up, you dad-blasted bunch of lazy buzzard bait. The sun's up and yer not. Move it!" His words bellowed across the small clearing.

The scruffy, bleary-eyed outlaw rolled from his place on the ground, grumbling and cursing. "Why'd'ya have to kick me? Not like we got cattle to rustle or money to spend."

"Yeah, Boss. What's the hurry?" A skinny, stoop-shouldered man slung his gun belt around his hips.

"He ain't *my* boss," muttered a third man sitting on his blankets.

Hinson turned with a roar and lunged at the outlaw, striking him in the mouth with his fist and knocking him back against the hard ground. "Anyone else wanna question my authority?"

No one spoke, and the other men scrambled around the camp, tossing branches on the smoldering coals and pulling out cooking utensils for breakfast. The next minutes passed in silence as each avoided their comrade still prostrate on the ground.

Finally, the man grunted, rolled to his side, and got an elbow under his body, pushing himself to a sitting position. "Sorry—*Boss*." He emitted the words with forced respect.

Bart's tense stance relaxed. "We don't got cattle to drive now, but we're gonna have plenty in a week or two."

The bustling activity came to a halt, and all eyes turned his way.

Hinson hitched up his belt, and his chest swelled. "I didn't drag you halfway across the country for our health, you know. I got me a plan, and if each of you varmints mind yer manners you might just come out rich. But there'll be no more bellyachin' or you'll get a two-by-six hole in the ground. Got me?" He stared at each one in turn until the men agreed. "Good."

He turned away and picked up his bedroll. He'd been hunting that gal for three years and finally got a fix on where she'd headed. Her purty face had been a draw all this time, but it sure didn't hurt that she'd fallen in with a rancher with a large herd of cattle. No sir. Didn't hurt none at all.

Chapter Twenty-One

....

Another week passed, along with another church service. Life settled into a routine. Angel spent her days working horses and tracking predators, and evenings visiting with her grandmother. The more time she spent with the older woman, the more her affection grew. Maria de Luca, for all her aristocratic poise, settled into ranch life as though born to it. She wasn't above helping Smokey in the kitchen, and Angel even caught the two laughing together while Grandmother dried the dishes.

Angel stood on the porch and took in a lungful of fresh morning air. It felt good to be alive. Travis hadn't said any more about finding a replacement, and she'd started to breathe easier. She'd been successful in cleaning out a pack of coyotes on the east side of the ranch, and now scouted the western side for the more elusive wolves. James had been nagging her to come, but after the incident with his horse she didn't feel comfortable having the boy tag along.

Libby stepped out the front door and walked to where Angel stood. "Have you seen James this morning?"

"No. He spoke to me before he headed to bed last night, and I'm afraid I may have upset him, so he's probably avoiding me today."

"Oh? What happened?"

Angel did a quarter turn and faced Libby. "He asked if he could track wolves with me today, and I told him no. After he ran his horse and nearly got himself killed I just figured…" She let her words trail off, afraid she'd overstepped her bounds.

Libby patted her arm. "Don't worry, you made the right decision. I had a long talk with him about the sheriff's concerns, and he denied sneaking off to town. But I'm not sure." She sighed. "Sometimes I wonder if it would've been better keeping him in San Francisco."

"I've never been to a big city, but wouldn't there be plenty of places where he could get into scrapes?"

"That's why I moved. Sometimes it seems like he's trying so hard to please me and be a good boy; then other times—"

"He has a lot of energy, Libby. Maybe he needs a job."

"A job? He does his schooling in the mornings and has chores. This fall he'll ride into town and attend school."

Angel shook her head. "I didn't mean like a job in a store. I was thinking about letting him get more involved in the ranch. Make him feel that he's useful and important. In another four or five years he could be going off on his own, and you want him prepared."

Libby's eyes clouded. "I hate the thought of him growing up. He's all I have left." She hunched one shoulder. "Except Travis, I mean. But James is my son, and it kills me to think of him leaving."

"I think he's been trying to show you he's not a child."

Libby nodded. "I know. It's just hard." She gave a half smile. "I'm going to see if he's out with the kittens again, since he's not in his room. Smokey will have breakfast on the table soon."

"Good idea." Angel watched Libby walk across the hard-packed dirt and slip inside the barn. She found it difficult to relate to Libby's feelings. Boys raised in the outlaw band were riding herd on stolen cattle at James's age, and some had already killed a man. Of course, they didn't have city-bred mothers worrying about them, either. What kind of a mother would she make if the time ever came? An

image of Travis flashed through her mind. He'd make a good father...
She lassoed her thoughts before they galloped away with her.

Libby emerged from the barn and hurried to the house, her
mouth twisted in concern. "He's not there, and his horse is gone."

Angel felt a tiny stab of worry but pushed it away. "Remember the
last time? He took his horse to the stream and staked him out on the
grass. I'm sure he'll return soon."

Libby mustered a smile. "You're right. And if he doesn't show up
in time for breakfast, he'll have to go hungry. James needs to learn to
be more responsible. He is thirteen, after all."

Angel bit her lip to keep from grinning. Libby was trying and
that's what mattered.

* * * * *

Travis pushed his chair back from the table and glanced at Libby,
working to quell his annoyance. "Still no sign of James? It's not like
him to miss a meal."

Libby shook her head. "I know. I wasn't worried at first, but now..."

Wren spoke up from his place at the end of the table. "How 'bout
I go take me a look-see, Boss?"

"Yeah," Arizona drawled and stood. "Me too. Can't have Miss
Libby worried about her boy all morning."

Travis looked from one man to the other. "You're right. Work
can wait." He turned to his foreman, who sat silent, his gaze fixed on
Libby. "Nate. You put the rest of the men to work, and I'll help the
boys look for James."

Nate dragged his attention back to Travis. "Sure. Let's go, fellas."

Angel touched Libby's arm. "I'm going too. I think I'll start down
at the stream."

"Thanks, Angel." Libby's pale face bespoke her anxiety.

Over the next few minutes the dining room cleared, while Smokey, Libby, and Grandmother stayed to put the room back to rights.

Travis had stuffed down his irritation in front of Libby. She had enough to worry over without knowing he'd like to rattle that boy's cage and make him think before he acted. No doubt he was lollygagging somewhere, with no thought for anyone else. This time he'd take a firmer hand with James. The boy needed a man-to-man talk, and that was Travis's responsibility.

He headed to the barn and climbed the ladder into the loft. Most likely he'd find the boy playing with the kittens again. "James? You up here?" He reached the top rung and stepped onto the hay-littered floor. "James! Speak up, boy."

Nothing. A movement caught his eye, and Travis tromped across the loft and looked behind the stack of hay. A black-and-white cat blinked at him, lifted her front paw, and started to clean it. Three kittens romped under the window, rolling and batting at each other's ears. No sign of James. Travis returned to the ladder and made his way to the floor of the barn, exiting the structure several moments later.

Libby waited outside. Wren and Arizona huffed around the corner at the same time Angel appeared. Wren caught his breath and sputtered. "His rifle's gone, Boss. I checked the gun cabinet in your office. The one you let the boy use is missin'."

Travis's heart jumped like a jackrabbit running from a coyote. Not good. Not good *at all*. "Why would James take a rifle?" He didn't realize he'd spoken aloud and cringed at the added worry it would cause Libby.

She clutched his arm, her grip tightening with each word. "He could hurt himself, Travis."

He patted her hand. "He's probably just target practicing."

"James knows he's not allowed to shoot unsupervised." Her voice cracked. "You've got to find him."

"We will." Travis faced his men. "Saddle up. Scout around and see if you can find his tracks. Wren"—he turned to the bowlegged man standing at attention—"find Nate and the others. I want every man on this."

"Yes, sir." Wren sprinted for the corral and grabbed a lasso.

Angel stepped close to Libby. "I'm saddling up and hunting too."

Travis furrowed his brow. He'd hired her as a tracker—with her skills she might have the best chance of finding the boy. "Fine. I want anyone who finds him to fire three shots in the air. What direction will you take?"

"I'll head over toward the butte. I've seen wolf tracks there. It's too far to hear any shots from there, so if I find him I'll have to get closer to the ranch before I alert you."

Libby gasped and covered her mouth with her fingertips. "You think he's hunting wolves? Alone?"

"I don't know, but we need to check." Angel squeezed Libby's hand. "We'll bring him back, Libby. But it might not hurt if you ask God to give us some help."

Chapter Twenty-Two

....

Angel left the ranch urging Bella into a hard trot. Her gut tensed. Something was wrong. She'd meant it when she suggested Libby pray, although why that thought occurred she couldn't be sure. Maybe something the pastor said about trusting God in times of need. This certainly qualified. She wondered if God would listen if she prayed with her eyes open.

Bella snorted and tugged at the reins, anxious to pick up the pace. They still had a couple of miles to cover and Angel loosened her grip, allowing the mare to move into a smooth, ground-covering canter. Sagebrush and low, flowering plants flashed on the edge of her vision, but she kept her focus on the butte looming ahead. The towering rock wall grew closer, but she spotted no indication of human life. Cattle dotted the landscape, spreading out over a swath at least half a mile long.

Angel reined Bella to a halt not far from the spring-fed pool and dismounted. She let her mare drink, then walked to the boiling spring and filled her canteen with the fresh, pure water. Slipping off the horse's bridle, she placed a halter on Bella's head and staked her on a long lead to a sapling near water and grass. She glanced around. Nothing. Maybe coming here was a mistake, but a sense of urgency pushed her forward.

She gazed up at the butte, remembering Travis's words the first time they'd ridden here. The other side of this rock was sloped, and climbing partway up afforded an excellent view. Riding boots didn't offer good hiking stability, but she'd climb it anyway. Good thing her arm had healed to the point of only being sore.

Angel checked the load in her rifle, cradled it in her arm, and started her trek up the hill. Loose shale littered the lower part of the rise and she skirted around it, gingerly picking her way over the outer edge. The ground grew firmer, and patches of grass and wildflowers dotted the area, interspersed with outcroppings of sharp rock and rounded boulders.

About halfway up she took a break and perched on a rock, setting her rifle on the ground. Most of her time was spent in the saddle, and hiking up a hillside left her short of breath. Only a hundred feet or so to go and she should have a good view of the surrounding countryside. She picked up her gun and finished the rest of the ascent, pausing to make sure of her footing before turning.

She surveyed the scene spread before her and emitted a small gasp. The rolling plains of Wyoming stretched out, the grass undulating like waves on a windblown lake. Magnificent mountains raised tight-fisted fingers to the sky in the distant haze, proclaiming their dominance over the flatlands at their feet. Clouds drifted across the azure sky, and she could make out diamond glints sparkling on the surface of a stream.

She tore her gaze away from the scenery, wishing she could sit on a boulder and do nothing but dream for the rest of the day. Not now. She'd promised Libby to bring James back safely. She scanned the area at the base of the hill and slowly moved her gaze farther away. Nothing moved but a calf romping a short distance from his mother. She continued to search until she could no longer distinguish the identity of the shapes, then covered the area from there back to the base of the butte once again. Still nothing.

Frustration mounted and left Angel feeling helpless. A secret part of her had hoped the prayer she'd prayed had touched God's ears, and maybe He was leading her. She'd fooled herself. God surely had better things to do than listen to someone like her. After all, she was hiding the truth from Travis and his family. Not even Grandmother knew how she'd been raised.

God didn't like liars. She was sure of that, so why should He answer her prayers? But what about James? Should the boy be punished and remain lost, possibly hurt, because God didn't see fit to listen?

Angel heaved a sigh and plucked her rifle off the rock. Time to head down the hill and search another area. She gave one last look over the landscape, dreading the downward descent in her slick-soled boots. Something moved from behind a clump of brush at the base, and she froze. James? No. It was low to the ground and gray. A shiver ran up her spine. A wolf. Either a lone wolf or a small pack had taken up residence on the outskirts of this herd of cattle. No wonder—it was easy pickings when the herd came in to drink.

She raised the rifle to her shoulder and sighted down the barrel. A movement out of the corner of her eye caught her attention and she eased her finger off the trigger. Another wolf? Slowly she turned her head a couple of inches and stared. James stepped out from behind a scrub tree, his rifle aimed at the wolf. Should she shout at the boy, or allow him to take the shot? If she didn't stop James from killing the wolf, would that be going against what Libby wanted for her son?

Once again Angel steadied the rifle and chanced a last look at James. Dark shadows circled only a few yards behind the boy, inching along and hunched low to the ground. The rest of the pack had found James.

Chapter Twenty-Three

....

Angel raised two fingers to her lips and whistled, then let out a piercing scream. "James! Wolves!"

James turned, looked up the hill, and lifted his arm to wave. He cupped his hands around his mouth. "Miss Angel, look!" He pointed at the wolf in the distance and gestured with his rifle. "I'm going to shoot him."

The hunkered shape behind the boy suddenly launched into a run. Angel threw her rifle up and squeezed off a shot. Her gun bellowed, echoing off the hillside. The wolf dropped to the ground in mid-leap and lay still.

James whirled around. The three remaining wolves backed up a few feet, snarling and snapping their jaws. Why didn't the devils run? They couldn't be hungry with the herd close by and no one hunting them. Fear surged through Angel's mind. One of them could've been bitten by a mad animal and passed the disease along to the others.

James yelled and turned to run, but the beast in the lead leapt after him, its tail extended. Angel lifted her gun and took aim, squeezing off another shot and bringing the brute down.

Off to the side and a short distance away, Angel heard a heavier gun boom and saw the third wolf hit the ground. Finally, the fourth took flight and ran the opposite direction from James.

She turned her attention to where the shot had come from. A dark bay horse trotted across the grassland, weaving in and out of the brush. Travis. Her heart leapt and her hands shook. She waved her rifle in the air. He responded, pointing to where James lay on the ground.

Angel raced down the hill, barely registering the boulders she darted around as she neared the bottom. Worry for James, along with intense relief at Travis's arrival, spurred her on. Her pace slowed as a new thought entered her mind. God had answered her prayer. He might care for her, after all.

Angel arrived at the bottom of the hill to find Travis and James waiting beside Bella. She didn't know whether to hug James or scold him, but one look at his pale, tear-streaked cheeks and she made her decision. She gathered him in a tight hug.

He shuddered and clung to her. "I'm sorry, Miss Angel. I won't never, ever do something like that again."

She patted his back and drew away a couple inches but kept her hands on his upper arms. "What made you come out here alone?"

James avoided her gaze and shrugged. "Don't know."

Placing her finger under his chin, she lifted it. "I think you do. Tell me."

He shrank away from her touch. "I wanted Uncle Travis and the men to respect me." His voice cracked on the last word. "Everybody thinks I'm just a kid, and they all boss me around."

Travis sucked in his breath, but Angel kept her attention on James. "Do you know why they do that?"

"'Cause I'm only thirteen?"

"Partly. But it's mostly because they care about you and don't want you hurt. Or killed." She motioned toward the dead wolves. "Do you know why those wolves attacked instead of running away after I shot the first one?"

"They were mad?"

She smiled at the irony of his words. "Yes, but not in the way you mean. They weren't angry, they were loco. Crazy. At least the two that charged you. I think they've been bitten by an animal with mad dog disease." Angel turned toward Travis. "Your uncle saved your life. You know that, don't you?"

James nodded but remained silent.

"He and your mother love you very much. You're right about something you said."

His eyes widened. "What?"

"You're only thirteen, and you aren't quite a man yet. But maybe your uncle and mother can find things you'd enjoy doing around the ranch where you'd be helping and still be safe." Angel released her hold.

Travis stepped forward and touched the boy on the arm. "Right now we need to get you home. Your ma is worried sick. But we'll think about the things Miss Angel said and talk about it later. All right?" He motioned toward the horse tied to a tree behind a big clump of brush a dozen yards away. "Now climb on and let's get home."

"Yes, sir." James gulped and trotted away.

* * * * *

Travis drew up in front of the house with Angel and James trailing behind. James slowed his horse's pace as they neared the ranch, probably dreading the meeting with his mother.

Libby peeked out of a window, then raced through the front door and catapulted down the steps. "James! Glory to God, you're safe!"

James slowly dismounted and wrapped his reins around the hitching post. He shuffled forward, meeting his mother's hug with a reluctant one.

Libby's shout brought Nate from the barn. "The boy's back? Hallelujah!" He raised his rifle in the air, then disappeared behind the barn. Three loud reports rent the air. Seconds later he returned wearing a wide grin.

Libby smiled and drew back from her son. She glanced from James to Travis and back again. "Are you all right?"

"He's fine, thanks to Angel's exceptional marksmanship." Travis leaned his hip against the hitching post. He blessed God for Angel's accurate aim. The last thing he'd want was more pain or loss in his sister's life; she'd had more than her share lately.

"Angel's marksmanship?" Libby's dumbfounded tone left no doubt as to her confusion. "What did she need to shoot?"

James shivered. "Wolves. They almost got me, Ma."

"I don't understand. What were you doing?" Libby grabbed his arms and gave a small shake. "You scared me, Son. I want some answers."

Travis held up his hand. "I'll explain. James rode to the base of the rocky butte to hunt wolves. Angel climbed up the sloped side. When I rode up, she was aiming her rifle at something below her. James waved his rifle and pointed at a wolf in the distance. What he didn't see was the rest of the pack moving in from behind."

Libby gasped. Nate grunted and moved closer to her side. She cast him a grateful look and turned her attention to Travis again.

"The leader of the pack charged and would've had James if Angel hadn't gotten into action so quickly and brought him down. She hit the second one, as well, and saved the boy's life."

Angel shook her head. "I didn't do it all. You got there in time to get the third one."

Travis eyed her. "I'd say we can all be grateful you're a crack shot."

A faint pink crept into her cheeks before she lowered her head.

He'd never met a woman so self-assured, yet so humble. The more he knew Angel, the more he saw to admire.

Libby's eyes pooled with tears. She let out a soft cry and wrapped her arms around Angel's neck. Muffled sobs emerged as Libby buried her face on Angel's shoulder.

"It's all right, Libby. James is safe," Angel said soothingly.

"I know. But he could've been killed." Several moments passed before Libby calmed and released her grasp. "How can I ever thank you?"

Angel patted her back. "No need."

Libby swung toward Travis, her brows drawn low. "You are *never* to let this woman go, you hear me, Travis? Never! I don't care if you didn't like the fact that she's a woman when you hired her. You can't replace her with someone else." She stomped her foot. "I won't have it!"

Travis took Libby in his arms as she started to cry again. "Don't worry, Lib, I have no intention of replacing Angel." He peeked over the top of her head and met Angel's wide eyes. "Not now or ever."

* * * * *

Angel's heart skipped a beat. Travis didn't plan on letting her go. But what had flashed in his eyes as they met hers? Confusion warred with common sense. She must have imagined the warmth and caring reflected there.

James tugged on her arm, bringing her back to reality. "Miss Angel? Thank you. I didn't tell you that before, but Ma's right. I don't want you to find another job, either."

The front door opened, and Grandmother stepped out. "What is all the shooting and shouting about?"

Angel sighed with relief. The emotional atmosphere hovering

over the small group had intensified, but everyone relaxed at the older woman's appearance. "James went for a little ride. But he's safe now and everything's fine. Nate was signaling the other men that James is home."

Maria eyed the drooping boy. "So. You run away, sí? Try to be a man like your uncle? My boy, he did that at your age. We tanned his britches when he got home." She tossed a glance at Libby. "I think you have a much kinder mama, and she is just happy to have you home, yes?"

James nodded. "I know."

Grandmother waved her finger in the air. "Good. It is a smart boy who sees these things and does not make excuses. Smokey is waiting with hot tea for me before he and I start supper preparations."

Shock kept Angel rooted to the ground as the older woman went back into the house. Grandmother was having tea and helping Smokey with supper? She glanced around the small circle of bystanders and relaxed. No one seemed to give the declaration any notice.

Nate tousled the boy's hair, then hooked his arm around the slender shoulders. "How 'bout you start riding with me from now on? If it's all right with your ma, that is." He glanced at Libby with a questioning expression. "I'd like to teach him how to take care of himself on the range. Not that Travis isn't a fine teacher, but maybe between the two of us…"

Libby tipped up her chin and smiled. "Yes, I'd like that very much." She turned to James and her voice grew stern. "You must obey Nate. Understood?"

"Yes, Ma. I promise. I'll never disobey or run off on my own again. Never."

Nate grinned. "That's a pretty big promise on the disobeying part, but I'll hold you to the other. And I'm adding something else. You're never to take a gun of any kind out on your own. Agreed?"

"Yes, sir."

"Good. Let's head to the barn and put up your horse. I'll bet he'd like a bait of grain and a rubdown." They sauntered off, and Libby's gaze followed the pair, a quizzical look softening her features. "That was good of Nate."

Travis smiled. "I think he cares for you, Lib."

"I beg your pardon?" Heightened color blazed in her cheeks.

"Yep. I've noticed him watching you the past few weeks. He's a good man, loves the Lord, and would make a fine husband."

"Hold on now." She held her hand up. "You're rushing things. I've been a widow less than a year."

"There's no hurry. Just figured you should know which way the wind's blowing." Travis grinned and kissed her cheek. "You deserve to be happy and so does Nate. It's a good idea for him to spend time with James."

She nodded slowly. "I agree. But beyond that? I'm not making any promises."

Angel gathered Bella's reins and lifted the drooping mare's head with a light tug. "Come on, girl. Time to give you a break too." The old feeling of being outside the circle settled over her as she walked away. What she'd give to be part of a family like this instead of constantly hovering on the fringes.

Chapter Twenty-Four

....

Bart Hinson grunted with pleasure. His small band of men had just crossed into Wyoming Territory. A passing drifter who'd worked on a ranch up north confirmed that the Sundance Ranch hired a young woman as a hunter some weeks earlier. Rumors had flown and speculation was rife as to what Travis Morgan was thinking. Bart smirked. He'd put money on why, and it didn't have anything to do with her being a good hand.

The woman could shoot, though, he'd give her that. It might pay to keep it in mind in the future. Her uncle taught her to use both a rifle and a pistol at a young age. Bart thought it stupid. Women should depend on their men to defend them. Nothing worse than a gun in the hands of a hot-tempered woman. He cleared his throat and spat. 'Course, he didn't intend to let her get close to a gun once he corralled her.

Too bad he'd never found José and killed him. The band had broken apart after that last raid, and the men he sent to track José never returned. Bart was sick of lying low and not making any money, but that would end soon. He'd have the cash he needed and the girl, all at the same time.

Another week, two at the most, and they'd reach the area near Sundance. He'd heard there was a band of outlaws working a few hours away at the Hole-in-the-Wall hideout in the canyon country, and of course, The Wild Bunch kept busy robbing banks and trains. He'd thought about falling in with one of them but decided against it. No sense bringing more men in on the deal. Besides, he'd kill any man who got close to the girl. No sir. Angel Ramirez was his property, and he aimed to keep it that way.

Chapter Twenty-Five

....

Travis stepped out of the barn, trying to contain his excitement at the surprise hidden inside. He grinned. Time to find Libby and James. Angel had taken the afternoon to work on her saddle, and he'd seen her walking to the house when he'd driven up in the buggy.

Travis poked his head in the door. "James? Libby?" He peered into the living area. Maria lay curled, sound asleep, on a sofa, a knitted shawl over her body.

He walked down the short hall and paused outside Angel's room. Quiet voices sounded through the door. He rapped lightly. "Angel? I'm looking for Libby."

Footsteps pattered across the floor, and the door cracked open. A pair of dark brown, sparkling eyes peered out. "Yes, she's here. Just a minute." The door closed, and a spate of giggles erupted.

What in the world? He hadn't heard anything like it since he was a schoolboy when the girls concocted some scheme. Moments passed, and no one returned. He lifted his hand to knock again but hesitated. Was he intruding on something personal? Travis took two long steps backward and turned, ready to dash back to the barn.

"Travis?" Libby stood in the open doorway. "I'm sorry, you needed me?"

"Uh. Yes. I have a present for James, and I thought you'd both like to be there when I give it to him. Do you know where he is?"

Libby lifted a shoulder. "Did you look outside? He kept pestering us, so I told him to find something to do."

"No. I came straight to the house." He hurried up the hallway and out the back door, the women following close on his heels. "James? You out here?"

Nothing moved, and no one answered. "James!" He halted and listened. Yipping came from the front of the house. "Oh no. Sounds like he found him." He broke into a run and dashed around the corner, skidding to a stop within sight of the hard-packed area between the house and the barn.

There on the ground lay James with a black-and-white, fluffy puppy, who was licking his cheeks and wiggling his entire body. "Aww, that tickles. Stop." Gales of laughter erupted from the boy. He sat up and wrapped his arms around the squirming pup. "What's your name, huh, boy? I'm going to ask Uncle Travis if you can stay."

Travis barely noticed Angel and Libby approach. He broke into a wide grin. "He came from a ranch between here and town. The rancher's dogs had a litter, and he didn't want them all. He's part sheepdog and smart. Call him whatever you'd like, he's yours."

James jumped to his feet and scooped up the pup. "No kidding? Whoopee!" The next few moments he danced a jig, kicking up dust. He set the puppy down, and it raced around James's feet, barking and jumping.

James paused in his play and turned. "But why did you get a sheepdog? We only have cows!"

Travis laughed. "That's just what they call his breed. They've had them for generations in countries that raise sheep, but they're good cattle dogs as well."

Libby sneezed and rubbed her nose. "You're sure about this, Travis? I didn't think you wanted a dog."

"I know, and I've regretted that hasty decision more than once." He turned to James. "But there are conditions."

James straightened, and his face took on a solemn cast. "Yes, sir. I'll do whatever you want."

"He's your responsibility. That means you feed and water him. The only time he can be in the house is at night in your room." His first impulse had been to insist the dog stay in the barn but realized James would worry about his new pet and probably sneak out to check on him. Better to have him under their roof. "That means you'll have to get up a couple of times in the night to take him outside. And work with him. I won't have him chasing the horses or cattle. Think you can do that?"

"Yes, sir." James flew across the intervening space, skidding to a halt in front of Travis. "Thank you, Uncle Travis. This is the best gift ever."

"It's your birthday in a few weeks and I was going to wait, but the pups are close to three months old and the farmer wanted them gone. So I decided to give him to you early."

"I'll take good care of him." James bobbed his head up and down. "I'm going to call him Dakota, after the new state of South Dakota that I've been studying about."

"That's a great name, Son. I think it suits him." Libby lifted her voice above the barking.

"Yeah, and Nate told me he used to have herding dogs, and he helped train them. I'll bet he'd teach me."

The puppy bounded to Libby's side, and she leaned over to pet it. "I'm sure he would." She turned a wide smile on Travis. "Thank you." Standing on her tiptoes, she placed a kiss on his cheek. "I hope someday you find a wife who deserves you." She cast a glance at Angel, then turned back to the puppy.

Travis's stomach dropped. What was Libby thinking saying that in front of Angel? Why, she'd think he'd put Libby up to hinting he needed a wife. He peeked at Angel. A tiny smile tugged at the corner of her lips. On second thought, Libby was right. A wife was exactly what he needed, and if he wasn't mistaken, he knew the perfect woman.

* * * * *

Contentment blossomed in Angel's heart. She'd been lonely for so long, but since Travis made his announcement a couple of weeks ago about not hiring someone to take her place he'd been softer—more approachable. For the first time she felt her life might amount to something. No more running from her past or the ghosts that haunted her nights. She'd found a home and people she cared about—she might even allow herself to dream that Travis might one day come to care about her, as well.

Angel watched the antics of the puppy romping with James. Mostly black with a white chest and a white snip on his nose, the dog was full of energy. What a wonderful thing Travis had done for the boy. So many men would've threatened and punished James for that last stunt he'd pulled, but Travis seemed to see beneath the reckless behavior and into the boy's heart. This puppy would help anchor him, give him a project to work with and more responsibility—a good thing for a youngster his age.

And Libby. Her throat tightened as she thought over the last hour spent in her room talking. She'd never had a friend besides her uncle—and never a woman she could open her heart to. This friendship was in the early stages, but Libby's acceptance felt genuine.

Joy bubbled inside, but Angel stuffed it down. It wouldn't do to get too comfortable in this new relationship. Things had a way of happening, and she couldn't trust that her current situation would last forever. But it had been over three years since she'd left the outlaw band, and three states separated them. Safety and security were within her grasp.

Over the past weeks she'd even found her heart opening to the preacher's words about God's love. Seeing this family interact and the kindness they extended to others made her willing to believe God might actually love her too.

She caught Libby's attention. "I'll check on Grandmother. If she's awake, she'd enjoy seeing James's new puppy. Would you like some tea?"

Libby nodded. "Maybe after a bit."

Angel smiled at the barking and laughing that escorted her back to the house. She stepped into the living area and tiptoed to where she could see the sofa. Empty. Rattling came from the kitchen, and she hurried that way.

Grandmother closed the door of the cookstove and looked up. "I hate to keep this stove hot, but it is the only way to get a decent cup of tea." She fanned her red face with her hand. "This weather, she is going to cook me, as well as the water. Soon we will not need a stove. We just set the water pot in the sun and voilá!" She flicked her fingers in the air. "We have tea!"

Angel chuckled and moved across to where the older woman stood. "I know. This time of day it would be nice to have something cold to drink."

"My piccolina, I have been hoping to talk to you but not here. Would you care to drive to town and sit with me at the hotel dining room?"

Angel wondered at the serious tone. "Are you feeling all right? I noticed you've been resting a lot lately."

"No, no. My health, it is good. Do not worry about this old

woman, little one." She clucked her tongue and shook her head. "It is other things I think on. Will you go with me? I would like a few minutes sitting at a table being waited on while we talk."

"Of course, Grandmother. I'll run to my room and change out of these dusty clothes. Could you ask Travis to hitch the buggy, or shall I?"

Grandmother flicked her fingers toward the hall. "You change, little one, and I'll ask."

* * * * *

Angel drew the horse to a stop in front of the hitching rail and waited for the cloud of dust to settle before she stepped down from the buggy and turned to help Grandmother descend. The silence during the drive unnerved her, giving Angel plenty of time to stew over what might be coming. Had Grandmother somehow discovered her past and planned to confront her away from the ranch? A peek at the older woman revealed nothing, other than a seeming interest in the single-story building nearby. Zane's Hotel was blazoned in gold paint on the glass pane of the door. Angel grasped the handle and swung it open, her heart hammering in her chest.

They walked through the lobby and into the dining room. The interior wasn't what Angel expected. Most eating establishments in the West were simple, basic, and not always clean. This was just the opposite. Linen napkins graced the small, cozy tables scattered around the room, boasting both glasses and teacups set at each place. Cheerful gingham curtains splashed red and yellow color to the sides of the two front windows, and a glass case of pies lined the space between. Everything was tidy, sparkling, and fresh, giving off an air of rest and refreshment.

Both women settled into their chairs and Grandmother smiled as she shook out the linen napkin and carefully spread it over her lap. "A touch of civilization out in the wilderness. It is nice, yes?"

Angel started to answer but paused as a matronly woman with a white apron tied around her waist and hair pinned back in a bun bustled up to their table. "Good afternoon, ladies, I'm Emma. How about cold tea to start with, or perhaps a cup of coffee and pie? Or were you looking for a late dinner? We have soup and bread, or I can bring you a menu."

Grandmother beamed. "Cold tea would be a wonderful treat, and perhaps a slice of pie."

Angel nodded. "The same for me, thank you."

Emma nodded and turned on her heel. She returned moments later with a tray and carefully set their order before them. "Enjoy, ladies, and take your time. Our evening rush won't start for another couple of hours."

Angel took a sip of the tea and sighed. "This is very good. They must have a root cellar where they store blocks of ice." She leaned forward and placed her hand over Grandmother's. "You were quiet all the way here. Is something troubling you?"

Grandmother's eyes took on a dreamy quality and she stared into the distance. "Home, *mia*. Italy. My husband's grave. Great-grandchildren. So much I must consider."

"Great-grandchildren?" Angel leaned forward. "You didn't mention that before. I thought your other son died without children."

Grandmother focused again on Angel. "Sí. You are my only grandchild."

"But…" Angel's mind whirled at the words. "I don't have children. I'm not even married."

"Sí. But you could be one day." She gathered Angel's hand in her own. "I want you to come to Italy with me. I know many good families—old families with young men who would fall at your feet. You would be the Bella of Venice. I would present you in a wonderful coming-out party. You would marry and give me great-grandbabies to love in my twilight years."

Angel swallowed the lump in her throat. She'd grown to care for this scrap of a woman who was her only link to her mother. But move to Italy? Leave everything? Her mind balked at the idea. She'd just congratulated herself on how smooth her life was going. Moving halfway around the world wasn't an option. But Grandmother had desires and needs. Could she deny this woman the one thing that would make her life complete?

Another thought ignited. If she left, there would be no danger of exposing her past. No one would know she'd been present when a Texas Ranger had been killed, or she'd ridden with a band of outlaws stealing a herd of cattle. Hope surged, and she gripped Grandmother's hand. She could start a new life and discover the places where her mother played as a child.

Angel's heart thudded to her toes. Travis and Libby. How could she leave the people she'd come to care for? She shook her head. It couldn't be done.

"Angel?" Grandmother lightly pressed her fingers again. "What is it? What are you thinking?"

"I don't know what to say. I'd never thought about you leaving, or going with you. I guess I just assumed…"

"I would stay forever, mia?"

"Yes."

"I have thought of that, as well. I like this country—and the people who live in this place." She flicked her wrist. "I came to find you and planned to return to my homeland immediately, but instead, I stayed. Partly because you needed time to know me, but also because I am drawn to the vastness and beauty of your country."

"Then stay, Grandmother. Stay and live here forever. We could still visit Italy."

"You would not return with me?"

Angel gently loosened her grip and sat back in her chair. "I'm not sure I could leave all that I know here, but I don't want to lose you. It feels like I've finally found my roots and am beginning to learn who I am—where I came from—and I don't want to let you go."

"Come, mia. I would not force you to stay. You could always return to your magnificent country if Italy does not please you. Will you think on it?"

Angel considered the request and slowly nodded. Confusion mixed with excitement swirled in her mind. "I will, but I can't promise I'll say yes."

Chapter Twenty-Six
....

Travis rubbed the base of his back. He'd spent parts of the past three days shoeing and trimming horses. Shoeing was one chore he didn't enjoy. He shaded his eyes against the sun's glare as the rolling beat of hooves reached his ears.

Nate galloped down the lane leading into the ranch yard and slowed his horse as he neared the barn. "Boss, I got bad news."

Travis tossed his hammer into the wooden box by his feet. "I've had a feeling something was coming. It's been too quiet."

"Yeah, I know what you mean. And I'm glad I left James behind today." Nate swung down from his lathered horse and tossed the reins over the hitching post. "I found shod hoofprints on the east side of the ranch that don't belong to any of our horses."

"Ah-huh." Travis waited, knowing more was coming.

"Cows are missing, Boss. Mostly two-year-olds and a few older."

Travis balled his hands into fists. "Cattle thieves, or did the stock wander to another pasture?"

"That's what I thought at first, until I stumbled on the tracks. Me, Charlie, and Bud followed 'em for a mile or so till we hit a rocky patch. The tracks are old, at least a week, so trailing them won't be easy. There are thousands of prints on this ranch, and the men were careful to hide their trail whenever they could."

"I'll talk to the sheriff. See if there's been any report of rustling in the territory over the past couple weeks. Looks like we'd have heard news of it." He took off his hat and wiped the sweat from his brow. "You think the Sundance Kid has taken to rustling as well as robbing trains?"

Nate shook his head. "Doubtful, Boss. Not on this small of a scale, anyhow. At least, there's been no word that I know of."

"We always lose a few beef per year to the Lakota tribe, but I can't see them taking a herd."

"Naw. Besides, they don't ride shod horses, and we rarely see them around here since the battle with Custer a few years back. I think we're lookin' at some low-down rustlers. I can send Arizona to our closest neighbor and see if they've been hit."

"Good idea. Tell him to hit the trail. I'll head for town."

* * * * *

Travis rode down the main street of town, veering around a wagon loaded with grain bags and crates, and barely avoiding a child who darted away from his mother. He reined to a stop, stepped down from his horse, and tossed the reins over the rail in front of the imposing brick courthouse. He needed to get to the bottom of this, and soon. Stepping onto the boardwalk, he entered the front door and made his way toward the back of the building to the sheriff's office. He gave a quick rap on the door and entered.

Sheriff Jensen looked up from a stack of papers on his desk. "Travis?" He stood, extended his hand, and waved at the chair across from him. "Have a seat. I'm glad you stopped in. I planned on taking a ride out your way today or tomorrow."

Travis groaned. "Not more problems with James?" He'd hate to have to take the puppy back if he discovered the boy had gotten into trouble.

The sheriff tipped back in his seat and shook his head, a rueful smile tugging at the corners of his mouth. "Just the opposite. I caught the little renegades who caused the trouble and scared the truth out of 'em. James has never been part of the mischief. There's a new boy who lives on the edge of town that bears a striking resemblance to your nephew. Same size, age, and hair color, but that's it. Just wanted to lay your fears to rest and assure his ma James hasn't done anything bad."

Travis let his breath out in a whoosh. One less thing to worry about—Libby would be thankful. "Thanks, Sheriff. Good to know."

"So that's not what brought you to town today?"

"No."

The sheriff leaned forward and propped his forearms on his desk, his gaze leveled at Travis. "I'm listening."

"My foreman rode in this morning from working the eastern edge of my ranch. Cattle are missing, and they found tracks of shod horses they didn't recognize. They followed the trail but lost it in a rocky patch. He thinks the rustlers split the cattle and took them different directions, hiding their tracks along the way."

"Huh. This the first time you've had a problem?"

"Yes. I wanted to alert you. Any other ranches hit?"

Sheriff Jensen shook his head. "Not that I know of, but I'll check. The West is growing, and it was bound to happen sooner or later. Men are always trying to get rich on someone else's hard work."

Travis pushed to his feet. "Thanks, Sheriff. I sent one of my hands to my closest neighbor."

"Good. We'll talk later." He walked Travis to the door. "The last thing we need is another Hole-in-the-Wall bunch of outlaws camping in our backyard. We'll root 'em out before they get a toehold."

Travis swung into the saddle and reined his horse around. He certainly hoped so. His herd had grown over the past three years and had achieved a size where he could enjoy a little financial freedom. That could change in a heartbeat.

"Travis. I nearly forgot." The sheriff lifted his voice above the sound of a stagecoach rolling past.

"Yes?" Travis stopped his stallion and turned sideways.

"There's been a gent asking about your new hand, Miss Ramirez."

"A gent? You get his name?"

Sheriff Jensen scratched his chin. "No, come to think of it, I didn't. Said he's her brother or cousin or some such. Got back from a long cattle drive and found her missing. Guess he's been trailing her for some time now."

Travis sucked in a sharp breath. Angel had never shared she had a brother, or a close cousin for that matter. Why would she withhold that information? His mind raced with the possibilities, and his hands grew clammy. This stranger came at the same time as the cattle disappearing. Could that be why she'd never mentioned this relative? "Did he tell you where he's camped, or did you point him to our ranch?"

"Nope. Something about him didn't set right. I told him I'd look into it. See if I could find any mention of a young woman of that description."

"So you don't believe he's related to her?"

"Didn't say that. He may be, but he had a shifty look about him—not trustworthy, if you know what I mean."

"Yeah."

"I'll let you be on your way. Tell Miss Ramirez if you're of a mind to."

"Thanks, Sheriff." Travis touched his horse with his spur, his mind awash with possibilities—none of which he liked.

* * * * *

Angel rode into the ranch yard bone-tired and heartsick. She'd not been in time to save a calf from a cougar attack and hadn't been able to find the cat. Mountain lions were private, oftentimes solitary creatures that kept out of sight as much as possible. It could take her days to hunt him down, and she dreaded the thought. This cat was more than likely the same one who clawed her arm. He didn't seem to have much fear of man, and she didn't like the idea of cornering him.

She swung down from her horse and slipped the reins over Bella's head. Her mare moved with a weary gait and Angel's heart contracted. Bella had been overused since arriving here, and as much as she hated to do it, she'd better ask Travis for another mount.

The sound of running steps swung her around. No longer did she reach for her gun, but she hated being caught off-guard. "James. Something wrong?"

"Yeah." His eyes were alight with excitement. "We've been robbed!"

"What?" Angel reached for the rifle secured in the sheath next to her saddle and withdrew it. "Are they still here? Where are the men? Is your mother all right?"

James' face fell, then he broke out in chuckles. "I didn't mean the house. Nate came home and told Uncle Travis that some of our cows are missing."

An icy chill swept over her body. The thought of anyone stealing cattle made her physically ill. Especially cattle belonging to Travis. "Is your uncle in the house?"

"Uncle Travis went to talk to the sheriff. He should be back soon. It seems like he's been gone a long time." He swiveled on his heel and dashed away then turned back. "I gotta help Ma with something. See you later."

Angel made her way into the barn, stripped Bella's gear, and rubbed her down. The hushed atmosphere and contact with her horse quieted the anxiety created by James's words. No sense in worrying about something she knew little to nothing about—at least not until she spoke to Nate or Travis. Then she could start worrying.

The pastor's words from last Sunday floated into her mind. He said something about the lilies and the sparrows. She struggled to remember. Oh, yes. That God clothed the lilies in splendor and fed the sparrows, so He'd take care of us, as well. She'd never known God cared about things like that. And the pastor proclaimed there was nothing too big or too small for God.

"Is that true, God? I'd really like to know." She whispered the words, and a gentle peace enveloped her. Did Bella sense the hovering presence of Someone else in the barn? "You feel that, girl?" She patted her horse's neck. "Do you suppose that's God?"

The peace deepened and tears sprang to her eyes. "I want to trust You, really I do. I'd like to know You the way Libby and Travis do, but I'm not sure what to do. Maybe You could help me if You have time?" She almost felt foolish speaking the words but something kept nudging her forward. "Thank You. Amen."

Chapter Twenty-Seven

....

Angel drifted on a cloud of calm for the next few days, in spite of her concern over Travis's cattle. The peace that surrounded her in the barn hadn't left, and while she wasn't certain it was God, the strong possibility comforted her. She wasn't ready to talk to Libby about it yet. Maybe she would if the feeling lasted, but right now she simply wanted to hug the newness to her heart and hope it didn't disappear.

She'd been hunting the golden panther for the past six hours, after another fruitless search yesterday. Not even a sign of tracks hinted at where the cat might be. Another half-eaten carcass surrounded by a pack of coyotes gave testament to the cougar's presence. The downed cow was a hefty two-year-old, too large and quick for the coyotes to kill.

Between the wolves, cougars, and rustlers, Travis was taking some serious losses. He'd reported the rustling to the sheriff, and Arizona brought a report back from their neighbor who'd been hit and suspected cow thieves, as well. There was talk of mounting a posse, but nothing had been done as yet.

Angel chafed at the thought of men stealing cattle from Travis. Why hadn't she thought of that when her uncle was involved all those years? Shame burned its brand on her heart, and she sank farther into her saddle. Deep down she'd always known it was wrong, but her love for Uncle José had overridden any guilt. Now she stood on the other end of the branding iron—men were stealing what *she* worked hard to protect—the very cattle that put food on the table of the family she'd come to love.

The word jolted through her, and she gripped her horse with her knees as a surreal feeling of being thrown off-balance washed over her. Love? Sure. She cared about Libby, James, and Travis. But love? Angel mulled over the word, thinking of all it entailed. Travis's visage rose in her mind, and her heart rate increased. Her hands grew damp, and she wiped one palm down her jeans. There was no way she could be in love. Why, she didn't even know what loving someone looked like.

A memory of affectionate voices from years past bobbed in her mind. Mama and Papa—laughing—hugging—talking to one another in hushed tones. Later, after Mama died of the fever, Papa would speak of her long into the evening hours. His voice reflected the longing, loneliness, and love he'd felt for his wife. Yes, she did know what love looked like—or at least, what it felt like. But did that type of feeling extend to Travis?

Bella snorted and sidestepped around a jagged rock in the path, and Angel brought her thoughts back to the task at hand. She felt something for Travis, and it was different than what she'd felt for José, or the friendship with Libby—she just wasn't quite sure in what way. This would have to wait for another time. The last thing she needed was to daydream and miss her opportunity of finding that cat.

She spent another three hours scouring the countryside, checking two of the waterholes and grazing areas the cattle frequented. Nothing. As much as she'd like to bunk under the stars and continue the hunt, she knew the family would worry. It would take a couple of hours to get back to the house at a steady trot, and she'd barely make it home for supper. A flick of her wrist and a nudge with her heel and Bella swung around. The mare perked up and gave a low nicker. Angel leaned over and stroked her neck. "You know where we're going, don't you, girl?"

The sun hung midway between the apex of the sky and the horizon. Nothing moved in the distance. Angel loosened her rifle in its scabbard. Taking chances while alone out here wasn't a good idea, especially with cattle rustlers in the area. It had been four days since the small herd was driven off, and no more cattle had turned up missing. The cowboys had been riding the range fully armed and ready to shoot if they encountered anything suspicious. Even though life had quieted down, Angel knew better than to trust the reprieve.

Something moved up ahead. She reined in her horse and studied the area at the base of a rock bluff. Had she imagined it, or had it been heat waves shimmering? No. There it was again. A man on a dark bay horse. A flash of light hit her in the eyes, then disappeared. She pulled her rifle and rested it across her saddle bow. It was possible one or more of the cowboys was using a spyglass in hopes of spotting rustlers.

He was too far to recognize, but she didn't know the horse. It could be one of their neighbors, as she wasn't far from the Winston place to the west. It was doubtful a rustler would be out here alone. Surely he wouldn't allow himself to be spotted, but she wasn't taking any chances. She kicked Bella from a trot into a canter, keeping her rifle steady as she rode.

The man wheeled his mount and headed the opposite direction. She was still a good half mile away. He seemed to disappear against the face of the bluff. She wasn't familiar with this area, as their cattle never ventured here with all the rock, brush, and lack of water or grass. If the stranger was a neighboring rancher, why not wait and talk?

When she arrived at the stone outcropping, it appeared to extend farther than she'd realized, both to the side and behind. Brush grew out of cracks in the rock, and small trees fought to maintain a tenacious hold. A scattering of pebbles and larger stones lay along the base, giving silent witness to the power of the changing season as ice and wind chipped away at the impressive bluff.

She rode for several moments before she spotted clearly defined hoofprints and three hand-rolled cigarette butts on the ground. He'd been waiting here for some time. For what? He couldn't know she'd come by. Was he simply resting his horse? He could be a cowboy passing through to Montana, but most cowhands she'd met loved to *palaver*, as they liked to call a lengthy chat. Maybe when she removed her rifle, he'd decided to ride on. She shrugged, wondering how he disappeared so completely.

Another hundred yards told the story. The tracks led inside a fissure in the rock face. It appeared to widen as it progressed and looked to be a natural tunnel formation. She'd tell Travis when she returned. She felt confident in her ability to track the man, but common sense forbade her. It could easily extend to a small valley on the other side, but it might end somewhere within the rock bluff. Either way, there was no guarantee the man was friendly. She'd follow her original plan and head home. But when Travis or one of the men came to investigate, she intended to be there.

* * * * *

Travis sat in his office, unable to concentrate on the ranch ledger. He shoved it aside and tipped back in his chair, resting his boots on the corner of his wooden desk. He still hadn't told Angel about the man who'd been asking after her in town. Why the clenching in his gut whenever he thought on the matter? He folded his arms across his chest. He'd let her know the next time they spoke.

His thoughts drifted to the first time he'd seen Angel in a dress and the two Sundays since when she'd worn yet another. She hadn't lost any of her allure, and he still found it difficult to keep from staring. The cowboys were equally smitten. All but Nate, who only seemed to have eyes for Travis's sister.

Libby deserved happiness. He knew she was lonely, but it never occurred to him one of his men might fall for her. He'd had no indication from her that she might return the sentiment, other than a blush and an almost too-vehement protest when he'd acquainted her with his suspicions. But his foreman was a strong, godly man who would treat a wife kindly and be a good influence in James's life. Maybe he'd find a way to help things along, if Libby and Nate didn't figure it out on their own.

He plunked his feet down on the floor, sudden resolve washing over him. Who was he to talk about figuring things out? He cared for Angel, and he hadn't given her so much as an inkling. What was he afraid of, anyway? Rejection? He shrugged. Maybe, although he hated admitting it. He'd had plenty of rejection from his father over the years—he should be used to it by now.

Could Angel possibly care for him in return? There was one person who might be able to tell him. Libby and Angel had been increasingly cozy ever since Angel saved James's life. If anyone had a glimpse into Angel's private thoughts, it would be his sister. He pushed to his feet and stalked to the door, jerking it open.

Maria de Luca stood there, hand raised ready to knock. She took a step back. "I am sorry, Signor Travis. If I bother you, I come back to talk another time."

Travis shook his head, as surprised as she. "Not at all, Maria." He swept open the door. "Please. Come in and have a seat." How ironic. He hadn't considered seeking out Angel's grandmother. He ushered her to a chair across from his desk, settled her into it, and took his place. "Would you care for anything to drink?" He started to rise, but she waved him back.

"No, grazie. I mean, thank you." She smiled. "Just to talk will be enough."

"Are you finding your needs met here on the ranch?"

"Ah, yes. Everyone treats me with much respect. I did not know Americans were so gracious when I come to this country. You are people with great strength and determination, as well as kindness."

"I'm glad." Travis leaned back and relaxed. Maria had added a delicate flavor to his household. When she'd first arrived he'd been a mite concerned, especially when Angel didn't take to her. But everything had worked out, and the two women had grown close. "What can I help you with?"

"I must speak to you about my granddaughter."

He sat up straighter. "Certainly."

"I am concerned for her future. She needs a home of her own. I grow old and will not always be here for her." Maria laced her fingers in her lap, and a rustling emanated from the dark brown silk.

"Yes, I can understand, but you're welcome to stay here as long as you'd like. I have no intention of sending Angel away. I'm very happy with the job she's done, and—" He took a deep breath, wondering if he should bare his heart to this woman before he did so to Angel. She could be an ally and maybe help sway Angel toward the suit he hoped to present. On the other hand, he had no idea how Maria or Angel felt about him as a possible suitor. "She's become a part of our family." There. That might hint at what he was feeling. All he could do was hope she picked up on what he was trying to say.

"You and your sister have been most kind, offering my Angel a home. But there is more to consider than just a home."

"Yes?" He wasn't sure what she implied.

"I want to see my granddaughter married. Hopefully with babies around her before I die."

Elation coursed through Travis's heart. He and Maria wanted the exact same things, and he had a feeling she'd come to him in hopes of reaching an understanding. He'd heard that many of the older generation from European countries still selected spouses for their children and grandchildren. While not unheard of in this country, it was becoming less common. "I understand your desire, Maria. I think that would be a good thing, as well." He smiled, sure of her next words.

"That is why—" She looked him straight in the eyes. "I take her back to Italy with me. There are many good families there with strong men to make a fine husband for my Angel. I ask your help to convince her to return there with me."

Chapter Twenty-Eight
....

Travis stared at the door where Maria had exited. He had no idea what incoherent nonsense he'd mumbled after she'd made her grand announcement. Angel leaving and returning to Italy? According to the older woman, Angel was seriously considering it, and Maria felt it would only take a little urging from him to convince her. She'd left satisfied that she'd achieved her goal, although he'd not made any promises. In fact, he'd been unable to do more than smile and stammer.

Why hadn't he declared himself then and there? Told her he was in love with her granddaughter and wouldn't allow her to leave the ranch, much less the country? A quiver started in his stomach and worked its way up to his throat. He wanted to bellow in frustration, but he held it in. He wouldn't speak to Maria about his desires until he'd approached Angel, and that couldn't happen soon enough to suit him.

Libby. He'd planned on talking to his sister when he'd been sidetracked by Signora de Luca. He frowned. Just an hour ago he'd rejoiced that Maria had come. Now he wished she'd never discovered Angel's whereabouts. He twisted his lips to the side. That wasn't fair. He'd made the decision several years ago to trust God with his future—all of it, not just an occasional piece. Who was he to decide who could come into Angel's life and who couldn't? When things got tough he still needed to trust, even though his inclination was to wrest control back into his hands.

Trotting beats entered the yard, and Travis peered out the window. Angel drew her black mare to a halt in front of the barn and swung to the ground. The air left his lungs in a whoosh, and he bolted to his feet. This might be the time he'd been waiting for. The men were still out on the range, and Libby was in the kitchen with Smokey. He jerked open his office door and headed outside, grim determination driving his steps. "Angel?"

She paused next to the opening of the barn and looked over her shoulder. "Travis. I was coming to find you as soon as I unsaddled Bella."

He paused, studying her. There was no light of happiness, no eager anticipation at the mention of coming to see him. Had he assumed too much about how she might feel? After all, they'd never broached the subject. "You have something to report?"

"I do." The words were short and almost sharp. "Give me a few minutes." She disappeared inside, leaving the barn door standing open behind her.

He wanted to follow her and pour out his heart—tell her how his thoughts dwelt on her so often each day, beg her to consider becoming his wife and not leave the country—but something held him back. Angel had seemed cautious, worried. Maybe he'd better hear her out first. Several minutes passed, and his impatience grew. He walked to the corral and leaned against the fence, watching the mares and colts grazing in the pasture.

A boot crunched on gravel behind him, and he turned. Angel stood several feet away, a curious expression clouding her face. As quickly as it came it disappeared, and she walked forward, resting her hip against the middle rail.

"What did you need?" He tried to maintain a casual tone, but everything within was in turmoil. Even in her work clothing she was beautiful.

Her wide, dark eyes shone with an indiscernible light, and her lips parted, but no words came. Her gaze lingered on his and time paused as longing swept over her face. Then she shook herself. "I think someone was following me today. If not following, at least spying on me."

The words were the last thing he expected to hear. All thoughts of romance disappeared. "Spying? Who?"

"I don't know; he was too far away. But I believe he had a looking glass."

"He didn't approach you?"

"No. He disappeared in a gap of the bluff, and I didn't want to follow him."

"Good. Don't go back there. There's no sense in taking chances."

She bristled and turned a scowl full on him. "I *will* go back out there. I'm hunting a mountain lion that's bringing down your calves. Besides, I can handle a gun as well or better than most men."

"That wouldn't stop someone from taking a shot at you from a distance, if they're of a mind to."

She plucked at a piece of dry bark still clinging to the corral rail and pitched it aside. "No one's hunting me, so there's nothing to worry about."

Travis hesitated then said what he knew he had to. "A few days ago, when I talked to the sheriff, he said someone's been asking about you."

Angel's hand stilled. "Did he say who?"

"The man didn't give his name, but he said he's a relative—cousin or something—and that you disappeared. Said he's been hunting for you and wondered if the sheriff knew anything about you."

"What did the sheriff tell him?"

Travis shifted his weight to his boot heel and leaned against the fence. "He didn't trust the man and didn't tell him anything. Told him he'd look into it." He watched her closely, but her expression didn't change. Her posture relaxed, but her fingers still clung to the wooden bar.

"I see."

"Do you have a cousin or relative that might be hunting you?"

"No. Must be a case of mistaken identity." She hunched one shoulder. "I'll show you where the rider sat his horse if you want to track him."

"Sure. As long as you're with me or one of the men. But I mean it, Angel. No more riding out alone until the rustlers are caught."

"But there haven't been any more cattle missing, and we don't know the man watching me is anything more than some lonely cowboy gawking at a woman."

"It doesn't matter. My orders stand." He turned away, frustrated at the way the afternoon had ended. He'd hoped to let Angel know how he felt about her, and instead he'd discovered her life might be in danger from some unknown rider. His love life would have to wait. Angel's safety was more important.

* * * * *

Three days later Angel sat the gelding she'd decided to work at the base of the cliff where the man had disappeared. She'd brought Travis, Nate, and Wren out here the morning after she'd imparted her news, and their tracking had hit a dead end. The canyon branched within the dark, overhanging cliff walls where little light sifted in, making it hard to follow the trail. The hard-packed, rocky ground added to the problem. No trace could be found, and there'd been no other sightings of the stranger.

Angel had ridden out today without Travis's knowledge. He assumed she planned on joining Nate, and she hadn't dissuaded him of the idea, preferring to go back to the rock bluff alone. The news Travis had shared about the man claiming to be a relative spooked her, and she'd been fighting a sick dread in the pit of her stomach ever since. Could the man who'd spied on her, and the one the sheriff spoke to, be one and the same? She didn't care for what that possibility opened, and she loosened the gun in her holster.

Only the tracks of Travis's horse and those of his men lingered at the face of the rock wall. No new cigarette butts lay on the ground. It was like the man had vanished—or decided he wouldn't be found. She swung off her horse, wishing yet again that she'd ridden Bella, but her mare needed rest, and some of the other stock needed work. She scouted along the base, stopping to kneel and run her hands over the dry grass.

Panic had gripped her at Travis's words. One man kept coming to her mind. Bart Hinson. His evil leer had lingered in her mind for the past three years. She tossed the handful of grass she'd plucked onto the ground and then swung into the saddle, suddenly anxious to leave this place. Nothing good would come of being here.

"Going somewhere?" A man's slow drawl came from the dark shadow of the cleft in the rock.

Angel's hand flashed to her gun.

"Don't even think about it. I already got mine aimed at your head." Bart Hinson walked out of the shadows, a Colt pistol gripped in his fist. "Ease that gun back into your holster, and turn around. Slow." He barked a sharp laugh. "You're a pretty woman, but I won't hesitate to kill you."

She released her hold on the butt of her gun, revulsion leaving a bad taste on her tongue. "I'd hoped you were dead."

"Ha. Nice seein' you again, too. Always did think you were too good for everyone else."

"I am. At least for the likes of you." She wanted to claw his eyes out. If only she'd had her gun drawn and ready. Nothing about this place had felt right, and now she understood why. She'd been an idiot to disobey Travis's orders and allow herself to fall into this man's grasp. He'd kill her as easy as look at her, and never think twice.

"You won't be singin' that tune for long." He leered at her, and Angel's skin felt as though it had been dribbled with hog slop.

"I'd suggest you clear out of this country. Ranchers don't take kindly to rustlers, and the sheriff has men hunting you."

"That's why I'm here, darlin'. You're going to help me with a little problem."

"I'm not helping you with anything, other than into an early grave." She stared at his gun hand, wondering what chance she might have if she drew and shot. Probably not much, unless she could distract him, and that was doubtful. All the years she'd known Hinson he'd been focused on self-preservation.

"That's what you think." He motioned with the muzzle of his pistol. "Keep your hands clear of your belt if you don't want a bullet in that pretty arm of yours. Come on now, rest them nice and easy on your saddle horn. There's a good girl." He leaned his backside against the rock. "You're going to help us steal your boss's cattle."

Chapter Twenty-Nine
....

Angel headed back to the ranch, shoulders slumped and a sick knot in her stomach. She laid the reins on her gelding's neck, confident the horse would find his way home. If only she'd gotten the drop on Hinson and could turn him in to the law. The man had seemed to read her mind, though, reminding her that she'd have some hard questions to answer on her own hook. She hadn't thought it through that far but realized he was right. The truth of her past would unfold if she alerted the sheriff to Hinson's presence.

Options flashed through her mind. Turn Hinson in and be exposed, or go along with his plan. Of course, she could always ignore him and hope he got caught, but he'd covered that as well. Either she helped him steal Travis's herd or he'd set fire to the house and kill the family.

He didn't know she cared for Travis, but somehow he'd discovered her grandmother had arrived. Hinson knew he held a winning hand. All she could do was pray the cowboys might corner him before he could implement his plan. But she had to start distancing herself. Leaving for Italy with Grandmother might be best—at least the Morgan family would be safe if she wasn't around.

But would they? Wouldn't Hinson still attempt a cattle drive whether she were here or not? Of course. The man was greedy at best and at the worst, pure evil. If she disappeared, he'd go ahead with his plans. That brought her full circle to helping him steal the cattle.

Her horse snorted, jerked his head up, and nickered. Angel grabbed her rifle and whipped it out of its sheath. She wasn't going to be caught off guard again. A man sat his horse in the distance, his hands resting on the pommel, his hat tipped back on his head. Travis. He must have discovered she wasn't with Nate. Letting him know about Hinson wasn't an option. She hated lying but didn't see any help for it right now. If Travis went after Hinson, he could be killed and she didn't want that on her conscience—not to mention her heart.

Travis picked up his reins and nudged his mount forward. He raised a hand. "I'm glad I caught up with you. I was hoping we could talk before returning to the ranch."

Angel's heart lurched. His expression was one of pleasure, not irritation at an employee who'd gone against his orders. The clamp on her emotions eased, and she rotated her shoulders. She'd have to do a good job of acting, but knowing the stakes, she'd do it. "I didn't expect to meet you out here."

"I needed a break from office work." A wide grin lit his face. "Besides, I have something to ask you."

Angel couldn't decide whether to spur her horse and run, or stay and take her chances. Something inside told her this wouldn't have a happy ending. "I'm sorry I rode off alone. I just needed a little time to think."

His smile faltered. "I didn't realize you had. I assumed…"

"I know. That I met Nate and Wren." Angel shook her head. "But as you can see, I'm fine." She finished in a rush, anxious to get the subject over and the truth—or most of it—out in the open.

"I'm thankful for that." He jerked his chin toward a tree nearby. "Let's get off and sit in the shade for a few minutes."

"All right." It was the last thing she wanted, but what could she do? She'd already tried to turn the conversation at her own expense and that hadn't worked. Whatever Travis had on his mind evidently wouldn't be deterred. She swung down from her saddle and dropped her reins, ground-tying her horse on the scant green patch under the tree.

Travis did the same and squatted with his back against the trunk.

Angel stretched out on a grassy spot a couple of yards away. For some reason she couldn't express, she didn't feel comfortable sitting too close. "What's on your mind?"

Travis's expression froze. His mouth opened, but no words came. He pursed his lips and rubbed his chin with the palm of his hand. "Sorry. I'm not quite sure how to say this."

"I guess just say it. I'm no baby."

His eyebrows rose. "You think I'm here to take you to task about something?"

"Aren't you?"

"Far from it. In fact—" He paused, then rushed forward. "I'm in love with you, Angel. I think I have been for a long time. I can't think of anything but you. Can't get any work done. I worry about your safety, and long to be with you when you're out of my sight." His deep blue eyes held hers. "I want to marry you, if you'll have me."

Angel didn't know whether to weep or dance with joy. She'd been running from her feelings for weeks, and his declaration solidified her own desires. More than anything she wanted to be his wife. If only she could say yes, fall into his arms, and be safe forever. She pushed up on her knees, then sank back, reality setting in. Bart Hinson stood in their way of happiness—possibly of life itself.

No way could she take a chance with Travis's life, not to mention Libby, James, and Grandmother. "I'm sorry, Travis…" She turned her head, unable to meet his entreating gaze. "I don't feel the same way." The words tasted like poison on her tongue, and she almost choked. She chanced a glance his way.

Hurt washed across his features. "But I thought"—he hesitated—"that you might feel the same. There's been something between us, and I don't think I imagined it."

She shrugged, hating what she was doing, but somehow she had to convince him. "You're a wonderful boss, and you've been kind to me since I arrived. But I'm considering returning with Grandmother to Italy. She might be right; there would be more opportunities there." Angel wanted to cry as her words settled between them like a massive boulder blocking a trail. "I'm sorry if I've hurt you."

Travis surged to his feet, his mouth set in a grim line. "I'll be fine." The words came out in a rough growl. "I've got my ranch and my family. I hope you'll be happy in Italy, Angel. We'd better get home."

They mounted their horses in a heavy silence. Angel trailed behind, not able to face this man she'd wounded. She wanted to curl up in a ball and cry but straightened her spine instead. If it was the last thing she did, she'd keep Travis and his family safe and bring Hinson to justice. Travis wouldn't want anything to do with her if he knew she'd decided to help the outlaw, regardless of the reason. But she'd made up her mind. Hinson would have his way—for now.

* * * * *

Travis slung his saddle over the rail on the inside wall of the barn and grabbed a curry brush. He wanted nothing more than to be off by himself. How could he have misjudged Angel so completely? Had he been so smitten that he'd assumed she felt the same? Her decision stung, pure and simple. And what was she thinking, riding off by herself after he'd given her orders not to? He'd let that go in light of what he'd wanted to say, but he'd deal with her willful attitude if she continued to work for him.

His hand slowed on the long stroke down his gelding's back. *If she continued.* She'd made it clear she planned to leave, but he had no idea when that might happen. Maybe he could talk to Maria, convince her to stay, tell her he loved Angel and wanted another chance. His spirit rose at the thought…and plummeted again.

Angel walked by, leading her horse to the outside corral without so much as a glance or a nod. She'd said she didn't care, and it was evident she'd told the truth. Why pursue a woman who wanted to be left alone? If she didn't return his feelings, there was nothing more he could do. He'd have to move on with his life.

Part of him wished she'd never ridden in asking for a job, but that wasn't fair. She'd done everything he'd asked of her and more. If it wasn't for Angel, James could be dead. He owed her too much to wish he'd never met her, but he didn't know if his heart would ever recover.

* * * * *

Angel lay on her bed wanting to die. Now that she'd lied to Travis, she'd be forced to travel with Grandmother once the cattle disappeared. The entire family would hate her if they found out what she'd done, and she could easily do time in jail—if not get hanged. She didn't know of any women who'd been hanged for rustling, but the swift justice of the West might not consider the fact of her femininity.

She couldn't do it. She wouldn't do it. Her heart leapt with hope, and she scooted up against the iron headpiece of her bed. There had to be another way. Maybe she could lure Hinson into a trap. But how could she turn him in without the law discovering she'd ridden on that last drive when the Ranger was killed? A deep groan tore from her throat. She'd tell Hinson she'd turn him in and hope he'd disappear. He'd told her to leave a note for him with instructions where to meet.

She burrowed her head in her pillow, willing darkness to come. A couple of hours later a knock sounded at her door, and Libby called her name. "Angel?"

"Yes."

"It's suppertime."

"I'm not feeling well. I think I'll turn in early."

"Can I help?"

"No. I'm mostly just tired. I'll be fine by morning."

"If you're sure." Libby hesitated. "Let me know if you change your mind."

"Thank you." Angel rolled over on her side as Libby's footsteps disappeared down the hall. She hated lying to her friend, but she couldn't face Travis in front of everyone. It wasn't *really* a lie, anyway. She *was* sick—heartsick.

Darkness seemed to fall more slowly than she remembered in years. She lit her lamp and removed a paper from the top drawer of her bureau along with a pencil. Long minutes passed while she considered what she'd say. Finally she wrote the words that could send Hinson into a rage, but it couldn't be helped.

I won't help you. Leave the country or face the law. Angel Ramirez

Now to rest until it was late enough to take it to the place he'd told her without getting caught. She'd have to walk Bella down the road at least a quarter of a mile before she mounted and picked up her pace. No way could she allow one of the sharp-eared cowboys to hear her.

* * * * *

Four hours later Angel crawled back into bed, emotional and physical exhaustion making her limbs shake. She'd done it. The note was pinned under a rock at the base of a large tree a mile from the gate leading to the ranch. Hinson or one of his men would find it in the morning. Now she just had to pray that somehow God protected the family, and the outlaw decided the risk wasn't worth taking. She fell into a restless sleep, but dreams of hangman's nooses and cattle stampedes haunted her night. Travis's horrified visage rose up to taunt her, and Libby turned her back and walked away.

Angel woke just before daylight, the images of the Morgan family fleeing from a fire still fresh in her mind. She shivered and jerked the blanket close to her chin, wanting nothing more than to escape into a dreamless sleep.

A strange smell tugged at her memory. Suddenly she threw back the covers and sat upright.

Smoke.

It couldn't be the fire in the kitchen stove, as they let that go out after supper during the summer months. She stepped to the window. Flames licked the wall of the lean-to connected to the far side of the barn—the section closest to the cowboys' bunkhouse. A trail of smoke rose in the air. Why hadn't anyone else smelled it?

She grabbed a shirt and trousers, slipped into them, and whipped open her door. If only Libby's and Travis's bedrooms were on the ground floor. Racing through the kitchen to the base of the stairs, she lifted her voice. "Travis! Travis! The barn's on fire." She grabbed the banister and took the steps two at a time, calling as she went. "Wake up! Libby, Travis! Hurry!"

A door slammed open, and Travis stood at the top, barely

discernible in the feeble light glowing behind him as dawn started to break. "Angel? What's wrong? I heard you calling."

Libby's door opened and she stepped out, wrapping a robe around her waist and cinching it. "What is it?"

"Fire. The barn. Hurry!" Angel bolted back down the stairs, satisfied at the sound of boots hitting the floor above. She grabbed the front door and flew outside, racing for the bunkhouse. Before she reached it, the door slammed open and the cowhands tumbled out, slinging gun belts around their waists and jamming hats on their heads. Angel skidded to a stop and pointed. "We might be able to stop it before it spreads." A sudden thought sent a shaft of fear deep into her heart. "Bella! The horses are in the barn!"

Footsteps pounded beside her as she ran. A masculine hand gripped the wood handle before she did and yanked it open. "Stay back, Angel. I'll get the horses." Travis's rough voice filled her ears, but she didn't hesitate. She dashed in on his heels. Smoke swirled in the dim light, making it almost impossible to see. Shouts from the men outside electrified her, and the screams of horses lent wings to her feet. Three long strides took her to Bella's stall.

The mare plunged backward, thrashing at the walls and rearing several feet off the floor. "Easy girl. Calm down. I'll get you out."

Travis pushed past her. "Get out of the way. I'm turning her loose. She's too terrified to lead, and she could hurt you." He swung wide the stall door and slapped the mare on the rump as Angel sprang out of the way. The frightened horse lunged for the opening and raced for the door, disappearing into the early morning light.

Bella wouldn't run far. She'd settle down, knowing where her grain came from, and make her way back to the corral. It only took a matter of minutes to help Travis set the other four horses free, and the two of them scurried out of the barn, coughing as they went.

Travis rounded on her as soon as they cleared the smoke-filled building and grabbed her arm. "I told you to stay out. You could've been hurt."

She jerked her arm free. "I'm a big girl, Travis, and Bella's my horse. I take care of my own." She waved at the men racing back and forth with buckets from the water trough where Libby and James took turns pumping. "Instead of arguing, I think we'd better put out the fire before it reaches the main part of the barn."

Travis spun around as though he'd forgotten the danger to his property, then dashed forward, joining the bucket brigade. "Men! Quit running and form a line. Pass the buckets down to the end. James and Angel. Bring them back to the man closest to the trough. Hurry!"

From what Angel could tell, the fire had smoldered at the base of a wall and the flames had burned halfway up. She'd noticed it before it engulfed the building. After an hour of dousing the wall the men slowed their frantic pace. Smoke drifted from a scorched area about twenty-five feet wide by six feet tall. Full daylight had broken, and the early morning sun shone on the dazed group. No one spoke for several moments, then pandemonium broke loose.

Wren pumped his fist in the air. "What in tarnation happened here?"

James stared at the cowboy and then looked at his mother, but she stood mute, just shaking her head.

Arizona glowered and slapped his hat against his leg. "Nothing good, I'll swear to that. Fires don't start themselves."

Grumbling sounded from several quarters and Travis swung around, staring at James. "Young man, come here."

James took a short step back. "I didn't do nothin', Uncle Travis. I swear."

Charlie walked over to the burned section and squatted on his heels. He waved a hand at Arizona. "Look for tracks, pard."

The cowboy sprang into action, and the two moved slowly from one corner to the next, disappearing out of sight.

Nate stepped over to James and draped his arm across the boy's shoulder. "You didn't get up in the night and come out here for any reason?"

"No, sir." James shook his head and peered up at the man. "I swear, Nate. I didn't do anything wrong."

Travis met Nate's eyes and nodded. "I believe you."

James slumped against Nate's side. "Thank you, Uncle Travis. I'd never do anything *this* bad. Honest I wouldn't."

Libby ran to her son, wrapping him in her arms. Nate stayed close, alternately patting the boy's back and stroking Libby's hair. She looked up at him, tenderness and gratitude lighting her face. "Thank you for believing him." Libby reached out, and his large hand engulfed hers.

Angel turned away, a deep pain filling her chest. Happiness warred with the pain—Libby needed a husband and a father for her son, but her own sense of loss bit deep. She felt someone's gaze on her, but she kept hers trained on the ground. Right now was not the time to see a look of longing on Travis's face. She knew she'd run to him and wouldn't let go, and that couldn't happen. Arizona was right. Fires didn't start themselves, and since there'd been no lightning that meant only one thing. Hinson had torched the barn.

"Boss!" Charlie's shout turned everyone around. He stepped around the corner and motioned. "Found something you'll want to see."

Travis and Nate led the way and the women and James followed. Arizona squatted on his heels, staring at something white ground into the dirt. He stood, nudged it with his toe, and leaned over. "Cigarette."

The single word dropped like a boulder falling from a cliff. No one moved and all eyes were trained on the small brown tube. It had been smashed flat by a boot toe after half of it had been smoked. Arizona held it higher. "No one on the ranch smokes, and this here cigarette's been rolled Mexican style. Not common around these parts."

Travis swung toward James. "I'm sorry for suggesting you did this, son. I was wrong."

James nodded silently.

"Who wants your barn burned?" Wren's words sliced the air.

"I don't know." Travis shook his head, deep lines of worry creasing his cheeks.

Angel choked back a gasp and covered her mouth. Thankfully no one noticed as they all continued to stare at the offending cigarette. Hinson had gotten her note early and made good on his threat. He must have had a man waiting near the tree, just out of sight. She should've known. What made her think she could get away without retaliation?

Charlie stooped over and took a few steps toward the back corner. "Looks like there's tracks here that some hombre tried to wipe out. They're not clear, but they lead off this way." He strode off, stopping every few yards. "He's headed into the brush, but there ain't much sign left. The gent's good at hidin' his trail, I'll give him that."

Travis jerked his head toward Arizona. "Go. Find the man who did this if you can and bring him back."

Arizona sprang into action and ran after Charlie.

Wren leveled a hard gaze on Travis. "What you want me to do, Boss?"

"Saddle up and check on Bud. No telling what's happening out on the range." He swung around and looked at his foreman. "Nate. You'd best go with Wren."

"Sure. We'll head out right now." Nate smiled at Libby and ruffled James's hair.

James raised pleading eyes. "Can I go with you? Please?"

"Not this time, boy. You stay here and take care of your mother. We need a man on the place to help guard the women." A grim smile broke his solemnity. "You think you can handle that?"

James straightened his shoulders and nodded. "Yes, sir."

"Good." He leaned over to whisper something close to Libby's ear, then stalked off toward the corral on Wren's heels.

"Angel?" a shaky voice called from the porch. Grandmother stood by a post, her anxious eyes focused on the barn. "What's happened? I woke up and heard shouts and smelled smoke."

Angel hurried across the clearing and up the steps. She wrapped her arm around the tiny woman's shoulders and pulled her close. "I'm sorry you were worried. There was a fire, but the men put it out."

"How did it start? Does anyone know?"

Angel hesitated, not sure how much to share. "It looks like some careless person dropped a cigarette too close to the dry wood." She hoped that would satisfy Grandmother and she wouldn't need to explain any more.

Grandmother nodded and tugged her sweater close to her chest. "Where's Smokey?"

Libby gasped. "Smokey? He's not in the kitchen?"

"No. I thought he'd be out here with the rest of the men."

Travis strode over. "You haven't seen him this morning?"

"No." Grandmother shook her head, small lines creasing her forehead.

Angel stepped toward Travis. "We'd better start looking. He'd be out here if he was all right."

"I agree. You check the bunkhouse, and I'll head to the privy."

They separated, and Angel stopped on the front porch of the bunkhouse, hesitating to enter the cowboys' private domain. A minute later, she pushed open the door and peered inside. Six beds lined the walls in sets of two each, one stacked above the other. A small table with chairs stood in the center, and a wood stove perched in the far corner with a stack of wood piled alongside. A deck of cards lay strewn across the middle of one table, and a book lay facedown on another. All of the beds had blankets thrown back, with some of the bedclothes trailing on the floor. Angel took in the room at a glance. Nothing in this area would hide a man Smokey's size, and all of the beds were empty. She backed out of the room and closed the door.

A shout sounded from behind the bunkhouse. Angel ran around the corner and skidded to a halt. Travis knelt beside Smokey's prostrate body, cradling his bleeding head in his arms.

Chapter Thirty

....

"Call Libby. Tell her to bring water and rags. I'll get Smokey onto his bed."

Angel did as she was asked, then helped Travis half drag, half carry Smokey into the bunkhouse. They hefted him onto the cot nearest the door. The bed sagged and creaked as his weight landed solidly in the middle.

The man moaned. His eyelids fluttered and he tried to sit up, then fell back against the straw-filled mattress. "What happened, Boss?" His voice came out in a husky whisper.

Travis leaned close. "I hoped you could tell us. You've got a gash on the back of your head. What hit you?"

"Not sure. Feels like it were somethin' awful hard, though, like maybe a gun butt." He groaned, and his eyes closed.

Libby rushed in carrying a basin of water with cloths draped over her arm. "Stand back and give me some room." Her no-nonsense tone took charge, and she bustled to Smokey's side. "Maria is heating more water, and James will bring it out."

Angel stood to the side, feeling out of place and useless. "What should I do?"

Travis turned to look at her, his expression showing he'd forgotten her presence in the turmoil. "Round up the horses we ran out of the barn. I'd hate to have them wander too far."

"Sure." Angel strode for the door and pushed it open, stepping into the smoke-tainted air. Her gaze roamed over the area. The barn door gaped, and gray tendrils still drifted from the charred boards on the side of the lean-to. Buckets lay where they'd landed, and patches of mud dotted the ground. Sadness swept over her spirit and she shook her head, hating what had transpired. A feeling of menace hung over the ranch. First the cattle gone missing, then Hinson's arrival, and now the fire and attack on Smokey. What would be next?

The front door of the house slammed open, and James scurried across the porch, a bucket swaying in his grip. Water splashed over the side. Angel lifted her voice. "Slow down there, or you won't have any left by the time you get to the bunkhouse."

James dropped to a walk, holding the bucket away from his leg. "Yes, ma'am." He ducked inside the cowboy's abode and disappeared.

Angel spotted Bella grazing a hundred yards or so behind a corral. She grabbed a lasso from a nearby post and hurried after the mare. Slipping the rope over Bella's head, Angel led her back to the barn, tying her to the hitching post outside. Angel wrinkled her nose at the smell as she stepped inside, but there was no help for it. She needed her saddle and bridle if she hoped to find the rest of the stock. Swiftly tacking up the mare, Angel swung aboard and headed down the lane.

A roan gelding lifted his head and snorted at her approach, side-stepping out of the way as she drew close. She shook out the lasso she carried and held it at the ready, urging Bella forward. A couple of swings dropped the loop over his nose and settled around his neck. She backed Bella, tightening her hold on the gelding. All of the riding stock was used to being roped, so he settled down and followed her back to the ranch. It didn't take long to round up the rest. She drove them back into the corral and closed the gate.

An idea had been niggling at her the past hour. There might not be any better time to implement it than now. She checked the load in her rifle, then swung back onto Bella. One way or another she had to make this right. Travis's family and cowhands were suffering because of her. Hinson had hunted and finally tracked her here. It was up to her to deal with the man.

* * * * *

Travis finished bandaging Smokey's head. He'd sent Libby back to the house after she'd dressed the wound, knowing she'd have her hands full fixing dinner. Maria would probably help, and James could certainly set the table. The men had left without breakfast, and his own rumbling stomach reminded him of the omission.

His thoughts turned to his cowboys, and he clenched his teeth. He prayed they'd find Bud alive and unharmed and no more cattle missing. The fire and the attack against Smokey left him stunned. Who would want to harm his ranch and why? Rustlers weren't usually this bold, and the ones who'd operated here in the past had only stolen unbranded calves—mavericks—that they could slap their own brand on without raising suspicion.

Travis thanked the Lord that Smokey's wound looked worse than it was. He'd lost some blood, but the gash wasn't deep. More than likely his head would hurt for a few days, but he'd be up and around in no time. In fact, he'd had to force the man to stay in bed and not get up to fix dinner. He seemed to be sleeping peacefully now, and Maria promised to keep an eye on him.

He walked to the corral and leaned on the bars. Looked like Angel had rounded up the horses. He'd best ensure the burned area was completely out. They didn't need smoldering wood igniting again.

James appeared on the porch and waved his arm. "Uncle Travis, Ma says to tell you dinner's ready. Could you call Miss Angel and let her know?"

Travis's head jerked up, and he stared at the boy. "She's not in the house?"

"No sir. I haven't seen her since you sent her to find the horses." James turned and reentered the house, letting the door bang behind him.

Strange. He let his gaze rove over the horses. No Bella. A quick check of the barn revealed her saddle and bridle were gone. She must have headed to where Bud had been keeping guard on the cattle. He frowned, not happy with the turn of events. Angel was a crack shot, but that didn't give him much comfort. He didn't want her tangled in a shootout with a bunch of cattle rustlers.

She may have turned down his proposal, but that didn't stop him from caring. A new thought crept in, and hope trickled through his heart. As long as she remained on the ranch there was always the chance she might change her mind. He headed back to the house, his gnawing hunger driving him toward the aroma of hot food drifting out an open window.

His boot landed on the bottom step when the sound of trotting horses came up the lane. Nate, Wren, and Bud reined in their mounts at the hitching rail. "Bud. Glad to see you're all right. Any problem with the herd?"

"No sir. Didn't see or hear anything all night. The men sure surprised me when they rode up and told me about the fire. Wanted us to get back in a hurry so's you'd know there ain't nothin' else the matter."

Nate leaned on his saddle horn. "We'll eat and get Smokey to put up some grub. A couple of us will head back right away."

Travis shook his head. "There's been more trouble while you were gone. Smokey got clobbered over the head. I found him behind the bunkhouse. Probably got attacked when he headed out early this morning."

A low rumbling started among the men, and Travis picked up more than one sharp retort. "Any of you run into Angel on your way back?"

Wren frowned. "No, Boss. You send her out to find us?"

"No. She headed out on her own hook after bringing in the horses. Maybe she trailed after Arizona and Charlie instead." Travis wanted to saddle up that moment and head after her. What was she thinking, trying to track the man who attacked Smokey and set the fire? She might be a varmint hunter, but that was a far cry from hunting an outlaw.

Nate swung down from his horse and looped his reins over the rail. "If she's not back by the time we're done eating, we'll go looking."

Wren and Bud chimed in, agreeing with the plan, and Travis held up his hand, motioning them inside. "Fine. Hurry up and fill your bellies. I want to find her before anything more happens."

Chapter Thirty-One

. . . .

Angel reined in her horse, not happy to see Arizona and Charlie in the distance. Her goose was cooked if they spotted her. They were heading cross country toward the ranch, traveling at a brisk trot. Arizona kept shifting in his saddle and swiveling his head, keeping a sharp eye on the countryside around them. He lifted a hand, reined his horse to a stop, and motioned her direction. Charlie shaded his eyes and waved. They turned their horses, trotting to within hailing distance.

Angel returned the gesture and lifted her voice. "I'm tracking a horse. I'll head back to the ranch right away."

Arizona glanced at Charlie. They exchanged words, and Arizona swung back towards her. "I'll help."

Panic gripped her. No way could she let any of the men come. "No. Travis wants you both back at the ranch. Smokey was attacked by whoever set the fire. I'll be in soon. I promise I won't go far."

He seemed to hesitate, then nodded. "All right, but hurry. Boss ain't gonna like it that I left you out here. I'll give him my report, and if you're not back shortly, I'm coming to help."

"Fine. Now go." She waved again and turned her horse. Relief surged at the cadence of trotting hooves.

Thirty minutes later she reined in Bella not far from the base of the bluff where she'd last seen Hinson, her rifle cradled across her lap. She wouldn't be caught unaware this time. In fact, if she could get the drop on the man, so much the better. "Hinson." She shifted in the saddle and raised her voice to try again. "Bart Hinson. If you're out there, show yourself." She tightened her grip on her rifle.

Something stirred on the edge of her vision, and she twisted in her saddle, raising her gun. A rabbit hopped a yard or two, then sat up on its haunches and stared. Her skin felt as though fire ants crawled across it. Someone was watching, but no matter how hard she searched she didn't see anyone. Angel worked to relax her tense muscles but didn't succeed. If the man didn't appear, what then? But what would she do if he did? For the briefest of moments fear gripped her stomach, making her almost physically ill, but she pushed it away. Her safety wasn't important right now. There were others at risk.

"God?" She lifted her chin and gazed at the wispy clouds drifting by on the gentle breeze. "I could use Your help here, if You don't mind. I know we're just getting acquainted, but I've heard people at church say You care about everything we care about. I'm not even sure I'm doing the right thing, but please help me in any way You see fit."

Nothing else moved. What now? Go back to the ranch and tell Travis the truth? But if she did, she'd have to tell him about her past. She nudged her horse forward. If someone was watching they'd probably follow. The bluff with the gushing spring and pool wasn't far away, and cattle dotted the area. The cowboys guarded the bigger herd on the far side of the range, and she doubted anyone was posted at the bluff. That might be a good place to lie in wait for Hinson.

Bella seemed to sense her need for action and broke from a trot into a canter. Angel loosened her reins and let the mare have her head. Within moments they moved into a hard gallop bordering on a flat-out run. The pace suited Angel's mood. Hard, pounding, and dangerous. They swerved around chuck holes and jumped small washes.

Finally, Angel decided she'd taken enough chances with her mare and slowed her to a trot. They'd covered a lot of ground in a short amount of time, and it would pay to approach the spring with care.

Nothing moved but the grazing cattle as Bella and Angel slowed to a walk. The midday heat radiated from the nearby cliffs, and sweat rolled down the side of her face. She plucked a bandanna from her pocket, wiped her cheeks, and knotted it around her neck. The water in her canteen would be tepid by now. She swung down from her horse and walked beside her to the pool. After letting Bella have her fill, she removed her canteen from the back of her saddle and held it under the flowing stream. The sound of the water soothed her agitation, and she smiled. She'd been foolish coming out here alone and thinking she could do anything to trap Hinson. From now on she'd leave the capture of outlaws to Travis. Her belly reminded her she'd missed dinner. Time to head back to the ranch.

"Hands up, lady," a coarse voice said behind her.

Angel froze, her canteen still gripped in her fist.

"I've got a six-gun trained on your back. Put your hands in the air if you don't want a bullet in your gizzard."

She raised her arms, retaining her hold on the canteen. "Hinson?"

"Naw. But he'll be along, don't you worry your pretty head. Too bad, if you ask me. I wouldn't a'minded a little private entertainment, know what I mean?" The last words broke on a laugh that sent a shiver up Angel's back. "Turn around. Slow."

She did as she was told, keeping her arms in the air. A man holding a Colt revolver stood about ten paces away. "I don't recognize you."

His hat shaded his face, but his eyes gleamed. "No matter." He shifted a large wad of tobacco from one cheek to the other, then leaned over to spit. He swiped at his lips with the back of his hand and leered. "Heard all sorts of things 'bout you from the others, though."

Angel shivered. If only she hadn't left her rifle on her saddle. There was no way she'd get her pistol out of her holster with him watching.

"Hinson thinks you're some kind of hand with a gun." He barked a sharp laugh. "Funny, you wearin' that iron on your hip. Ain't never seen no woman wearin' a six-gun before." He flicked his wrist. "Toss it on out here. I reckon it's mostly for show, but no sense takin' chances. Pick it out nice and easy with your fingertips and drop it at your feet."

She did as he said, pinching the butt of the gun between her thumb and finger and lifting it clear of the holster. She started to lean over and place it on the ground.

"I said drop it." His voice sharpened, and he took a step closer.

Angel released her hold, and the gun hit the dirt.

"Now kick it away from you. This direction."

Once again she obeyed his orders, seething at her helplessness. The gun skittered out of her reach and slid close to the outlaw's feet. "Now what?"

"We wait. Sit on that rock and don't move." He pointed at a nearby boulder and watched while she moved over and sat. "I can see why Hinson wants you. Yes, sir."

"Wants me? He wants Travis Morgan's cattle."

"A lot you know. The cattle are payment to the rest of us for ridin' along. As far as he's concerned, we come to get you."

* * * * *

Travis stared at Arizona and Charlie. "You let her ride off on her own?"

Red crept up Charlie's neck, and he uttered something under his breath.

"Speak up, man. Whatever you've got to say spit it out." Travis didn't care how harsh he sounded; he'd personally throttle these two if anything happened to Angel.

"Arizona wanted to stay, but she told us you wanted us both back pronto. Said she was tracking one of the horses and would be right back."

"Yeah, Boss. I told her I didn't want to leave. I'll head back." Arizona jerked his horse's head around.

"Hold it!" Travis's sharp retort made the man jump. "We're all heading out. I don't know what she's up to, but something's not right. She brought the horses in before she left."

Arizona's face crumpled. "She lied to me?"

"Looks that way, and I aim to find out why." Travis turned to the silent cowboys standing around. "Mount up, men, and make sure you're armed."

* * * * *

Angel couldn't move. Hinson wanted her? The man had made her skin crawl when she lived at the stronghold, but she figured he'd forgotten her by now and found another woman. She shot up another frantic prayer toward heaven, hoping someone was listening.

Hoofs pounded the ground behind her, and she turned. Four dusty men rode around the corner of the cliff. Rifle barrels glinted in the sun, and Bart Hinson broke into a grin. "You got her." He gestured to the man holding the gun. "Mount up. We're heading out."

"Where to?"

"You want those cattle, don't you?"

The outlaw jumped to his feet, a broad smile creasing his darkly tanned face. "Right smart, we do. But we'd best hustle before someone comes lookin' for this one." He gestured toward Angel. "I got her gun off'n her, Boss, but it's probably just for show. She's some humdinger of a looker. Woo-whee!"

Hinson lunged forward. He whipped his arm backward and let loose a mighty swing. His fist connected with the man's jaw, snapping his head back. The outlaw fell with a grunt, hitting the ground hard and lying still. Hinson swung around and stared at the group of mounted men behind him. "Anyone else want to say something about my woman?"

No one spoke, but each head shook a negative response.

Angel almost gagged. She stiffened and rose to her feet. "I am *not* your woman, Hinson, and you'd do well to remember that."

"That's what you think, little lady. Why you figure that old, fat cowhand only got his head busted instead of killed?"

She shrugged, determined not to give him the satisfaction of trying to guess.

"I done that for you." He grinned.

"Like you tried to burn the barn? For me?" She took a step forward, her hands balled into fists. She wanted to punch him in the gut. Better yet, she itched to get her hands on a gun.

"Sure. Just for you." Hinson gave a raw laugh. "And don't you forget it. I burned that barn and hit that man to show you I meant business. I coulda just as easily plugged that youngster when he made a trip to the privy this mornin'."

She shivered. Hinson had seen James outside? How long had the man been watching the ranch? "I'll help you get the cattle. I'll even take them to the next territory if that's what you need. Promise you won't hurt anyone else."

"No promises. You'll do what I say without bellyachin'. Get on your horse and move out. Now."

Hope flickered in Angel's heart. Her rifle was still in her scabbard.

The other outlaw had taken her pistol but hadn't thought to remove her rifle. If she could keep that side of her horse away from Hinson, she might have a chance. She picked up Bella's reins and her mare snorted and danced sideways, turning the rifle away from the outlaws. Angel shot up a prayer of thanks and swung up, settling into her saddle. All she could do was hope they'd be so focused on moving the cattle before anyone arrived that they wouldn't think of checking to see if she was still armed.

Chapter Thirty-Two
....

Travis, Nate, and the four cowboys settled into a rolling canter, traveling in a straight line toward the only herd of cattle they hadn't yet checked—the ones grazing at the big spring. How could he have been so careless as to let Angel leave the ranch? Sure, he was tending to Smokey and assumed she was occupied in the house, but he should've known better. Angel was the most stubborn, independent—he sighed—beautiful, free-spirited woman he'd had privilege of meeting, and he couldn't bear to think of anything happening to her.

They'd all come loaded for bear. If the man who attacked Smokey laid a hand on Angel, he'd live to rue the day. Men were hanged in the West for accosting a lady, and they'd apply necktie justice before the day was out.

Raven snorted and jerked at the reins, seeming to sense his rider's impatience. "Easy, boy." Travis hauled in his own frustration and reminded himself he was a law-abiding citizen. The thought galled him. He was also a man, and he wanted to pummel anyone who got in his way of bringing Angel home. Travis allowed himself a grim smile. Pummeling would be forgiven easier than hanging.

Nothing stirred against the horizon. The silence rubbed at his nerves. Crows should be soaring on the warm drafts of air, cows bawling, or the occasional coyote or fox scurrying across the trail, but all lay still. He lifted his heart in supplication to God, begging that He keep Angel safe. If he had to get down on his knees to convince her not to return with Maria, he'd willingly do so. Placing an ocean between them wasn't an option.

Travis motioned to the men to fan out across the grasslands. Nate fell away to his right, with Charlie and Bud beyond him. Arizona and Wren galloped off to the left, and he made note of more than one rifle removed from the scabbard. He loosened his own, feeling the muscles in his gut tense with anticipation. It wouldn't be long before they'd be within sight of the spring. Maybe they'd complicated this entire situation and Angel was doing what she'd claimed—tracking a stray horse. Sure, she'd rounded up the ones from the barn, but what was to say another hadn't gotten free from a fence or a pen? He'd look like a fool chasing down a woman who wasn't in danger, but he didn't care. His instincts told him different, and he'd trust those over a possibility any day.

* * * * *

Angel swung wide around the herd of cattle, ever aware of the watchful eye of Bart Hinson. He or one of the other men stayed close beside her. Hinson's taunting gaze had gone to her rifle, and a smirk crossed his flat face. He'd raised his brows but didn't speak. There was no need. She got the message: touch it and die.

She wondered if part of him almost hoped she'd try so he could teach her a lesson. Strange that he seemed obsessed by her as well as revealing the need to conquer. At this point she wouldn't tempt him to reach for a gun or tie her to her horse. She'd bide her time until an opportunity afforded, then pray that God's hand would be extended in her hour of need.

What must Travis and Libby be thinking? She should've been back a couple of hours ago. Would they be looking for her by now?

Part of her longed to be found, but her sensible side shook off the need. Lives would be lost if the cowboys appeared, with no guarantee someone she cared about wouldn't be among them.

How had she gotten herself into this mess? If only she'd swallowed her pride and taken her chances with the law—and with Libby and Travis's ability to understand and forgive. Angel glanced at the rough-looking man riding a black gelding a stone's throw away. His attention wandered to a rogue steer dashing out of the herd. She dropped her head and allowed her shoulders to sag, hoping he wouldn't see her as a threat. His horse's hoofs beating a staccato against the hard ground brought a small smile to Angel's lips, but she kept her head bowed.

A slight tug on the reins turned Bella a little farther to the side, and she slowly dropped behind a few paces. If only she could fall far enough back to make a dash for it. Most of these men could plug her with a rifle even on a running horse, but she had to try. She'd seen the possessive look in Hinson's eyes. Getting shot in the back was preferable to falling into his lecherous grasp.

Hinson had his own hands full at the moment, keeping the back edge of the herd bunched. The greedy outlaw had tried to snatch too many cattle for the number of rustlers hazing the edges of the moving melee.

She fell farther back along the fringes on the outside edge, keeping a wary eye on the rustler assigned to watch her. Her hand rested on the butt of her rifle. She eased it out of the scabbard and dangled it against Bella's offside.

A shout went up from one of the men. "Riders coming!" The outlaws riding closest to the rear swiveled to gaze behind them, and as one man, they shucked their guns from holsters and scabbards.

Hinson pivoted. A curse ripped from his throat, and he bellowed at the top of his lungs, "Get these cows moving, men, and shoot while you ride." Gunfire exploded, and the cattle surged ahead in a mass, charging through the brush.

Angel looked over her shoulder. Both relief and dread washed over her heart. Travis and a long line of cowboys raced their horses a few hundred feet behind the now stampeding herd. Travis had his gun drawn, and the grim-faced cowboys each held a rifle or a six-gun in their hands.

Cattle bawled as the wild-eyed beasts ran unfettered. Horns clashed against one another and foam from their open mouths whipped behind them in the wind. A large brindle steer jostled his way through a tight clump of cattle, head high and his gaze trained on the outlaw to his right. The mad animal seemed intent on overtaking the horse, his head and wide-spread horns swinging with each leaping stride.

Angel watched mesmerized as the scene played out. She wanted to cheer for the steer in his dash to run down the rider but felt ashamed of the bloodlust welling up inside. The man didn't seem aware of the crazed animal so close on his heels. A sudden swing of the steer's head, and one of his horns caught the bay gelding in the haunch, sending the horse tripping, then rolling onto the ground. The rider flew clear, landing on his neck. His body lay sprawled with his head at a crooked angle. The horse lunged to his feet, racing off in the opposite direction.

Hinson turned his hard gaze on the rider and swore. He yanked his horse around and spurred him toward Angel. "Get over here. Now!" His pistol came level with her chest. "You're riding next to me from here on." He motioned with his gun. "Get a move on before those riders catch up."

Angel whipped up her rifle. There was no time to aim. Bella lunged forward as she leveled her rifle. She prayed her bullet wouldn't find his horse instead of his chest. The mare swerved just as the gun bucked in her grip, the bullet tugging at his sleeve as it passed. She laid her reins and spurs into Bella's sides, and the startled mare leapt forward, charging through the brush. A shout sounded behind her, easily recognizable as Hinson. Angel guided her mare around rocks and roots churned up by the cattle.

The pound of hoofs drew closer, and she chanced a backward glance. Hinson. She swung Bella in a wide circle, heading toward the charging, bellowing herd. The risk of injury would increase the closer she came to the cattle, but it seemed her only hope of evading the outlaw.

She shot up a prayer for safety—first for her horse, then for herself. No way did she want to go down under the trampling mass of horns and hooves, or see her horse maimed.

Shots reverberated off to the side and behind her, but Angel kept her focus on the charging cattle lunging on each side of her horse. She urged Bella forward, trying to keep pace with the terrified animals bellowing their fear. Calves raced beside their mothers, barely able to keep their feet.

Her thoughts went to her grandmother and sorrow engulfed her. She'd never told Maria she loved her—never expressed her gratitude that she'd come so far to find her. If she survived this frantic race and returned to the ranch, that was the first thing she'd do.

A steer darted in front of Bella, and Angel hauled back on her reins. The quick-footed mare sat on her haunches and skidded, but another, smaller cow slammed into her hip, nearly toppling the mare into the mass of animals rushing by. Somehow Angel got Bella's head up and helped her regain her balance. Fear surged through her body, and her breath quickened.

Where was Hinson? Had the man given up, or better yet, been shot by one of the pursuing cowboys? She kept Bella moving at a fast trot and peered around her. Her spine stiffened, and she froze.

A pistol gripped in Hinson's hand was aimed at her heart, and only a dozen cows separated them.

Angel's heart rate quickened. The man meant to shoot. He spurred his horse toward her, releasing a cursing roar.

A brush of her heels sent Bella lunging forward. She lifted her rifle and snapped off a shot, praying she'd hit her mark. The man jerked and blood blossomed on his arm, but he kept coming.

An answering shot rang out. Sharp pain ripped through the fleshy part of her shoulder.

A bellow of fierce satisfaction flew from Hinson's mouth.

Angel gripped the saddle horn, struggling to maintain her seat and not slip into the darkness tugging at her mind. Bella settled into a trot and moved to the side toward a scant patch of grass. The last thing Angel remembered before sliding from her saddle was the grinning Bart Hinson moving up alongside her mare.

Chapter Thirty-Three

....

Travis hauled back hard on his horse's mouth and slid to a stop, horror rising inside. Angel had fallen from her horse, and a man was swinging down alongside her. His cowboys had already accounted for one dead rustler, and the herd of stampeding cattle took care of another. Arizona and Wren were hard on the heels of two who had fled, and his other cowhands were heading off the exhausted cattle. That left the hombre standing over Angel.

White-hot anger filled him. He'd seen Angel wing the rustler and the man pull his pistol, getting off a shot before Travis could so much as lift his gun.

He lashed Raven's sides. "Yaw!" The big black leapt forward, and Travis lifted his pistol. The rustler bent over Angel's prone form, and Travis let loose with a round. It fell short, clipping the grass alongside the man's leg.

The big man jumped sideways, and an ugly oath rolled from his mouth. He turned, gun in hand.

Travis kept his horse moving, guiding him with one hand and using his knees to urge him forward, while his other hand kept a firm grip on his gun. Another fifty feet and he'd be close enough to land a shot.

Ping! The whip of a bullet zipped past his ear. Another report sounded, louder this time, and his hat flew from his head. His scalp burned, and something warm trickled down the side of his face. He pushed the discomfort aside and raised his pistol again. Angel. What if his bullet hit Angel instead of the rustler? Holstering his weapon, he leaned low in the saddle, his mind racing. Another minute and he'd be there.

The outlaw leaned over Angel one last time, then swung away and grabbed his horse's reins, pulling him to the side. He put his foot in the stirrup and started to rise. Travis called for more speed. Raven jumped a small wash and barreled across the clearing where Angel lay.

Travis dragged the stallion to a stop and catapulted from his saddle, launching himself and hitting the rustler full force. Raven trotted away, and the outlaw's horse jumped sideways, almost trampling the men as they somersaulted across the ground.

Travis rolled onto his knees and pushed to his feet. He leaned down and grabbed the man's shirt. The rustler groaned and slowly pulled his gun from his belt. Travis kicked it out of his hand, then yanked him to a standing position.

Suddenly, the outlaw lashed out with his good arm. His doubled fist caught Travis full in the stomach. Pain shot through Travis's middle, and he doubled over. Another blow landed on the back of his head and he fell to his knees, struggling to shake off the throbbing. If this man got away, they'd probably never find him again. He had to pay for what he'd done to Angel. The cattle didn't matter, but Travis had a horrible feeling he'd lost the woman he loved. He threw all of his strength into standing and made one last charge, throwing his arms around the man's knees and knocking him to the ground.

They tumbled across the ground, fists pounding and boots kicking. Travis landed several hard punches to his opponent's body. The rustler seemed to lose steam, and his swings grew weaker, only occasionally finding their mark.

Hooves entering the clearing gave Travis a renewed burst of energy. One of the other outlaws might be returning. It was time to end this. He drew back his arm and let loose with a mighty swing, connecting with the man's bloody face. A loud crack echoed as Travis made contact with his chin, and the outlaw fell unconscious at his feet.

Travis leapt forward and scooped up the pistol he'd kicked out of the way and turned, holding it in front of him.

Nate swung down from his horse a few yards away. He dropped the reins, cast a glance at Travis, and rushed over to Angel. "How bad is she?"

"I don't know. This hombre shot her and was getting away when I rode in."

"Yeah, I saw you finish him off." Nate leaned over the prostrate girl. "She's bleeding bad."

Travis tore his bandana from around his neck. "Give me yours." He held out his hand and grabbed the one Nate held out. "No good. They're both filthy. You got anything else?"

Nate jogged to his horse and came back a moment later, holding a clean towel. "I keep an old one in my saddlebag."

"Tear a piece off. We've got to stop the bleeding and get her to the ranch."

As soon as Nate finished, Travis grabbed the cloth, opened the top buttons of her shirt, and pressed it against the wound high up in her shoulder. "Tear the rest in half and knot it together."

Nate did as instructed and handed the long piece to Travis.

"Now help hold her up so I can get this wrapped around her chest." They worked together for several long minutes without speaking. Finally, Travis sat back on his heels as Nate carefully laid Angel back on the ground. "The bleeding could start up again, but we've got a chance. How about the men?"

Nate looked up. "Arizona and Wren shot another of the rustlers, and they captured the last one. Wren took a bullet in the arm but it's not serious. Looks like we've got two to take to the sheriff."

"Good. You, Arizona, and Wren get this carcass loaded on a horse, but make sure you tie him good and proper. We don't want him waking and getting away."

"Looks like you winged him. Want I should tie up the wound?"

Travis grunted. He didn't care if the man died from blood loss, but the sheriff might appreciate a live prisoner over a dead one. "Yeah. But I didn't shoot him, Angel did. Just before he clipped her."

Nate's mouth firmed in a harsh line. "Plucky girl, our Angel. Wish she'd shot him dead center, though."

"Yeah, but I'd hate to have his blood on her hands. Find Charlie or Bud and send one of them to town for the doctor. Tell him I don't care if he has to ride the horse into the ground. Get there fast and get the doc back to the ranch."

"You taking Angel?"

"Yes." Travis stood. "Help me get her into the saddle, and I'll sit behind her. I'm praying Libby and Maria will be able to pull her through."

Nate nodded. "I'll be praying, as well. God loves her. Don't forget that."

Travis wiped his hands down his pant legs. His fingers had started to swell, and he hoped he'd be able to hold Angel and the reins, but he wasn't giving this precious cargo to anyone else. "I won't. On second thought, send Bud after the doc and have Charlie come with me. Just in case I need him."

"You got it." He turned to leave then swung back again. "How 'bout the cattle?"

"They don't matter right now. Once we get these two to the sheriff and take care of Angel, you and the men can return and bring them back to the pasture near the spring." He leaned over Angel and signaled Nate to come close. "Help me lift her." He turned to his foreman. "I can't lose her, Nate. I'll string up that low-down rustler myself, if she dies."

"Hold onto your faith, Travis. God hasn't failed you yet, and I don't think He's going to start now."

Chapter Thirty-Four

....

Travis waited for Charlie to dismount in front of the ranch house, then slipped off his horse, keeping his arms around Angel. Charlie stood on the other side, balancing her until Travis drew her into his arms.

Travis lifted his voice in a shout. "Libby. Maria. We need you out here."

The front door banged open, and Libby ran across the porch. "What's happened? How bad is she?"

"She's been shot. Lost a lot of blood. It's not good, Lib."

Libby gasped. Her fingers came to her mouth, and she straightened. "All right. Let's get her inside to her bed." She turned to the gaping boy standing on the steps. "James. Ask Maria to heat water and then find clean rags. Tear up some of our towels if you have to, but make sure we have plenty."

Maria came out as James bolted back inside. "*Dio mio*! Oh please, God, help us!" A sob broke from her lips, and she seemed to wilt against the nearby post.

Travis cradled Angel in his arms and made his way past Maria. "Hurry, now. There's no time for tears if we're going to save her. Help Libby."

Maria nodded and held open the door. The next minutes passed in a haze as Travis carefully laid Angel on her bed. Libby waved him from the room. "We've got to take her clothes off, Trav, and wash the dried blood from the wound so we can see what we're dealing with."

Travis waited outside Angel's door, pacing up and down the short hall. It felt like a lifetime but must've been only thirty minutes later when Libby stepped out of the room. Travis swung toward her, fear warring with hope in his chest. "Well?"

Libby took his hands and pressed them between hers. "I can't tell much, but it doesn't appear that the bullet hit any vital organs. Did you send for the doctor?"

"Yes. Bud went after him. I don't know what's taking them so long, but they should be here soon." He stalked to the front door. James's puppy set up a frantic yapping outside on the porch and, moments later, Travis heard horses traveling at a rapid gait up the lane. He stepped onto the porch and patted the dog while keeping an eye on the road. "Good boy, Dakota. You might make a decent watch dog, yet."

Bud and the doctor reined their horses in at the rail and swung from their saddles. The doctor untied his bag from behind the cantle. "Bud tells me Miss Ramirez is hurt again. Gunshot, is it?"

"Yes. She got shot trying to save our cattle from a band of rustlers."

The doctor labored up the steps and headed for the front door. "I know where her room is. I'll send your sister out with a report once I know anything." He bustled into the house, letting the door bang shut behind him.

* * * * *

Angel woke to the smell of blood and dirt. Memories rushed back almost faster than she could field them. The capture by Hinson. The cattle drive. Travis and the cowboys coming up behind the herd and opening fire. Hinson's look of purpose and arrogance as he sighted down his gun at her heart. The sting of the bullet as it penetrated her body and she fell from her horse. Sinking into unconsciousness knowing the outlaw was nearby…

Where was she now? She rolled her head against something soft. Not the ground. She tried to touch it, but her arm wouldn't move. Teeth-grinding pain shot through her shoulder, and she moaned.

"There now, honey, don't try to move. You're home." Libby's voice, soothing and comforting. "Can you open your eyes?"

Angel struggled to comply and finally fluttered her lashes a couple of times, trying to focus on the person hovering above her. She licked her lips. "Libby?" The question came out with a croak.

"Shh." Libby smoothed the hair off her forehead. "You're safe. You need to rest."

"Travis?"

"He's safe as well. All the men came home."

Angel plucked at the covers with her free hand. "I don't want to see him yet. Please."

"Whatever you say, honey. Don't fret now."

"Hinson?"

Libby puckered her brow. "I don't know who that is."

"The outlaw leader—" Angel struggled to speak and tried to swallow. "Who stole Travis's cattle. Is he dead?"

"No. They captured him and took him to the sheriff's office, along with another one of his men."

Angel sank against the pillow and moaned. She'd only winged the man when she'd taken a shot at him but had prayed he'd be killed in the fray. He'd spill his guts to the sheriff to save his own hide. It was only a matter of time until she landed in jail.

Libby reached for a glass on the table next to the bed. "Here.

Drink." She slipped her hand under Angel's neck, lifted her head, then eased her back against the pillow. "No more talking. The doctor says you're going to recover, but he still needs to get the bullet out. You're weak from blood loss and need to stay in bed a few days, but otherwise, you'll heal."

"How long has it been?"

"Just a few hours."

Angel nodded and closed her eyes, then opened them a little. "Thank you."

Libby smiled. "For what?"

"For caring about me."

* * * * *

Sometime later Maria exited Angel's room carrying a pan of red-tinged water. Travis took it and hefted it outside the back door, then reentered the kitchen. "Does Doc need more?"

"No. He is done dressing the wound." Maria sank into a chair and wiped her forehead with the back of her sleeve. "Such agony that young one went through as the doctor probed for the bullet. But she did not speak a word—just clenched her teeth and closed her eyes."

"She's awake?" Travis wanted to race down the hall and see for himself, but he clamped down on his emotions. He had no idea what her condition was or when it might be safe to see her.

"Sí. But the doctor tells Libby that Angel must rest and not be disturbed." She laid gentle fingers on his sleeve. "I am sorry. I see your worry. You care for her, no?"

"I do. Very much." Travis patted the wrinkled hand. "I love her, Maria, and I asked her to be my wife, but she turned me down."

"But why? I have seen her eyes when she looks at you. I thought—perhaps…"

He shrugged. "So did I. She said she doesn't care for me in that way, and she's returning with you to Italy."

"Ah. That is the first time I have heard this, Signor. It would not be the right thing for her to do."

He raised his brows. "You wanted her to come live with you."

"Sí. But not at the expense of her happiness. She runs from something. I have felt that for some time now. Maybe it is fear. Maybe it is love. I do not know. I think it will be up to you to find out." She smiled and stepped away. "I go to help Smokey with the meal, and later I will sit with my granddaughter." Her bright eyes sparkled. "I do not know how that man ran his kitchen before I came." She tsked over the last words and disappeared into the kitchen.

Libby opened Angel's door and ushered the doctor out before her. "Thank you for coming. You'll stop by again in the morning?"

"Certainly." He turned to Travis. "I should take a look at that graze on your head."

Travis held up his hand. "I'm fine. A bit of a headache is all, but Libby will tend to it."

"That's a plucky young woman."

"So Signora de Luca told me."

The doctor nodded and shifted his bag in his hand. "I'll see you tomorrow." He strode to the door and stepped outside without looking back.

Libby moved up alongside Travis. "There's something you need to hear."

"Oh?" Travis wrenched his thoughts from Angel and focused on Libby. "What's that?"

"Angel said something rather strange."

Travis's senses went on alert. "Strange how?"

Libby hesitated and twisted a strand of hair between her fingers. "She knew the outlaw's name that you captured. Did you tell her?"

"No." Travis frowned, trying to think back. "She was unconscious when we discovered their names. How would she know Bart Hinson?"

"I don't know. I told her he'd been captured, and she seemed to wilt."

He stepped away and headed down the hall. "That does it. I'm getting to the bottom of this."

"Wait, Travis." Libby's stern voice hit him square in the back.

He halted and did a quarter turn. "What?"

"Angel told me she doesn't want to see you."

His heart plummeted. "Did she say why?"

"No. She simply asked that you not come anytime soon. I think it's important you respect that request."

"Fine." He spun on his heel and stalked past her.

"Where are you going?"

"It's high time I paid a visit to the sheriff. Maybe this Bart Hinson can shed some light on Angel's behavior."

Chapter Thirty-Five

....

Angel sat up against the headboard and creased the blanket just above her waist. A week had passed since she'd been shot, and her wound was healing nicely. For the last several days the only people she'd seen were Grandmother and Libby. One time James poked his head in the door to say hello, but Libby shooed him away.

A couple of times she'd heard Travis's voice in the hallway outside her room, but he'd never attempted to enter. She longed to know if he'd come to see her but couldn't bring herself to ask. As soon as she was well, the sheriff would be at their door. If Travis didn't already know about her deception and sordid past, he would soon enough. She couldn't bear to see his disappointment and hurt.

She'd watched Libby and Grandmother closely but hadn't seen any sign of censure. That could change any time. If only she'd been able to leave with Grandmother before Hinson arrived in Wyoming territory.

It was a good thing she hadn't accepted Travis's proposal—the risk of being found out was too great—and she couldn't imagine the shame she'd feel if she'd married him and the outlaw had appeared.

No, it was better this way. Travis would go on with his life and find some good, solid, Christian woman to marry. Even though she'd come to believe that God was real and loved her, she didn't have the clean background Libby and Travis had, and could never measure up to what he deserved in a wife.

A quiet knock sounded at her door, and she turned toward it. Hope surged in her heart, but dread followed quickly on its heels. "Come in."

Libby stepped inside. "The doctor is here."

"Oh." Angel didn't know whether to shout for joy or sink in despair. Once she got out of bed, the end would come soon. If only she could stay here forever, safe in Travis's home. "Send him in."

* * * * *

Travis paced in front of the barn, worry gnawing at his gut. The cowboys had stayed clear of him lately, and he couldn't blame them. He'd been as crotchety as a hungry bear coming out of hibernation. Nate had taken over most of the ranch duties, and even James had stepped into the gap, offering to help. The boy had been working with his pup and the dog appeared to be turning into a good herding animal. Looked like his nephew and Dakota might grow up to be a first-rate fit for the ranch, after all.

He mulled over all he'd learned the past four days. The trip to the sheriff hadn't been enlightening. In fact, the officer of the law had been close-mouthed, stating he had questions for Angel of his own.

At first Travis had fumed at Angel's rebuff, then sorrow and longing set in. Did she dislike him so much, or was Maria right about Angel running from something? Looked like it had to do with her past, and from all appearances, it could poison her future.

The front door slammed. Doc Simmons walked across the porch and headed for his buggy. Travis sprinted across the clearing. "Hold up there, Doc. What did you decide about Angel?"

The doctor paused and brushed at a fly. "She's healing well. I told her she could get up tomorrow and sit in the living room or at the table for short spells, but she's not to tire herself. I have a feeling that young woman would saddle her horse and go back to scouring the brush for varmints if someone didn't hold her down."

Travis grinned. "She would at that. Don't worry; we'll keep an eye on her."

"Good. See that you do." The doctor swung into his buggy and picked up the reins. "I'll check back in a couple of days, but I don't think she'll need me past that. Good day, Travis."

"To you, as well." He raised his hand and stepped back out of the cloud of dust kicked up by the wheels. Angel would be up tomorrow. She could no longer hide in her room. He had a few things to say to that young woman, and he'd be jiggered if he'd let anyone stand in his way.

* * * * *

The following morning Angel shuffled carefully into the living room, leaning on Libby's arm. She hated looking like a weakling who couldn't walk on her own, but the past days in bed had left her as feeble as a newborn fawn. At least Doc Simmons agreed to let her get up. As much as she wanted to keep hiding in her room, she was sick of staring at the same four walls. Guilt niggled at her mind. She couldn't complain about her forced confinement. Libby and Grandmother had been wonderful, and Smokey had cooked some of the finest meals she could imagine.

"Little one. You are out of bed!" Grandmother peered into the room and smiled. "May I bring you a cup of tea? Smokey has the kettle on, and I would love to join you."

Angel sank onto the sofa with a soft grunt. "That would be nice."

Libby touched her hair and then withdrew. "I'll leave the two of you alone."

"There's no need. Why don't you join us?"

Libby gave a quick shake of her head. "Nate's waiting outside. We're taking a walk by the creek."

"Ah." Angel felt at a loss for words. She hadn't thought about Nate in days. "Have a wonderful time."

"Thank you." Libby slipped from the room at the same moment Grandmother entered. She carried a tray with a teapot, napkins, and two cups and saucers.

Angel reached for the tray and winced. "Ouch. Guess I'm not ready for that yet. I'm sorry I can't help."

"Nonsense. You sit and rest. I love pouring tea and waiting on my favorite granddaughter."

Angel grinned. "Aren't I your only granddaughter?"

"Yes. But I am very certain you would be my favorite if I had many more, so hush." Grandmother's eyes held a merry twinkle. She set the tray on a low, round table between them and picked up the teapot, pouring the steaming liquid into the cups. She placed the cup and saucer within easy reach of Angel. "So. I have much to tell you, now that you are better."

Angel straightened. Grandmother had already informed her a couple of weeks ago that she planned to return to Italy. What else could she have to share? "All right. I'd love to hear your news." She folded her hands in her lap.

Grandmother set her cup down. "I have made a decision." She paused, letting the words bounce around the room and settle. "I will stay here. I do not go back to my home country."

"What?" Angel gripped the arm of the sofa, delight sparking in her heart. "Here? In America? On the ranch? What changed your mind?"

"Slow down, mia. One question at a time, sí?" She crossed her arms, but a warm smile lit her face. "Yes, in America. Maybe on the ranch; that is yet to be decided." She tossed a smile toward the kitchen before her gaze darted back to Angel. "Why? Let us just say there are…interesting people in this land." Her smile widened. "And, my darling girl, you are the most important reason of all. Your heart is here." She waved her hand in the air. "You do not wish to leave, and I do not wish to return without you."

"But Grandmother, Italy is your home. Won't you be lonely if you stay here?"

"No. I have you, and others, who I have come to care about. Besides, I understand things about you that I did not see when I came."

Angel lifted the cup and took a sip. "What kind of things?"

"You are a strong woman, my Angel. That did not happen by accident. Your parents and uncle had much to do with your growth, but so did this magnificent land of your birth. You and the land, they are one. Do you see that? Just like you and Travis."

Angel choked on the tea and nearly toppled the rest of her drink onto her lap. She set it down, wiped her mouth with a napkin, and raised her gaze. "I'm not sure why you think that, but Travis and I—" She shook her head, not sure how to continue. Her heart hurt just saying his name.

Grandmother grasped the arms of her chair and pushed to her feet. "It is time to quit running, little one. You need to face who you are, and where you have come from." She looked over Angel's head at something behind her, and back at Angel. "Someone is here to see you. We will talk more of this later, if there is still need." She leaned over, placed a gentle kiss on Angel's cheek, and stood, sweeping from the room.

Chapter Thirty-Six

....

Angel shifted in her seat and tried to peek over her shoulder but couldn't quite twist that far. Tiny stabs of pain assaulted her and she sank back against the sofa, letting it cradle her body. "Who's there?" Libby would've said something by now, and James didn't know how to keep quiet. A small shudder shook her. *Travis.*

"Hello, Angel. May I join you?" He walked around the end of the sofa and stopped a stride away, his hat clutched in his hands.

Panic set her heart to thumping. "I suppose. Although I'm a bit tired and was thinking about going to my room."

"I understand. I'll try not to take too much time." He glanced around the room, then settled into the chair Grandmother had vacated. "How are you feeling? I haven't had a chance to talk to you since your injury."

Angel shifted in her seat, suddenly uncomfortable. She prayed he wouldn't question her about the cattle raid. "Better, thank you. It's nice to be up." She stifled a groan. Here she'd just said she wanted to return to her room, then implied she'd rather stay up.

"I'd like to ask you some questions." He propped his boot on top of his knee and leaned back in the chair.

A knock sounded against the archway, and Libby entered. "Sorry to disturb you, but Angel has a visitor."

Angel didn't know whether to feel relief at the reprieve, or dismay at the chance of something worse happening. "Who's here, Libby?"

Travis rose from his seat and took a step forward. "Sheriff Jensen. I didn't expect to see you today."

The sheriff strode into the room and met Travis's outstretched hand, giving it a hearty shake. "Sorry I didn't send word, but I was coming out this way and decided it might be wise to stop by. Doc Simmons mentioned he'd given Miss Ramirez permission to be up. I hoped to speak with her." He nodded at Angel. "If you don't mind, Miss?"

Angel clenched her teeth and tried not to bolt from her seat. Her body began shaking, and she couldn't seem to stop.

Travis gazed at her, alarm written across his face. "I don't think that's a good idea, Sheriff. Miss Ramirez isn't feeling well. She needs to go back to her room." He leaned toward Angel and held out his hand.

A flood of peace washed over Angel's heart. She'd asked God more than once to help her straighten out her life. Maybe He was giving her a chance to do so now. "Thank you, but I believe I'll stay and speak to the sheriff."

His brows rose, and he straightened. "I'll leave the two of you alone then."

She held out her hand. "Don't leave. I'd like you to hear what I have to say."

He hesitated and nodded. "All right. Sheriff." Travis waved at the empty chair. "Have a seat."

Sheriff Jensen sank into the padded leather chair. "I appreciate this, Miss Ramirez. I'm hoping you can clear up some confusion caused by some rather, shall we say, unusual accusations Bart Hinson has lodged against you."

"Hinson?" Travis gripped the arms of his chair. "That no good, low-down rustler? You'd believe anything that man has to say about Angel?"

"Hold it." The sheriff held up a warning hand. "I didn't say I believe him, only that he's made some strange statements. That's all."

Travis settled back in his seat but kept his grip on the chair. "All right. But I won't tolerate any disrespect."

"Understood." He turned to Angel. "Hinson claims you were part of his band a few years ago. That you rode with him and his men on more than one occasion when they rustled cattle. Can you explain that?"

Angel laced her fingers together and gripped tight, hoping to quiet their shaking. "I can. My uncle raised me in an outlaw band after my parents died."

A gasp sounded from the open doorway; something hit the floor and shattered. Angel turned to the side and groaned. Grandmother stood frozen, gazing at the shards of broken glass at her feet. "I am sorry. I did not mean—it slipped, somehow."

Travis leapt to his feet and hurried to her side. "Please don't worry, Maria. I'll ask Smokey to clean it up."

"No, no. I should do it, not him." Grandmother stooped over, but Travis grasped her arm.

"I think you should sit down and hear what Angel has to say." He glanced over her head at Angel, and she gave a slow nod. "It wouldn't be fair to ask you to leave now."

"All right. If you are sure, my dear?" Grandmother turned an entreating gaze on Angel.

"Yes. You need to understand. Come," she patted the seat on the sofa next to her, "sit by me."

Grandmother made her way around the broken cup, and Travis took his seat, not seeming to care about the mess.

Angel coiled her fingers around Grandmother's hand and squeezed. "I'm sorry I haven't told you this before. I didn't want to hurt you. I see now that I have, in spite of everything."

"No, mia. It was just a surprise, that is all. Please, go ahead with your story." Grandmother sat a little straighter.

"After Mama and Papa died, Uncle José took me in. Papa had worked with him rounding up unbranded mavericks running loose on the range. Papa and José knew that wasn't a crime, and the pay was good. After Papa died, José couldn't work alone, and he needed to provide for me. He met a man who promised him big money if he'd fall in with their band. The job lasted for several months. Finally, they moved to a new spot and started again, and several men joined the group."

Sheriff Jensen sat forward. "Was Bart Hinson part of that group?"

Angel shook her head. "No. He came later. After a while, José noticed an occasional branded calf mixed in, but the boss assured him they'd be cut out and returned to the range. My uncle believed him and forgot about the calves. Weeks later, it happened again, with the same explanation. After a few months, José began to wonder. The boss laughed and said Uncle was a fool to believe they'd only sell unbranded mavericks. He claimed José was in too deep to back out, as they'd been stealing branded stock for over a year and he'd be hung along with them if they were caught."

Travis nodded. "There's many an honest cowpoke that started that way, and ended up getting greedy. Why didn't your uncle saddle up and ride, rather than stay and keep at it?"

"Fear for me. By this time I was ten years old, and he knew it wouldn't be long before I'd be turning men's heads. If he tried to leave, the outlaws might kill him, and I'd be left unprotected. He decided to stay and work with the rustlers."

The sheriff laced his hands around his knee and leaned back. "Hinson claimed you rode with them on their raids. That true?"

"Only once, on the last one. Four years ago José got worried. Hinson broke into my room one night, and my uncle found him standing over my bed as I slept. He was drunk and hadn't touched me. That's the only reason José didn't kill him on the spot—that and because Hinson had several men who'd sworn their allegiance to him. Killing Hinson would have gotten my uncle killed and left me alone."

"Makes sense, but I'm a mite surprised your uncle still didn't plug him." The sheriff shrugged. "So what happened to make you ride with the men?"

"A few months after finding Hinson in my room Uncle José decided I should leave the band. He told me to pack my saddlebag and be ready to ride." Angel shuddered as the memories rushed over her. "We drove the herd through the early hours of the morning, and shortly after first light a posse rode up on our tail, led by a Texas Ranger. They opened fire, and I fled for the brush. José followed but was shot." She choked on the words and placed her fingers over her lips.

Grandmother patted her arm. "There, there, mia. It will be all right. Just go slow and tell us only what you must."

"No. I need to tell you all of it." Angel sucked in a sharp breath. "Hinson shot a Texas Ranger in the back."

Grandmother fell against the back of the sofa. "Oh, dear heavens!"

The men remained silent, but their eyes were locked on Angel.

She plucked at a thread on the edge of her shirt, then raised her gaze and met the sheriff's. "I bound José's wound, and he went back to the fight. He told me he'd buy me as much time as he could and keep Hinson from following me. The entire posse died that day, and some of the men. I made for the hills. I've been running ever since, at first disguised as a man and hiring out as a varmint hunter from New Mexico to Wyoming territory." She shot a glance at Travis and tried to smile. "But I got sick of being a boy and decided to live as a woman when I got to this ranch. Travis almost didn't hire me, but I'm so thankful he decided to take a chance."

A pinched smile worked its way across Travis's lips. "So am I. But I wish it hadn't been under such awful circumstances."

Sheriff Jensen nodded. "I agree. But I need to know one more thing. What were you doing with Hinson's men when they stole the Sundance Ranch cattle?"

Travis edged to the front of his chair. "I'm satisfied she wasn't helping them steal my stock. Can't we let it go at that?"

"No. We need the entire story."

Angel licked her lips. "I agree. Hinson gave Uncle José the slip and started hunting me not long after the band split. He found me on the range and told me I had to help him steal the cattle, or he'd kill all of you. He had one of his men set the fire and attack Smokey. I knew he was capable of murder, so I agreed." She shot a look at Travis. "I knew it was wrong, but I was so afraid for the people I'd come to love. I prayed, asking God to take charge of my life and help me, and He did. That's all. I guess I'm guilty of cattle rustling."

Sheriff Jensen turned to Travis. "You told me she took a shot at Hinson when you rode up, is that correct?"

"Yes, sir. She hit him."

"So Miss Ramirez was trying to prevent the theft of your cattle, not aid in the rustling. That the way you see it?"

A slow grin chased away the fear that had lodged there seconds ago. "It sure is, Sheriff."

The sheriff pushed to his feet and plucked his hat from a nearby table. "My business here is finished." He gave a slight bow. "Ladies, enjoy your day. And Miss Ramirez, I hope you recover quickly. We'll need you to testify at Hinson's trial, although no doubt he'll be found guilty and hanged." He placed his hat on his head and walked to the door without looking back.

Chapter Thirty-Seven
....

Travis stared at the sheriff as he disappeared through the doorway, then pushed to his feet. "Guess I shoulda seen him out." He ran his hand over his hair, still feeling a bit muddled at Angel's story.

Grandmother cleared her throat, and Travis blinked a couple of times. "Young man, help me to my feet. I will find Smokey and get that mess cleaned up. You should take my granddaughter outside in the fresh air, is that not right?"

He scratched his chin and smiled. "Yeah."

Maria leaned over, whispered something low in Angel's ear, and brushed the hair off her forehead, placing a firm kiss there. "Quit running, little one. It's time to trust God."

Travis heard the words with only half his mind. He still couldn't quite take in everything he'd heard. Angel had been raised in an outlaw gang, and Hinson had been after her all this time? A slow rage built in his gut and threatened to choke him. He shook himself and pushed down the anger. No need to let hatred take root in his heart. God would judge the man's sins.

Angel sat still, staring at her hands twisted in her lap.

Travis wanted to haul her to her feet and envelop her in a hug, but he didn't know if she'd accept his touch. Hadn't she made it clear she didn't care for him the way he cared for her? A sudden thought struck him. She'd been running from her past for years. Was it possible her rejection had been due to her fear of discovery? And hadn't he just heard her say she'd lied to protect the people she loved? Hope emerged like a butterfly trying to escape a cocoon.

"Angel? Will you spend a few minutes outside on the porch?"

"I suppose." She didn't look up but put her good arm under her and tried to push up off the sofa.

Travis held out his hand. She hesitated, then placed her small one in his. He didn't let go once she got on her feet but tucked her hand under the crook of his elbow and squeezed it against his side. "Come on. Smokey will come in soon, and I'd like to get outside before he decides to start visiting."

Angel nodded but kept silent. They made their way through the house and out the front door. She sank onto the end of a porch swing with a high back and sighed.

Travis looked at the space next to her with longing. He hooked his toe around the leg of a chair, pulling it close, and sank onto it. "Angel?"

She kept her head down and didn't respond.

"What are you afraid of? The sheriff said you're in the clear. He's not holding you responsible for your uncle's decisions or what happened with Hinson. Shouldn't you be celebrating?"

She shrugged. "I suppose."

"What is it?" He touched her hand, but she drew back and tucked it between her legs. Frustration welled up inside. "Why won't you look at me, or let me touch you? Maria told me she's not returning to Italy, so I know you're not leaving. What's wrong?"

Angel raised tortured eyes to his. "I figured you and Libby would hate me. Grandmother forgives me because I'm her daughter's only child. Why should either of you?"

He sat back in his chair and stared. "There's nothing to forgive."

She wrung her hands in her lap. "I deceived you—I didn't tell you the truth about my past." She shivered. "I let that man steal your cattle and hurt Smokey. I asked God to forgive me and I think He did, but I don't deserve your forgiveness."

He took her hand, and this time she didn't resist. "None of us deserve to be forgiven, but God does it all the time when we ask Him to. As far as I'm concerned, you did nothing wrong. But if it makes you feel better, of course I forgive you." He squeezed her fingers, raised her hand to his lips, and pressed them against her palm.

Her chin jerked up, and she gasped. "Travis?"

"Honey, haven't you figured it out?" He placed another gentle kiss on her palm. "I'm in love with you. I told you before, but I don't think you believed me, or you were too frightened to accept it. I'm hoping you'll find it in your heart to care about me a little in return."

Her hand trembled in his, and her eyes pooled with tears. "I do care."

Travis's heart beat like a runaway horse, and he struggled to breathe. "How much, Angel?"

She looked him full in the face and didn't answer but slowly lifted the hand cupped over hers to her lips. Keeping her gaze locked on his, she pressed her lips against his knuckles. "That much."

Travis smiled and gave a slight shake of his head. "Ah, that's a good start. But I had something a bit—bigger—in mind." He stood and settled down beside Angel, keeping hold of her hand. He extended his other hand, placing it on her good arm, and turned her toward him.

Her deep brown eyes glowed. "Bigger? I don't understand."

"Let me show you." Travis loosened his hold and placed his fingertips under her chin. "You are the most stubborn—" He leaned in close and touched his lips to her forehead. "Independent—" Another kiss found its way onto her cheek. Travis could feel the heat in her skin and smiled. "Beautiful—" This time he hovered over her mouth for a second, then bent to touch her lips, drinking in their sweetness.

She loosened her hold on his hand and slipped one arm around his neck, drawing him close.

The kiss continued and deepened, and Travis felt his control starting to slip. He tamped down his desire and withdrew a few inches, then reached up and touched her face. His fingers lingered on her soft skin, stroking down her cheek and stopping at her chin. More than anything he longed to get lost in another kiss. "I need to ask you something, and this time I hope you'll give me a different answer."

Dreamy eyes gazed into his. "What?"

"Marry me. I love you, Angel. You're everything I've ever hoped for in a wife, and more. I'd be eternally happy if you'd say yes."

"Yes." She leaned into him and raised her lips.

Travis couldn't resist. He met hers with an eagerness he wouldn't deny.

Angel was the first to pull away this time, her face rosy and a smile tipping up her thoroughly kissed lips. "How about Libby?"

"What about her?"

"She might not want me moving in permanently. I don't want to upset her. She *is* the lady of the house, you know."

Travis shook his head. "You don't have to worry about Lib. Nate proposed to her. He told me she turned him down."

Angel gasped. "What! Why?"

"She didn't want to leave me alone. He told me to hurry up and throw a lasso around you, so he could tie the knot with Libby." Travis grinned. "She'll be only too happy to move to her own house. Of course, the men and I will have to help build them one, but I think he's earned it."

"I can't cook, you know." Angel cocked her head to the side. "Are you sure you don't want to back out?"

"That's why I hired Smokey." He started to lean forward again, but she placed her hand against his chest.

"You haven't noticed?"

He raised an eyebrow. "What?"

"Smokey and Grandmother."

"Huh?" He felt like he'd been bucked off a bronco.

She giggled and nodded. "I think they've fallen for each other, and that's why she doesn't want to go back to Italy."

Travis threw back his head and laughed. When he finally came up for air, he pulled her close and placed his cheek against hers. "Good. We'll build them a house too, if we need to. It will be nice to have your grandmother close by, and Smokey can keep on cooking for all of us." He placed a gentle kiss on her lips. "Any more reasons you can't marry me?"

She shook her head, and her good arm crept around his neck. "Can't think of a single one, Signor Morgan. I'm plumb out of excuses. This Angel has come home for good."

Author's Note

....

Each book I've written for the Love Finds You™ series has been carefully researched as to place, setting, and time period, but this one was a little different. Due to an unexpectedly quick deadline, I did not have the chance to visit the museums and historical society in the town, take photos of the surrounding area, or do the in-depth research that typically accompanies one of my books, but I believe you'll enjoy the story just the same.

None of the characters in the book are based on real people other than Butch Cassidy and the Sundance Kid. The businesses mentioned in the town of Sundance were actual businesses, and the Church of the Good Shepherd Episcopal church was built in 1889.

Other than Sundance, The Wild Bunch, and the Hole-in-the-Wall gang, there is only one character in the book that's real—the puppy Dakota. So far I've featured three of our family's dogs in my books. The first was my daughter and son-in-law's shepherd Hunter, who died of cancer a year ago; he appeared in *Love Finds You in Last Chance, California*. Then came Buck, a black lab we owned many years ago, who appeared as Art Gibbs's dog in *Love Finds You in Bridal Veil, Oregon* (Art was my great-grandfather and did have a big black dog, but we're not sure of his name). Dakota was a Border Collie/Australian Shepherd rescue puppy we got fifteen years ago who passed away almost a year ago. We miss them all, and I'm thrilled they'll live on in my stories.

I'd had the idea for this book but only knew there would be a young woman raised in an outlaw band. I had no concept what she looked like or what her name might be. While drifting off to sleep one night, I saw a distinct picture of a black-haired woman in her early twenties with small bones, fine features, and wide, dark eyes. She proceeded to say, "My name is Angel. Angel Ramirez." So, there you have it. I didn't name Angel; she introduced herself to me.

I'd love to hear from you, so pop over to my website at www.miraleeferrell.com and drop me a note.

About the Author

....

Miralee Ferrell grew up in a small town and married Allen, her high school sweetheart. They raised two children, who both serve the Lord. After they left home, she prayed about filling her time. In 2005 she received the answer. While at church the pastor prayed with her, stating he believed God was calling her to write and be published. After praying, she embarked on a new adventure. Two years later her debut novel, *The Other Daughter,* released, and since then five more novels have followed.

Miralee serves as president of the Portland, Oregon, chapter of ACFW. She speaks at women's groups, libraries, historical societies, and churches.

Allen and Miralee have been married for thirty-eight years. They live on eleven acres in Washington State, where they love to garden, play with their dogs, and go sailing. Miralee also rides her horse on the trails near their home with her daughter, who lives nearby.

You can visit Miralee's website to find out more about her books and her life, and find photos of the towns she's visited while doing research for her Love Finds You™ books.

WWW.MIRALEEFERRELL.COM

**Want a peek into local American life—past and present?
The *Love Finds You*™ series published by Summerside Press
features real towns and combines travel, romance,
and faith in one irresistible package!**

The novels in the series—uniquely titled after American towns with romantic
or intriguing names—inspire romance and fun. Each fictional story draws on
the compelling history or the unique character of a real place. Stories center on
romances kindled in small towns, old loves lost and found again on the high plains,
and new loves discovered at exciting vacation getaways. Summerside Press plans
to publish at least one novel set in each of the fifty states. Be sure to catch them all!

Now Available

Love Finds You in Miracle, Kentucky
by Andrea Boeshaar
ISBN: 978-1-934770-37-5

*Love Finds You in Snowball,
Arkansas*
by Sandra D. Bricker
ISBN: 978-1-934770-45-0

Love Finds You in Romeo, Colorado
by Gwen Ford Faulkenberry
ISBN: 978-1-934770-46-7

*Love Finds You in Valentine,
Nebraska*
by Irene Brand
ISBN: 978-1-934770-38-2

Love Finds You in Humble, Texas
by Anita Higman
ISBN: 978-1-934770-61-0

*Love Finds You
in Last Chance, California*
by Miralee Ferrell
ISBN: 978-1-934770-39-9

*Love Finds You in
Maiden, North Carolina*
by Tamela Hancock Murray
ISBN: 978-1-934770-65-8

*Love Finds You
in Paradise, Pennsylvania*
by Loree Lough
ISBN: 978-1-934770-66-5

*Love Finds You in
Treasure Island, Florida*
by Debby Mayne
ISBN: 978-1-934770-80-1

*Love Finds You
in Liberty, Indiana*
by Melanie Dobson
ISBN: 978-1-934770-74-0

*Love Finds You in
Revenge, Ohio*
by Lisa Harris
ISBN: 978-1-934770-81-8

Love Finds You in Poetry, Texas
by Janice Hanna
ISBN: 978-1-935416-16-6

Love Finds You in Sisters, Oregon
by Melody Carlson
ISBN: 978-1-935416-18-0

Love Finds You in Charm, Ohio
by Annalisa Daughety
ISBN: 978-1-935416-17-3

Love Finds You in
Bethlehem, New Hampshire
by Lauralee Bliss
ISBN: 978-1-935416-20-3

Love Finds You in North Pole, Alaska
by Loree Lough
ISBN: 978-1-935416-19-7

Love Finds You in Holiday, Florida
by Sandra D. Bricker
ISBN: 978-1-935416-25-8

Love Finds You in
Lonesome Prairie, Montana
by Tricia Goyer and Ocieanna Fleiss
ISBN: 978-1-935416-29-6

Love Finds You in Bridal Veil, Oregon
by Miralee Ferrell
ISBN: 978-1-935416-63-0

Love Finds You in Hershey,
Pennsylvania
by Cerella D. Sechrist
ISBN: 978-1-935416-64-7

Love Finds You in Homestead, Iowa
by Melanie Dobson
ISBN: 978-1-935416-66-1

Love Finds You in Pendleton, Oregon
by Melody Carlson
ISBN: 978-1-935416-84-5

Love Finds You in
Golden, New Mexico
by Lena Nelson Dooley
ISBN: 978-1-935416-74-6

Love Finds You in Lahaina, Hawaii
by Bodie Thoene
ISBN: 978-1-935416-78-4

Love Finds You in
Victory Heights, Washington
by Tricia Goyer and Ocieanna Fleiss
ISBN: 978-1-60936-000-9

Love Finds You in Calico, California
by Elizabeth Ludwig
ISBN: 978-1-60936-001-6

Love Finds You in Sugarcreek, Ohio
by Serena B. Miller
ISBN: 978-1-60936-002-3

Love Finds You in
Deadwood, South Dakota
by Tracey Cross
ISBN: 978-1-60936-003-0

Love Finds You in
Silver City, Idaho
by Janelle Mowery
ISBN: 978-1-60936-005-4

Love Finds You in
Carmel-by-the-Sea, California
by Sandra D. Bricker
ISBN: 978-1-60936-027-6

Love Finds You
Under the Mistletoe by Irene
Brand and Anita Higman
ISBN: 978-1-60936-004-7

Love Finds You in Hope, Kansas
by Pamela Griffin
ISBN: 978-1-60936-007-8

Love Finds You in Sun Valley, Idaho
by Angela Ruth
ISBN: 978-1-60936-008-5

Love Finds You in
Camelot, Tennessee
by Janice Hanna
ISBN: 978-1-935416-65-4

Love Finds You in
Tombstone, Arizona
by Miralee Ferrell
ISBN: 978-1-60936-104-4

Love Finds You in
Martha's Vineyard, Massachusetts
by Melody Carlson
ISBN: 978-1-60936-110-5

Love Finds You in
Prince Edward Island, Canada
by Susan Page Davis
ISBN: 978-1-60936-109-9

Love Finds You in Groom, Texas
by Janice Hanna
ISBN: 978-1-60936-006-1

Love Finds You in Amana, Iowa
by Melanie Dobson
ISBN: 978-1-60936-135-8

Love Finds You in
Lancaster County, Pennsylvania
by Annalisa Daughety
ISBN: 978-1-60936-212-6

Love Finds You in Branson, Missouri
by Gwen Ford Faulkenberry
ISBN: 978-1-60936-191-4

COMING SOON

Love Finds You on
Christmas Morning
by Debby Mayne and Trish Perry
ISBN: 978-1-60936-193-8

Love Finds You in
Nazareth, Pennsylvania
by Melanie Dobson
ISBN: 978-1-60936-194-5

Love Finds You in
Sunset Beach, Hawaii
by Robin Jones Gunn
ISBN: 978-1-60936-028-3

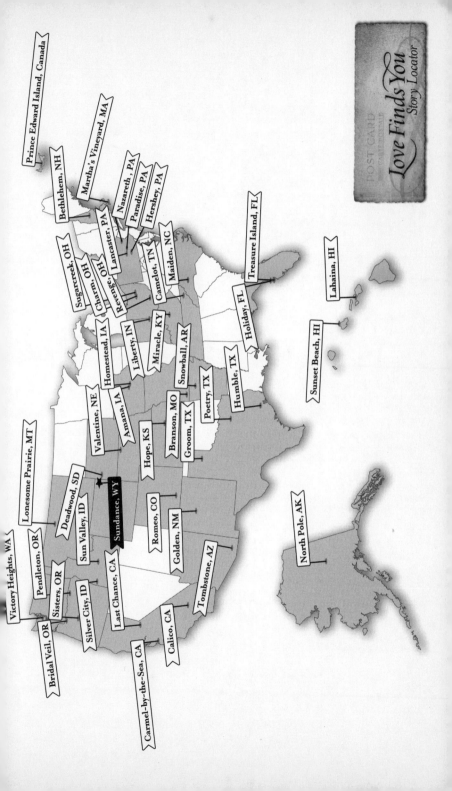